Oral Robbers

Freaky Florida Mystery Adventures, Volume 3

Margaret Lashley

Published by Zazzy Ideas, Inc., 2020.

Copyright

For more information, write to: Zazzy Ideas, Inc. P.O. Box 1113, St. Petersburg, FL 33731

This book is a work of fiction. While actual places throughout Florida have been used in this book, any resemblance to persons living or dead are purely coincidental. Unless otherwise noted, the author and the publisher make no explicit guarantees as to the accuracy of the information contained in this book and in some cases, the names of places have been altered.

What Readers are Saying about Freaky Florida Mystery Adventures ...

"I read a lot, and Kindle suggested your book. This book is laugh out loud funny. Is everyone in Florida crazy? I have read Tim Dorsey, Carl Hiaasen, and Randy Wayne White. Those writers are funny but they need to watch out for you."

"I read the whole book in two days, something I've never done before! I just couldn't wait to find out what was going to happen next!"

"Margaret Lashley has a knack for creating funny, small town strange, off the wall, but so endearing type of characters."

"If you enjoy laugh-out-loud comedy, this book is for you!"

"Plenty of mysteries and slap stick humor with a backwoods redneck cousin thrown in the mix. I almost felt like I was reading a cross between Terry Pratchett and Piers Anthony."

"The twists and turns of the story line kept me eagerly turning the pages to see what would happen next and kept me thinking as well. Loved the small town feel of the book and the very real to life characters. Great start to a new series!"

Prologue

I made it through my first official "investigation" with Nick Grayson without getting fired or taking an extended dirt nap.

In other words, I accomplished two of the three goals I'd set out for myself. The third—not falling for the guy—well, that one's still a little sketchy.

Traveling with Grayson in his ratty old Winnebago means he's always close.

Irritatingly close.

And every time we bump into each other, I get this weird, electric feeling.

Is it love? Is it hate? Is it an ungrounded electrical socket?

I really can't say for sure. But I read somewhere that love and hate sit side-by-side on the emotional scale—and that the true opposite of love is *indifference*.

Indifference is definitely *not* what I feel for Grayson.

Maybe the right word is *grateful*—albeit, begrudgingly so.

Grayson snatched me, kicking and screaming, out of my dead-end life as a second-rate mall cop. Then he shoved me, head-first, into his crazy, disco world of monster a-go-go.

Investigating reports of the unexplained with Grayson can be bizarre.

Dangerous, even.

But boring? No.

I *totally* give him that much.

Chapter One

"Hold still, Drex. And take that Tootsie Pop out of your mouth."

"Why?"

I glared into the eyes of Nick Grayson. He was my boss, private-eye instructor, and current owner of the world's cheesiest moustache.

We were in a sleazy motel off US 19, just outside New Port Richey. I was in bed, propped up on mysteriously lumpy pillows. Grayson, a physicist turned conspiracy-theory nut, was hovering over me, pasting electrodes onto my scalp.

His eyes gleamed maniacally as he hooked me up to his electroencephalogram machine. His plan was to scare whatever miniscule amount of wits I had left right out of my half-shaved noggin.

Fun times.

The last time Grayson strapped me to his EEG contraption, he'd shocked me to the core with a video of gray-skinned aliens being ambushed by military-style Rambos. After the mysterious militia freed three kids from glass holding tubes, they'd freed the aliens of their oversized heads.

Not pretty. Not pretty at all.

As I lay there, I still had no idea whether that bizarre video was real or not. I wasn't sure Grayson knew, either. And, for the time being, it didn't matter. Half an hour ago, I'd experienced something that had scared the bejeebers out of me even more—and it hadn't come from Grayson's test program.

I sat up in bed and frowned at Grayson. "Why can't I keep the Tootsie Pop?"

Grayson glanced up from fiddling with a knob on the EEG monitor. "You might choke on it. Besides, it's a crutch, Drex."

I scowled. "A crutch?"

Grayson locked his mesmerizing green eyes on mine. Dressed all in black, the wiry, fortyish man with the washboard abs had a mysterious hold on me. At times, I wanted to kiss him. Other times, I wanted to run from him—screaming. But most times, I felt compelled to follow his lead, glued to his side by my own twisted curiosity.

"An oral fixation," he said, studying me like I was his favorite new lab rat. "Like smoking. Or chewing gum. Typically brought on by insufficient breastfeeding during infancy."

My eyes narrowed. "Are you saying I have *mommy* issues?"

He smirked. "If the sucker fits ...."

I shot Grayson some side-eye. "That's rich coming from a guy with two navels. As far as *I* know, *you* came out of a test tube."

Grayson's eyebrows wagged below his stubble-covered head, which was usually covered by a black fedora. "An excellent argument for why I *don't* have mommy issues, I'd say. Now lose the Tootsie Pop and lay down."

I plucked the sucker from my mouth and put it in an ashtray on the nightstand. Cringing with disgust, I cautiously laid back onto the mystery-stain pillows. "Satisfied?"

"Yes." Grayson glanced at the used red Tootsie Pop. "But if *you* were, you wouldn't need *that* thing."

I scowled. "Just fire up your gross-out program before I change my mind."

Grayson's right cheek dimpled, a sure sign that a deviant smile lurked beneath his bushy black moustache. He snatched my Tootsie Pop from the ashtray and stuck it in his mouth.

Gross.

His right cheek bulged as he clicked a key on his laptop computer, then handed it to me. The screen blinked to life in my hands. On it, a yellow emoji face grinned above the words, "Welcome to My World!"

The ludicrous cliché was so on target I nearly laughed out loud. Grayson certainly lived in another world, all right. And, like some sort of pseudo-Stockholm Syndrome victim, I was slowly becoming part of it.

I'd just finished the first two weeks of my internship with Grayson. It had been a crazy ride—akin to costarring in a low-budget remake of *The X-Files.*

In redneck Florida.

In a rundown RV.

Let's just say, I wasn't expecting a call from Hollywood anytime soon.

"Okay. Here we go," Grayson said.

I glanced over at him. Something about his expression triggered my fight-or-flight response.

But it was way too late to make a run for it now.

Besides, it wasn't exactly like my life was brimming with other possibilities. Who else but Grayson would've taken on a reluctant, wet-behind-the-ears private-eye wannabe like me?

I'd been under the influence of vodka when I'd ordered a detective correspondence course from a late-night infomercial. And I'd been so angry I couldn't see straight when I'd handed over my family's auto repair business to my cousin Earl.

Suffice it to say, at 37, I was a tad behind schedule on my plan to retire at 45. Broke, angry, and recovering from being shot in the head, I'd been headed for a meltdown.

Instead, a meltdown found me.

Grayson's arrival at my auto-repair shop in his busted Winnebago had been the catalyst that had spawned the perfect storm—a tornado of emotions powerful enough to blow the remnants of my old life to smithereens. When he'd offered to provide the two years of training I needed to become a real private investigator, I'd jumped at the chance—and into his RV.

And now, here I was, in a sleazy hotel room, my shaved scalp glued by electrodes to a mind-altering machine invented by, quite possibly, a madman.

But, in all honesty, nobody had forced me to drink Grayson's crazy Kool-Aid. I'd made my very own pitcherful, spiked it with vodka, and willingly downed every last drop.

I blew out a sigh, slapped on a determined face, and gave Grayson a thumb's up. He nodded, then turned his attention back to the display panel on the EEG machine.

I glanced down at the computer in my lap and braced for impact. My job was to observe the macabre images that would soon be popping up on its screen. Grayson's task was to monitor my alpha brainwave activity during the test. The more alpha waves I produced, the more relaxed my nervous system was.

The concept behind Grayson's self-designed program was to help him—and now *me*—gain control over the physical reactions any sane person instinctively experienced when encountering the weird, the freaky, and the blatantly bizarre.

As Grayson had so artfully enumerated, "Screaming, pissing one's pants, fainting, and/or running for one's life aren't particularly helpful tactics when it comes to investigating unexplained phenomena."

He was right. Thanks to his tutelage, I'd already gained first-hand experience with all of the above. As a result, I was now eager to up my game.

"I'm ready," I said. "Let her rip."

Grayson nodded. "Okay. Here we go."

The screen on the laptop blinked. The yellow smiley face disappeared. In its place came the image of a cute, golden-haired little girl prancing in a field of daisies.

"Good. The baseline's set," Grayson said.

The next image appeared. It was the little girl again. This time, her mouth morphed into an evil grin, complete with a set of blood-dripping Dracula fangs.

My pulse quickened. I glanced up at Grayson.

He was staring at the monitor. His eye ticked like he was experiencing the early stages of Tourette's.

My alpha waves must've taken a hit.

I took a deep breath to calm myself. A moment later, the screen changed to a vintage, black-and-white video clip of *Nosferatu,* rising straight up from his coffin like the world's creepiest post-mortem erection.

Geez. Nosferatu doesn't mean "hideously ugly vampire" for nothing.

My heart skipped a beat. I breathed through it.

"Good," Grayson said, his eyes glued to the EEG display.

The image on the screen switched back to full color. A green-skinned, yellow-eyed vampire lunged toward me, snapping his bloody fangs at me like a ravenous piranha.

Breathe deep. It isn't real.

"You're not telling yourself it isn't real again, are you?" Grayson asked.

I flinched. "Why would you say that?"

"Because your alpha waves are remaining unusually high. Either you're mastering this, or you're still in denial."

I bit my lip. "What's so wrong with denial?"

Grayson eyed me. "Well, for one thing, in the case of a *real* encounter, it could get you killed."

I rolled my eyes at the ceiling. "I mean *besides* that."

Grayson frowned. "Don't you value your life?"

Maybe I would if I actually had *one.*

I shrugged. "Sure."

"Humph," Grayson grunted, and turned back to the EEG monitor.

In a way, I envied Grayson. The man had a distinct mission in life. He was absolutely certain that unknown creatures were hiding out in the nooks and crannies of rural Florida, and that, one day, we would be the ones to prove it.

In the past two weeks, we'd definitely shared some undeniably odd experiences. But whether what we'd encountered had been real or merely hoaxes, hallucinations, or the residual effects of brain damage, was still up for debate as far as I was concerned.

I'd yet to come across anything I could, with absolute certainty, say was "the real deal."

But then again, my life to date had presented me with very few "real deals." Instead, I'd honed my cynical chops on dead-end jobs, cheating boyfriends, and a mother who'd scammed me out of knowing my real father.

And now, here I was, hitching my wagon to a man who got his jollies searching for freaks of nature.

The irony made me nearly laugh out loud.

Was *I* Grayson's latest freak, or was *he* mine?

Chapter Two

Like most of my life to date, things were going more than a tiny bit off-plan. But this time, for once, the misdirection was in my favor.

By now, Grayson and I should've been in Ruskin, Florida, investigating a story about killer tomatoes.

But this morning, as we'd watched Plant City's humongous strawberry water tower disappear in the rearview mirror, my P.I. mentor had given me the choice between the Ruskin tomato gig and checking out some sketchy dealings going on in a nursing home in New Port Richey.

Having been to Ruskin before, choosing the nursing home had been a no-brainer. Grayson, on the other hand, had apparently had his heart set on the homicidal fruit.

In an effort to maintain what he called, "a professional level of democratic decision-making," Grayson had challenged me to a thumb-wrestling match. Winner take all.

He'd failed to inform me of his secret weapon. The double-jointed jerk won best two out of three in no time flat.

Deadly tomatoes, it seemed, had been about to become an imminent part of my future. I'd been contemplating asking Grayson for a rematch when a call buzzed in on the old ham radio mounted under the Winnebago's dashboard.

Someone was calling Grayson's nutter hotline.

Little did we know then that our destiny was about to be changed by a bucktoothed weirdo with a blond mullet hairdo and a giant wimp of a dog named Tooth.

What he told Grayson and me would soon have us seeing red—but tomatoes would have nothing to do with it.

Chapter Three

I was rubbing my sore wrestling thumb when the unexpected transmission crackled over the ham radio, sending an electric buzz through the cab of the vintage RV.

"Oh gee double-oh seven to Mr. Gray. Come in, Mr. Gray. Over."

I recognized the squeaky voice instantly. It belonged to one of our new conspiracy-chasing allies—a *Wayne's World* wannabe we'd dubbed "Operative Garth."

The thought of the skinny, bucktoothed redneck and his secret junkyard compound made me smile. All in all, Garth was a good egg, as far as cracked ova went.

"Double oh seven?" I laughed and shot Grayson a look. "Is that prepper code for geek or nerd?"

Grayson's lips curled slightly as he reached under the dashboard for the radio. He unhooked the microphone and held it to his lips. "Gray here. Over."

"News flash," Operative Garth said. "Caught more buzz this morning about Banner Hill. Another vet reported missing this morning. Over."

"So, it's not an anomaly after all. Thanks for the intel, OG." Grayson replied in a tone that was serious, yet somehow mocking. I suddenly suspected I might be the foil in a new Leslie Nielsen movie.

Naked Nerd 33 1/3.

"My honor, Mr. Gray," Garth squeaked. "Over."

"Same MO?" Grayson asked. "Over."

"Yeah. Disappeared without a trace. Over."

"Any speculation on causation? Over."

"Money's on organ reapers," Garth responded. "Or body snatchers. Any theories? Over."

Grayson's right eyebrow flat-lined. "Too soon to speculate. But a third victim definitely thickens the plot. Keep in contact OG. Reward if tip pans out. Over."

"Cool!" Garth blurted. A moment later, he hastily added, "Over."

I imagined Garth grinning like a donkey, pushing his thick, black-framed glasses up on his pug nose.

"So, what gives?" I asked as Grayson hung up the mic. "I thought we were going to Ruskin."

"That's three veterans in less than a week. Vanished like Draino down a dump hole. Something's definitely up."

I eyed him skeptically. "Why? Is three some kind of magic number?"

Grayson kept his eye on the road. "Three drops the probability of random coincidence to near zero."

My brow furrowed. "But who in their right mind would kidnap veterans from a nursing home?"

"Exactly," Grayson said, nodding thoughtfully. "No one. Unless they had a good use for them."

A good use for old men? Now there's *a probability of near zero.*

"What about body snatchers?" I asked. "You know, like Garth said."

Grayson shook his head. "Not likely. As far as we know, they were still alive when they were taken."

My nose crinkled at the thought. "Organ reapers?"

"Doubtful. These guys are too old to be of any use for organ transplants."

I lifted my ball cap and scratched the auburn stubble growing in atop my shaved head. I knew Grayson wouldn't be satisfied until there was some screwball angle to the chase. I, on the other hand, just wanted to hang on for another 102 weeks to complete my P.I. internship.

"What about ritual sacrifice?" I offered. "To satiate demonic lust?"

"Hmm. A buffet of human organs." Grayson rubbed his chin as he pondered the idea. "You hungry?" He turned to me and smirked. "How about liver and onions for lunch?"

I shook my head.

Only you, Grayson. Only you.

Chapter Four

Like asteroids colliding in space, Operative Garth's intel had sent Grayson and me careening off on another trajectory. After a quick stop for gas, we'd shifted gears and direction, setting Ruskin and its murderous crop of tomatoes aside for another season.

The disappearance of a third veteran from a New Port Richey nursing home had piqued Grayson's curiosity. With his weird-o-meter recalibrated, for once the universe had redirected us in my favor.

Our new destination required us to head west, toward the Gulf coast. I-4 would've been the most direct route, but definitely not the most reliable.

It was late November. Tourist season was in full swing.

We both knew all too well that I-4 would be clogged with Thanksgiving holiday traffic. With millions of white knuckles wrapped around fake-leather steering wheels, this time of year the only blessing from God that Floridians could count on was a rental-car invasion of biblical proportions.

Given the annual plague of travelers hell-bent on getting to Disney World for a relaxing family vacation, one tiny fender-bender could set off a road-warrior-style apocalypse.

So we took SR 39 north instead, and headed toward Zephyrhills.

After driving by cow pastures, rundown rural churches, and an ugly stretch of sprawl missing its urban, we hung a left on CR 54 and headed west, where we were treated to yet another string of trailer parks, strip malls, housing developments, and dollar stores littering the landscape like hurled garbage.

It was the side of Florida never featured on a postcard.

By the time we reached the outskirts of Zephyrhills, both of us were mesmerized by monotony, and hungry as all get-out. Thankfully, it was my turn to pick a place to eat.

When I spied Sargent Pizza, I practically yelled in Grayson's ear.

"Stop here!" I jabbed a finger at the low-rent pizza joint. Its checkered past as a failed convenience store was as obvious as a girdle on a goose.

Grayson frowned. "Why there?"

"I'm in the mood for pepperoni," I said. But that was a lie. I'd have chomped down on a lawn-clipping sandwich at Katie's House of Kale if that's what it would've taken to ensure liver and onions wasn't on the menu.

THE INTERIOR OF SARGENT Pizza appeared to have been fitted out entirely with furniture stolen from somebody's dead grandma.

Grayson sat across a scarred oak table from me, sipping coffee and waiting on his anchovy pizza. The only other patron in the place was some lady languishing in a corner booth. Judging by her outfit, she was either a hooker or she was blind and had been dressed by one.

"How much further to New Port Richey?" Grayson asked, adjusting the floral cushion tied to his chair by a dirty bow.

I knew his question was just a ploy to make me practice using my smart phone. But after perusing Sargent Pizza's menu and finding no organ meats on offer, I was feeling smugly generous.

I pulled my cellphone from my purse and punched a few buttons, trying not to let my fear of technology set my teeth to grinding. To my surprise, with very little prompting, a map with several routes and timeframes popped up on the screen.

Huh. Maybe Google Maps wasn't designed explicitly to spy on me in my underwear, after all.

I showed the routes to Grayson. "Looks like maybe another hour or two, give or take traffic."

Grayson gave me a quick nod, then removed his fedora and rubbed the stubble growing in on his head. Like me, we were both sporting a buzz cut. Mine, hidden under a ball cap, was courtesy of an over-exuberant ER staff when I'd been struck in the forehead by a ricochet bullet a few weeks ago.

Grayson's shaved head was self-inflicted—an attempt to achieve more accurate results from his EEG contraption. Or, at least, that was the story he'd told me. And, so far, he was sticking to it.

Grayson opened his laptop, but before he could click the power button, the pizza arrived. It was delivered to our table by a short, roundish man in his late fifties. Shockingly, the guy was sporting a moustache bushy enough to give Grayson's a run for its money.

I secretly found myself worrying that the close proximity of two Freddie Mercury-style moustaches might set off some kind of planetary disturbance that could end the world as we knew it. Then I secretly worried why in the world I would think such a thing ....

I've either sustained serious brain damage, or Grayson and his conspiracy theories are turning my mind to mush.

"Enjoy," the waiter said, leaning closer to Grayson as he set down the pizza.

I cringed and held my breath as the moustaches grew nearer and nearer to each other—just in case my theory had any merit ....

But then, as suddenly as he'd appeared, the waiter turned and left. No black hole appeared. No rift in the time-space continuum occurred. The guy didn't even leave a greasy skid mark.

I breathed a sigh of relief—and caught a whiff of cheese and freshly baked crust.

Maybe the heavenly aroma somehow counteracted The Moustache Effect. Or maybe I've officially gone insane ....

I glanced down at the pizza. It was as big around as a bicycle tire, and took up most of our table. Half the pie was garnished with pepperoni. The other half was rendered inedible by blackish-gray strips of dead fish.

Anchovies. Yuck.

"Looks good," Grayson said, and folded his laptop closed, oblivious to how close we'd come to planetary annihilation.

I shot him a look. "At least *my* half does."

"What've you got against anchovies?"

"Nothing. Just a rule my Grandma Selma taught me. Never order fish from a roadside restaurant that used to be a 7-11."

Grayson shrugged. "Suit yourself." He took a bite from an anchovy slice. His face went slack.

"Something wrong?" I asked.

"No." He forced a smile and another chew.

I smirked and picked up a slice from the pepperoni side. The melted mozzarella stretched like rubber all the way from the pan to my mouth.

Grayson discretely spit his mouthful into a napkin. "Trade you a slice."

I smirked. "Not a chance."

"Come on. What's it worth to you?"

I took another bite. "Mmm. This is *delicious.*"

His eyes fixated on my side of the pizza. "One slice. I'll let you pick the radio station."

I licked my lips and stared him square in the eye. "Let me drive the RV."

Grayson nearly choked on his own air supply. "What? Not a chance!"

I might've had mommy issues, but Grayson was totally OCD. And when it came to driving his RV?

Total. Bloody. Control. Freak.

"Why not?" I argued. "We're traveling backroads. Come on. Let me drive. That way, you can ... you can work on your computer."

I watched Grayson mull it over as he stared at my pizza. I knew his hesitation. It wasn't because the ratty old RV itself was worth much. The outside of the 1967 Winnebago looked like a traveling algae farm that had somehow survived a Cat 4 hurricane.

No. His concern was about what was on the *inside*.

Grayson had spent lord-knows-how-much money converting the RV's small bedroom into an electromagnetic monster trap, complete with steel walls, caged windows, and eight massive deadbolts on the door. He'd also crammed the cabinets in the Minnie Winnie with all kinds of spy equipment and secret potions and stuff. To Grayson, that junk was probably irreplaceable. Not to mention, the hoarder had stashed stacks of cash behind the paneling in the walls.

I smiled and chewed my pizza patiently. For once, I had the upper hand on Grayson. I met his mesmerizing green eyes with calm, serene clarity.

Grayson, you're obsessive-compulsive, a control freak, and a hoarder.

The thought made me stop chewing.

Huh. That makes three *things. According to Grayson's own logic, that means the random probability that he isn't a neurotic whack-job is officially zero.*

I studied Grayson as he considered taking another bite of anchovy pizza. The cheese hanging off his moustache wasn't helping his case regarding my whack-job theory.

I took a sip of Dr Pepper and smirked. "I have a valid Florida driver's license, in case you're wondering."

Grayson crinkled his nose. "I know."

"Then what's the problem? Just let me drive your crappy old RV, already."

He shook his head. "No can do."

"What's it gonna take?" I asked, reaching for another slice of pepperoni pizza.

"Three slices," he said.

I jerked my hand back. That was the rest of my half of the pizza.

What do I care? I won!

"Done!" I said.

Grayson flinched. "And you have to call me Mr. Gray."

One side of my mouth hooked skyward. "Like one of your nerdy operatives? No way."

"Yes, way. For a week."

I sneered. "One day."

He frowned. "Five days."

"Once," I said. "Final offer."

Grayson smiled in a way that made me feel as if I'd somehow managed to come out on the short end of this wager.

"Okay, then. Let's hear it," he said, and reached for a slice. "Call me Mr. Gray."

THE RV'S TRANSMISSION crunched like a handful of nails thrown into a garbage disposal.

I winced. Like an idiot, I'd turned the key in the ignition after the motor was already running.

I glanced over at Grayson. He was grimacing as if he'd been shot in the heart.

"Sorry," I said. "Stop hovering! You're making me nervous!"

I shifted into reverse, and slowly, carefully, inch by inch, backed the hulking old RV out of the parking space and into a lamp post.

Grayson closed his eyes and groaned.

"It was just a light tap," I said, trying to believe it myself. "I've never driven a rig this big before."

Grayson let out a painful-sounding sigh. "It's only twenty-four feet long, Drex."

"I'm used to driving the Mustang," I said. "This thing's got no visibility."

Grayson closed his eyes and took a deep breath. "I guess you have to start somewhere. But have mercy on me and the poor girl." He thumped a fist on his chest. "Any more screw-ups and I'm gonna refund your pizza."

I bit my lip, then carefully steered the RV out of Sargent Pizza's parking lot. I took a right, heading east on CR54.

"Geez," Grayson said. "I thought you said you knew how to drive. We need to go *west*. You should've turned *left.*"

I kept my eyes on the road. "I know. I just want to make one quick detour. For supplies."

Grayson's right eyebrow flat-lined. "Twenty feet down the road and already I'm regretting this, big-time."

"Relax, Mr. OCD. I've got this."

Grayson's brow furrowed. "I don't have obsessive-compulsive disorder."

Rich, coming from a man who folds his Tootsie-Pop wrappers before putting them in the trash.

"Who said anything about obsessive-compulsive disorder?" I lied. "OCD stands for Officer, Commander and Detective."

Grayson's lips twisted to one side. "Sure it does. What kind of fool do you take me for?"

I gave him a sweet smile.

With that moustache? How about Borat?

Chapter Five

"See? That wasn't so bad," I said to Grayson as we hauled our shopping bags out of the Walmart supercenter on Gall Boulevard. Given the hordes milling about the place, I surmised we'd stumbled upon the cultural epicenter of Zephyrhills.

Grayson munched a handful of Cheetos he'd plucked from a bag as big as his torso. "Pardon me, lady. Do I know you?"

"You *wish*." I laughed and tousled the brand-new wig atop my head—an auburn, shoulder-length bob.

The burgundy-hued polyester flop-top wasn't the finest wig in the world, but compared to a ball cap or being bald, it made me feel like Sophia Loren. And, given my track record, there wasn't any point in sinking too much money into a quality hairpiece, anyway. The first two hadn't survived much more than a day each, thanks to Grayson's penchant for "unconventional fieldwork."

My first wig had been snarled into a sticky, duct-taped rat's nest during a scheme to entrap Mothman with the womanly wiles of seduction. The second one had been blown to bits by a stoned doomsday prepper sporting a kewl set of grillz.

As I strutted along in the Walmart lot, I hoped this third wig would stick around awhile—at least long enough for me to outgrow looking like a stunt double for *G.I. Jane*.

"You know, that hairstyle really does suit you," Grayson said. He took my hand and pirouetted me around in the middle of the asphalt parking lot.

As I spun, I felt it again. That odd, electric buzz I got in my gut every time Grayson touched me.

Unnerved, I broke free of his grasp.

"Thanks," I said. "Appearances are important. That's why you should lose that cheesy moustache, Grayson. You look like you got lost in Kazakhstan on your way to meet The Village People."

"Ouch." Grayson winced and pressed a hand over his heart as if he'd just taken a bullet. "So much for unconditional love."

"You're such a jerk," I said, pretending to laugh off his comment.

But it wasn't all that funny. In my heart the strange bedfellows of elation and terror were taking turns short-sheeting each other.

I couldn't decide which scared me worse—Grayson's electric touch, or the fact he seemed utterly content to throw away his life chasing imaginary monsters.

But then again, maybe that's what we all do ....

I yanked the RV's passenger door open. "Get in, Groucho," I quipped. "I'm taking you to Elfers."

One of Grayson's bushy eyebrows rose a notch. "Elfers?"

"Yes." I rattled one of my shopping bags. "And if you're a good boy, I'll even give you a green Tootsie Pop for the ride."

WHILE I DROVE WEST on CR 54, Grayson disappeared into the back of the RV with his Walmart purchases. One of them was a pouch of live mealy worms for Gizzard, the pet lizard he kept in a terrarium on the banquette table. We were just outside Zephyrhills when he came climbing back into the cab.

"You know what mealy worms taste like?" he asked as he flopped into the passenger seat.

I grimaced. "No. And I don't want to know."

"Suit yourself. But I find your lack of curiosity disconcerting." He fished his laptop from the floorboard, powered it up, and kept his eyes glued to it all the way to the next town.

Smart choice, since it was pretty much like the last one.

Sadly, like so much of "new" Florida, the once-quaint town of Westley Chapel had bourgeoned into yet another soulless collection of strip malls, dollar stores, and chain restaurants that spread outward, like a fungal infection, from where its original heart had been cut in half by I-75.

Still, despite its lack of planning or originality, compared to my tiny home town, Westley Chapel sparkled as glam as a Vegas show-girl—complete with fancy traffic lights and a genuine KFC!

As we passed a drive-thru convenience store, I thought of big fat Artie plopped in his chair at the Stop & Shoppe back home in Point Paradise. A wave of nostalgia passed through me like gas from a bad bean burrito.

Being born and raised in Florida, I guess so-called progress would always be a mixed bag.

I set my jaw to sullen resignation and drove onward. A mile or two later, the terrain went feral. I breathed a sigh of relief. Ahead lay miles of flat, unbroken scrubland—a hodgepodge of oaks, pines, palmettos and tangled underbrush.

Now *that* felt like real Florida to me.

I GLANCED OVER AT GRAYSON. He was happily tapping away on his laptop. He'd barely glanced up as we passed through the tiny towns of Odessa and Seven Springs. I wondered what he was working on, but decided not to disturb him.

Eventually, we wound our way toward the gulf coast and the promised land known as Elfers.

"We're here," I said as we passed a small roadside placard announcing our arrival.

Grayson looked up. His face collapsed with disappointment. "This is it?"

"What were you expecting? A fairyland village?"

Grayson shot me an earnest look. "Is that so wrong, Drex?"

Uh...yeah.

"Ghosts of a bygone era," Grayson said as we buzzed by a gray, wooden shack. "According to my Google search, Elfers is home to 13,612 residents and zero registered sex offenders."

"Really?" I asked. "How many *un*registered ones?"

Grayson grinned. "Good one. But I guess you can't believe everything on the internet. It also says the median home sales price here is zero."

I smirked. "So people either never leave, or they give away their homes and flee."

"Perhaps. Or maybe elves never die, and therefore, never have to sell."

"Huh?"

"Oh! Pull in over there," Grayson said, and pointed across the street to a strip center called Elfers Square.

I shot him a look. "You serious?"

He shrugged. "We're here. Might as well see what the Elfer buzz is all about. I created this survey, see?" He shoved his laptop screen at me.

Elfer buzz? Survey? Shoot me now.

I shook my head. But from the childlike excitement on Grayson's face, I knew there was no point in trying to argue with the man. If I'd learned anything in my 37 years, it was that idiocy trumped reason every time.

I sighed, pulled into the strip center, and spent the next hour pissing and moaning like a spoiled brat while Grayson interviewed prospective Winn Dixie shoppers about their encounters with elves.

Yes, my life was just that fabulous.

Chapter Six

I was hiding out behind a stack of Winn-Dixie brand pork-n-beans, trying to distance myself from any affiliation with Grayson. I took another furtive peek around the tin cans. He was around ten feet away, standing by a barrel of cantaloupes.

Clad in black jeans, black shoes, a black shirt, black moustache and black fedora, Grayson looked like Mr. Peanut's evil twin hawking a dubious, new product.

Planters' dark-roasted nutcase.

Grayson glanced my way. I flinched.

He held up his little recorder for my perusal. The gleam in his eye made me question my own sanity.

Interviewing grocery shoppers about elves?

But then I got a look at the person he was talking to and felt relatively sane—comparatively speaking. The first victim in Grayson's inane interview scheme was an elderly man wearing a straw hat and overalls, without the courtesy of an undershirt.

So that's what happened to Tom Sawyer.

"I done lived here all my life," the old man informed Grayson proudly. "But I ain't never laid no eyes on no elf." He scratched his armpit hair and explained to Grayson that, "Elves wouldn't care nothin' for this town no how, seeing as how short they is."

"Can you elaborate?" Grayson asked.

"I don't rightly know," the old man said. "Is that some kind of dance?"

I nearly groaned out loud.

"Never mind," Grayson said. "Just tell me more about the elves."

"Well now," the man said, "you see, a goodly portion of Elfers floods ever' time the Anclote River swells up with rain."

After a pause, Grayson prompted the man. "Yes?"

"Well, it's purty obvious, ain't it? Any elves livin' in this here vicinity would've surely drownded by now."

I shot Grayson a sideways smirk.

Sounds perfectly logical to me.

With the calm, cheerful attitude of a true professional, Grayson thanked the old redneck. He shook his hand, wished him a pleasant day, and proceeded to stick his recorder in the face of an elderly woman in a faded, flour-sack dress.

She blinked at him behind pink, cat-eye glasses wedged tightly onto her doughy, Cabbage-Patch-Kid face.

"How are you today, lovely lady?" Grayson asked.

"Fair to midl'in," the old woman answered.

"May I have a moment of your time?"

"I guess. Long as it don't cost nothin'."

Grayson shot me a thumbs up.

I rolled my eyes and ducked back behind the stack of bean cans. After making a full orbit around their sockets, my eyes landed on a display of kosher dill pickles. I studied them for a moment, carefully considering which size jar—half-pint, pint, or quart—would do the most effective job of knocking Grayson unconscious.

I decided on quart-sized.

I picked up a jar, tested its weight in my hand, and glanced around the pork-n-beans at my dubious P.I. partner. He was still talking to the old woman.

"Madame," he said, "I wonder if you might help me solve the mystery of Elfers' moniker."

The old woman squeezed a cantaloupe and eyed Grayson as if she suspected he might be missing a chromosome. I could totally relate.

"Now you listen here, sonny," the woman said, wagging a crooked finger at him. "Elfers weren't named after some nonsensical creature. It was named after my first cousin's grandfather's wife's favorite uncle."

"What?" Grayson leaned in closer. "Are you saying you're related to elves?"

Good grief! The man must be some kind of idiot savant—minus the savant part.

"No!" the old lady hollered. Her puffy face turned nearly as pink as her glasses. "I ain't no elf, you weirdo!" she yelled, and reared back and walloped Grayson in the chest with her giant vinyl purse.

The impact sent him reeling back into a stack of grapefruits.

"Now git!" she yelled as Grayson scrambled to regain his footing. "And shave that sorry old moustache of yours!"

If I hadn't been doubled over in laughter, I'd have surely peed my pants. As I gasped for breath, a grocery clerk went whizzing by me in Grayson's direction.

I instantly sobered up. Like a professional, I assessed the situation. Carefully and calmly, I returned the jar of pickles to the shelf.

Then, I bolted for the door like my wig was on fire.

I cleared the exit in under four seconds, then hauled ass for the RV. Grayson came flying out a few seconds later, looking as if he'd just robbed the place. He ran up to the driver's side and grabbed for the door handle.

"Scoot over!" he yelled through the closed window.

I smiled and pressed the lock on the door. "No way."

Grayson yanked the handle once, shot me a look, and scrambled for the passenger door.

I smirked as he climbed inside. I was in command of the driver's seat *and* the keys. And even Grayson had to admit, possession was nine-tenths of the law.

"Smooth move, Ex-Lax," I said.

"Just shut up and drive."

AN HOUR OR SO AFTER our hasty getaway from Elfers, I was still grinning from ear to ear. I'd bested Grayson. Again.

Even better, I hadn't hit a lamppost peeling out of the strip mall parking lot. But best of all, I'd MacGyver'ed a new use for a quart-sized jar of dill pickles.

Yeah. All in all, I was feeling pretty good about myself.

But I should've known better than to gloat.

Like my Grandma Selma always said, "Crowing over victories can send the pendulum of life swinging back to wallop you upside the head."

I wish I'd heeded Grandma's words. Or, at the very least, learned how to duck.

Chapter Seven

We were cruising along US 19 just a few miles shy of New Port Richey when it happened.

One moment I was staring at a huge circus tent with a banner for the Baptist Evangelical Resurrection Path Seekers. The next thing I knew, I was staring into a dark, empty void.

In the blink of an eye, the windshield—and everything else—had gone pitch black.

My entire world had been swallowed up by darkness, as if someone had slapped duct tape over my eyes and covered my head with a sack.

I gasped.

I'm blind!

Then I remembered I was driving and nearly swallowed my tongue.

I'm driving blind!

A horn sounded to my left. I jerked the steering wheel and screamed, "Grayson!"

My fingers clamped down on the steering wheel. Somewhere to my left, another horn blared out a passing warning.

"I can't see!" I screamed as brakes squealed to my left.

"What'd you say?" I heard Grayson ask to my right.

"I said I can't *see!*"

"Wha?!"

Suddenly, a mild electric shock went up my arms as Grayson's hands settled over mine on the steering wheel. His voice, calm and steady, whispered instructions into my ear.

"Listen carefully, Drex. Everything's fine. Let up on your grip. I'll steer from here on out."

Panic scrambled my brain.

Should I trust my life to a man who believes in elves?

Elves!

"Are you sure?" I squeaked.

"Yes. Let up on the gas, Drex."

Grayson's words felt warm and comforting against my neck. I eased up a bit on the gas pedal.

"Good," he whispered. "That's it. I've got the wheel now. You can let go."

"Are you sure?"

"Yes, I'm sure."

Reluctantly, I surrendered my grip on the steering wheel. A moment later, I bounced blindly along to the staccato joggle of the RV as it ran over a dozen or so roadway reflectors.

Slowly but surely, our velocity was slowing. I breathed a tiny sigh of relief.

Suddenly, the RV bounced. Another horn blared from the darkness on my left.

I grabbed for the steering wheel and screamed, "Grayson!"

"Gently on the brake now," he coaxed calmly. "Bring us to a stop. Easy does it."

I stomped the brake with all my might. My chest collided with Grayson's arms on the steering wheel.

"Ung," he grunted. "It's okay. We're safe. Good job."

He cut the ignition.

As the RV sputtered out, my body collapsed inward.

"Th ... thank you," I stuttered.

"What happened?" Grayson asked.

"I ... I'm not sure," I said, blinking wildly.

"Another vision?"

"No. Everything just went ... black."

I felt Grayson's hands gently cup my face. "Can you see me?"

"No." Fresh panic shot through me.

"Ease up, Drex. Stop trying so hard."

I blinked my wide-open, straining eyes. Nothing.

"Sit back," he said soothingly. "Close your eyes. Breathe."

I did as Grayson instructed, hanging onto his every word. His voice was the only familiar anchor I had left in the world.

Is this it for me? Has that stupid vestigial twin in my brain taken my sight for good? Crap! What am I going to do?

I was about to burst into tears when I felt Grayson's hand on my shoulder.

"It's a good thing you're not German, Drex," he said.

"What?" I whispered into the darkness. "Why?"

"Because then you'd be a not-see."

I groaned. Then I swallowed hard. Then I laughed despite myself.

"Let's just sit here for a while, cadet," Grayson said, and took my hand.

I concentrated on the warm, mild current of his touch. Slowly, my racing pulse returned to normal. Black turned to dark gray, then to a bluish haze, as if I were looking through a Vaseline-smeared lens.

As my vision cleared further, the first thing I made out was Grayson's blurry moustache in front of me.

I'd never seen anything so beautiful.

His face was inches from mine, watching my every move.

"You had a vision, didn't you?" he asked.

I shook my head. "No. It was more like ... I dunno ... a flavor."

His bushy eyebrows drew closer together. "A *flavor?*"

"Yeah. A ... *taste*."

I made a sour face, then raked my teeth over my tongue. I rolled down the RV window and spit the foul taste from my mouth.

Grayson leaned forward in the passenger seat. "*That's* a new one. What exactly do you think you 'tasted'?"

"I'm not sure." I grimaced from the lingering, unsavory film in my mouth. "I think it was ... the flavor of *evil*."

Grayson's left eyebrow arched. "Intriguing. And what, pray tell, does evil taste like?"

I shrugged. "I dunno. Tingly. Metallic. Like sucking on an old battery."

"Stick out your tongue," Grayson said.

"Why?"

He leaned forward, reached into the glove compartment, and pulled out a baggie of what looked like Q-Tips in vials.

My nose crinkled. "What are you doing?"

"Collecting samples, of course. Now stick out your tongue."

I blew out a breath. Grayson had gone from caring to clinical in two seconds flat. "Honest to God. I don't get paid enough for this."

Grayson stared at me, an incredulous look on his face. "You don't think I'm going to miss the opportunity to gather empirical evidence on evil itself, do you? Think about it, Drex. If I can proffer actual physical evidence of the physiological changes brought about by ectoplasmic enc—"

"Just shut up and do it," I said, and stuck out my tongue.

Chapter Eight

"I suppose we can rule out Viagra," Grayson said. "How about pregnancy?"

I stared at him blankly as we switched places and he climbed into the driver's seat of the battered old RV. "What are you talking about?"

"The cause of your temporary blindness," he said. He turned and shot me a look. "What did you *think* I was talking about?"

"With you, there's no telling," I muttered, then studied the windshield. "But to answer your question, no, I'm not pregnant. And I didn't take Viagra."

"Any other drugs or chemical stimulants?" he asked, cranking the engine and pulling back onto the road.

I plucked a blue sucker out of my mouth. "Only if you count Tootsie Pops."

"Sugar *is* a gateway drug. But as yet, it's not been proven to directly induce blindness, as far as we've been told. Unless, of course, you count diabetic retinopathy."

"No way," I said, and I chewed my lip from concern. "What else do you think could've caused me to lose my sight?"

Grayson pursed his lips. "Ocular migraine, perhaps. Did you experience any numbness or tingling?"

"Only on my tongue."

"Hmm." Grayson drove on for a minute. The ugly urban sprawl better known as New Port Richey came into view. "Amaurosis Fugax."

I glared at Grayson. "Did you just insult me?"

"What? No. Amaurosis Fugax is a sudden reduction in blood flow to the eyes."

My brow furrowed. "You mean like a stroke?"

"Similar, but no. Not technically. Did you have any loss of feeling on one side? Any trouble speaking?"

"No. You were *there*, Grayson. You heard me yelling."

"Right." Grayson shot me a smirk. "How could I forget *that?*"

"Har har har."

"Okay, okay." Grayson pulled up to a red light. "So, no stroke. Let's go back to the bad taste in your mouth. Could you describe it in more detail?"

I sighed. "I don't know. Like I said before. Tingly. Bitter. Metallic. Like a mouthful of old pennies."

"Pennies." Grayson lolled the word around on his tongue. "Exposure to mercury or lead could cause that, but it seems unlikely."

"Why?"

Grayson studied me for a moment. "Because I'd probably have experienced the same exposure."

I frowned. "Maybe you did. Maybe you're about to go blind, too." I looked down at the steering wheel.

Grayson smirked. "Nice try, but you're not driving again."

The light turned green. Grayson stomped the gas. The g-force sent me slumping back into my chair.

"You brush your teeth regularly?" Grayson asked, shifting into second gear.

"I beg your pardon?"

"Poor oral hygiene could account for the bad taste. Interesting side factoid. Did you know that when you brush your teeth, it's the only time you clean part of your skeletal system?"

I closed my eyes and shook my head. "No." And I didn't want to know.

"Okay, so you brushed your teeth," Grayson continued. "Dementia could also cause changes in taste perception. You're not holding anything back on me, are you?"

I shot him a sour look. "If I had dementia, how would I know?"

Grayson laughed. "I guess that leaves illicit drugs or vitamin supplements."

My back stiffened. "Vitamins?"

Grayson glanced my way. "Yes. Some supplements contain heavy metals like copper, zinc, chromium, and whatnot."

"Oh." I reached into my purse and pulled out a bottle. "Like these?"

"Flintstone vitamins with extra iron," Grayson said, grabbing the bottle from my hand and reading the label out loud. "Well, what do you know? Yabba, dabba do."

Chapter Nine

"Could vitamins really be the cause of whatever happened to me?" I asked as Grayson pulled the RV into a low-rent motel off US 19 called the Dilly Dally Motor Court.

"The metallic taste in your mouth, yes," he said, pulling up to the motel office. He parked and cut the ignition. "Loss of eyesight, I don't think so."

He unfastened his seatbelt and studied me with his piercing green eyes. "But there *is* one thing that could cause both."

"What?" I asked, not entirely sure I wanted to know.

"Pregnancy. Are you sure there's no chance you've got a hot-cross bun in the oven?"

I scowled. "Not unless I'm the Immaculate Conception, 2.0."

Grayson laughed. He rattled the jar of vitamins at me. "When's the last time you had one of these babies?"

"Right after lunch."

"Which one did you take? Barney, Fred, Wilma or Pebbles?"

"I don't remember." I chewed my lip, then realized Grayson was having a laugh on me. "You can be a real turd, you know that?"

Grayson smirked. "Just trying to make you smile. After all, laughter is the best medicine, they say."

I sneered. "Not when it's delivered by a quack."

Grayson snorted, then mocked offence. "The ingratitude!" he huffed, then flung open the RV door.

The thought of being left alone panicked me. What if I went blind again? "Where are you going?" I asked.

"To get a room. I think it's time to put that faulty noggin of yours through its paces."

I cringed. "Not more *Mystery Science Theater 3000!*"

"No. Something way better."

Grayson waggled his eyebrows like Groucho Marx, and suddenly I knew what "something way better" meant.

"Wait!" I said.

But it was too late. Grayson hopped out and slammed the RV door behind him.

As he disappeared into the motel office, I noticed he'd left the keys dangling in the ignition. I contemplated the odds of me going blind again if I stole the rundown Winnebago and made a mad dash for Poughkeepsie.

Probably considerably less than the odds of me being pregnant by immaculate conception. But then again, you never know....

Before I could make up my mind, Grayson reemerged from the motel office with a key chained to a wooden paddle. The look in his eye made me instantly curse my own indecisiveness.

In less than ten minutes, I would find myself lying in a lumpy bed in a sleazy hotel room with electrodes pasted to my head—the hapless Guinea pig of a slightly mad physicist with a pimped-out EEG machine.

Ain't life grand?

Chapter Ten

The green-skinned demon in Grayson's computer program snapped its bloody fangs at me again, then the laptop screen blinked out with a static buzz.

As the horrific image faded, it was replaced by the silly, smiling face of the cartoon vampire, Count Chocula. Above the breakfast-cereal icon's head, a conversation bubble read, "Have a chocolaty scrumptious day!"

I let out a sigh. Another of Grayson's bizarre desensitization training sessions had come to an end.

"So, we're done?" I asked, suddenly craving cereal. I sat up in bed and felt the tug of the dozen electrodes pasted to my head like a Medusa starter kit.

Grayson looked up from the EEG machine's display monitor. "Yes. You did well, considering."

"Considering what?"

"Your incident today. I don't see any brain anomalies on the printout. At least, no *new* ones."

I scowled. "Is that some kind of crack?"

He stared at me quizzically, like an emotionless Spock. "Is *what* some kind of crack?"

"The brain anomaly thing."

"You *do* have the vestiges of a twin lodged near your pineal gland, remember?"

I flinched. I remembered, all right. "Do you think that's what caused me to go blind?"

Grayson shrugged. "It's a possibility. But, I'm curious. Why *now?* And why only *temporarily?* The mass on your brain might be partially responsible, but I find your ingestion of vitamins intriguing."

I sneered. "*That's* what you find intriguing about me?"

Grayson continued his analytical monologue, seemingly oblivious to my comment. "Some element—or elements—of the supplement must've acted as a catalyst, precipitating interaction between otherwise inert substances."

My upper lip hooked toward the ceiling. "What?"

Grayson glanced over at me and held up the jar of vitamins.

"Pebbles go bam-bam on your brainstem."

"Oh." I sat up and tugged off an electrode pasted to my right temple. "Grayson?"

"What?"

"Thanks for being so cool during my ... uh, *incident*. While I was driving, I mean. I know you didn't want me to. I shouldn't have .... Anyway, you saved us. I could've gotten us both killed."

"All in the line of duty," he said softly, then grinned at me like the Cheshire Cat who ate the LSD canary. "Besides, the risk was worth it."

"What do you mean?" I asked sourly.

He wagged his eyebrows. "Now I never have to let you drive again."

I scowled. Grayson chuckled and went back to studying my test results. I pulled off a few more electrodes, then I blew out a breath.

"Nosferatu. Dracula. Count Chocula. What's up with the vampire theme?"

"One ghoul at a time," Grayson replied, his attention still on the EEG monitor.

I rolled my eyes. "Grayson, if I ever got a straight answer from you, I think I'd faint."

He glanced over at me. "Good thing you're in bed, then."

"Ugh!" I pulled off another electrode. "What've you got planned for your next program? Mummies?"

Grayson winked and tutted at me. "Come now, Drex. Mummies are for sissies. Everybody knows that."

I got up and headed to the bathroom for a hot shower and to scrub my stubbly head clean of electrode paste. I turned back toward Grayson. "So, what now?"

"I think you should call it a day." He grabbed the RV's keys from the cheap nightstand beside his threadbare twin bed. "I'll go pick up some dinner. What are you in the mood for, battery breath? Oh! I know. How about a fried Energizer bunny—and an 'alkali-ic' drink to go with it?"

I stared at him blankly. "I bet you've been waiting your entire life to say that to somebody, haven't you?"

Chapter Eleven

Quick travel tip: If you ever go in search of the nostalgic highlights of old Central Florida, sunrise over the parking lot at the Dilly-Dally Motor Court in New Port Richey is one that should by all means be *avoided*. Unless, of course, the alternative is to be trapped in one of their grungy rooms with a travel companion who sings in the shower like Barry Gibb with his nuts in a vice ....

I hauled my butt off the cold, concrete curb and stared at the artless still-life before me.

Cigarette butts on asphalt at dawn. A post-apocalyptic abstract.

I checked my cellphone. I figured I still had around five or six minutes before Grayson finished his earsplitting aria. I shoved my phone back into my pocket and shuffled across the motor court parking lot to the dreary lobby. Inside, I downed a cup of crappy coffee and perused the giant rack of gleaming tourist-trap flyers.

One in particular caught my eye.

It had a Sasquatch on it.

I picked up the flyer and began pondering three of the great mysteries of life.

Who knew the headquarters for skunk ape research was in Ochopee, Florida? Who knew there was a town on Earth called Ochopee? Who knew what Ochopee stood for? Eight Spanish urinations?

I let a few minutes tick by as I reflected on these burning questions. I was about to leave when another one of Grandma Selma's sayings popped into my mind.

"An ounce of prevention is worth a pound of government cheese."

I got up and hid the Skunk Ape Research brochures behind the mini-fridge, just in case Grayson wandered in later. Then I poured a couple of fresh cups of stale coffee, and joggled my way across the parking lot and back to the motel room.

I set the coffees on the ground beside the door and reached for the wooden paddle I'd stuck in the back waistband of my pants. The room key was fastened to the paddle like a ball and chain on an old-time convict.

I shook my head. Who would want to steal a key so they could return to this place was beyond my current mental capacity.

I opened the door and tentatively poked my head inside our cigarette-scented room. Mercifully, Pavarotti had finished his morning sonata. I bent down to pick up the coffees and blanched.

A lizard was using one of the coffees as a heated swimming pool.

Correction. A lizard was using Grayson's coffee as a heated swimming pool.

I plucked the little reptile out of his brown bubble bath and set him on the sidewalk to dry off. Then I slipped inside and parked my keister in the vinyl chair that had the smallest split in its seat.

I fired up Grayson's laptop and was slurping stale coffee and perusing local nursing-home websites when he emerged from the bathroom wearing his signature black jeans and blue hospital booties.

Yep. Livin' the glam life, all right.

"What was the name of that nursing home Garth mentioned?" I asked. "Bunker Hill?"

"Banner Hill." Grayson rubbed his chin. "I wonder if any more vets went missing last night."

I glanced at Grayson's killer abs and smooth, muscular chest and felt something inside me stir. Then I remembered the guy had swabbed my tongue for evil and interviewed hillbillies about elves. My swizzle-stick went limp.

"I didn't see anything about it on CNN," I quipped.

Grayson nodded. "Good one, considering you haven't had any coffee this morning."

I lifted my paper cup. "What do you call this?"

"That's not coffee, Drex. That's brown water."

I stared at the weak brew and crinkled my nose. "That's an insult to brown water."

"Hopefully the coffee's better at Banner Hill."

I looked up at him. "We're going there?"

"Yes."

"Right *now?*"

"Of course not. I need to put on a shirt and shoes first."

"Fine," I said, picking up the other coffee cup. "But first, you've gotta try this. It's really not that bad."

Chapter Twelve

"That looks like the place," I said.

Grayson whistled long and low. "You sure?"

"Yeah. I recognize it from the website."

Grayson pulled the RV to a stop in front of a single-story, red-brick building. White, concrete-block additions had been cobbled onto both sides of the main structure. A string of small outbuildings sprouted like toadstools over a half-acre campus of asphalt parking lots and intermittent strips of patchy, threadbare lawn.

A huge oak tree shaded Banner Hill's front yard. Under it, a few droopy-seated park benches languished in the shade. Overall, the place reminded me of a third-world elementary school that had fallen from the sky onto a post-war parking lot.

A couple of old guys in wheelchairs were lined up along the brick wall outside the front door, smoking and squinting like geriatric peeping-Toms, the mid-morning sun filtering through the oak tree's thick branches.

"I don't think Banner Hill is gonna make the cover of *Architectural Digest* anytime soon," I quipped.

When Grayson didn't reply, I turned to face him. He hadn't cut the ignition. Instead, he was staring at the steering wheel, chewing his bottom lip.

"What's up?" I asked.

He shook his head and glanced over at the building. "Something doesn't feel right."

"Why? Were you expecting a welcome committee?"

"Not exactly." Grayson studied me for a moment with his unreadable green eyes. "Where are the reporters, Drex? Three vets missing, and not a single media van, cop car, nosy neighbor, nothing."

I cringed. Grayson had yet again had to point out the obvious to me.

"Maybe nobody reported them missing," I said, mostly in an attempt to save face.

"Hmm. I suppose that's possible." His eyes shifted back to the building. "But why?"

"Where did Garth get his intel about guys going missing?" I asked.

"From the guy who cuts his hair."

I nearly choked. "We're here based on the ramblings of a barber who thinks mullets are still a valid fashion statement?"

Grayson pursed his lips. "Not exactly. The barber's grandfather is living here. His name is Melvin Haplets."

"Oh."

"According to Melvin, the men here are slowly fading away."

I glanced at three old men lined up in wheelchairs by the front door. "Uh ... isn't that the whole point of this place?"

"Disappearing without a trace isn't." Grayson's gaze fell back on me.

"No. You're right," I said, ditching my snarky attitude. "Do you have any working theories?"

"One." Grayson held out two fingers, forming a V.

"Victory?" I asked.

"No."

"Veterans?"

"No."

"Vanishing?"

"No."

"Okay, Grayson, I give up. What, then?"

"Vampires."

I nearly choked. "Vampires? Get real!"

"Don't be so quick to discount vampirism," Grayson said. "Florida has a rich history of believers."

"Yeah? Name one."

Grayson smiled. "Okay, if you insist."

Oh, crap. Here we go again. Another of Grayson's drive-by "factings."

"Back in 2000, a guy from Tampa calling himself 'The Impaler' ran for the senate. He also made a bid for president of the United States in 2004 and 2008, telling reporters he wanted to become the first vampire president."

I cringed. "You're making that up."

"Nope. I listened to the TV interview myself. I've got to say, The Impaler had some well-thought-out opinions on capital punishment and veterans issues. Must've brushed up on things when he served on the Executive Committee of the Hillsborough County Republican Party. You know, before he went over to 'the V-side.'"

"One lone case," I said.

"Hardly," Grayson laughed. "Nowadays, people say they see vampires everywhere. Not long ago, a guy in Cape Coral was caught on video climbing atop a police cruiser and gyrating to the sweet tunes of *Rich Girl*."

I frowned. "Are you saying all Hall & Oates are vampires?"

"Hmm. I never thought about that."

"Ugh! So, what's your point, Grayson?"

"Well, after the guy finished his dance number atop the cruiser, he tore off the windshield wipers for good measure. Then he jumped down, grabbed an American flag, and waved it around until he was taken into custody. According to the Lee County police affidavit, the man's solo act was inspired by 'a woman with fangs.' The man claimed she'd threatened him and scared him out of his home. He was absolutely convinced a human sacrifice involving vampires was about to occur."

"That didn't really happen, did it?"

"Sure did. The Lee County Sheriff's Office released the video. I saw it myself."

"Geez. Did they find out why he got on top of the police car?"

"Yes. He said he was 'looking for the Sheriff of Nottingham to help him stop the slaughter of small children.'"

I cringed. "There couldn't be any truth to that, could there?"

Grayson shrugged. "Who knows? They never caught the vampire woman who was allegedly harassing him."

"Or the meth lab that sold him the drugs." I shook my head. "Okay. Two totally isolated instances. That doesn't mean Florida's overrun with vampires."

"Then how do you explain the old guy in Daytona Beach who burned down his own house after screaming vampires were going to get him?"

"What?"

Grayson nodded. "It happened. And the guy was probably the same age as the old men sitting over there."

Grayson pointed back to the old guys smoking on the front porch of the nursing home.

"Really?" I asked.

"Absolutely."

"What happened?"

"The old guy went berserk. He broke out a few windows with his cane, then threw some ceiling insulation on the stove to really get the party started. Once the place was going up in flames, he grabbed a knife and started shouting, 'The vampires are going to defend themselves.'"

I shook my head. "That really happened?"

"Yes. And from what I hear, the house was a total loss. But on the bright side, nobody got hurt. And, he avoided being Baker-Acted because they couldn't prove he was incompetent."

"So ... the old man was sane?"

"Apparently so. So, do you need any more proof vampires are alive and well? I've got plenty more examples."

"No. That's enough." I frowned and shook my head. "Geez. What's the world coming to?"

"The same as always," Grayson said. "The world's always had its prophets, Drex. Some go down in history as heroes. Others just go down."

"So, what do we do now?" I asked. "Should we go interview Melvin Haplets?"

"That's the idea. But I doubt they'll let us just wander in." Grayson put his hand on the door handle. "I've got a plan. Leave your Glock behind and follow my lead."

Grayson pushed open his door, hopped out of the RV, and slammed the door behind him.

"Wait!" I said, fishing through my purse for my gun. I shoved it under my seat and scrambled after him. "What plan?" I called out.

"We're brother and sister," he said as I sprinted to catch up with him as he marched up the sidewalk. "We're looking for a new home for granny."

"Okay, we're siblings," I said to his back. "But what if they don't have any rooms?"

Grayson spun on his heels and eyed me as if I'd just confessed I was made of cream cheese. "According to my calculations, Drex, they should have at least *three* fairly recent openings."

My shoulders sagged. "Oh. Yeah."

He turned back toward the facility. "Keep up, and keep sharp."

"Yes, sir," I said, then mentally kicked myself in the ass.

Elf surveys and bathroom booties be damned. Nick Grayson might've been a kook about some things, but when it came to detective skills, he had me beat by a redneck mile.

Chapter Thirteen

Grayson saluted as he passed the clot of old men congregated in wheelchairs outside the main entrance to Banner Hill. I offered them a weak smile as I passed by. One smiled back. The others stared, zombie-like, at some point of interest apparently only they could envision.

Just inside the entryway, a middle-aged woman with a mousy brown helmet of hair sat stoically, entrenched at her station in the cheap office chair behind the reception desk. Her tired face, beige polyester dress, and dreary disposition matched the nursing home's decor so perfectly that for a second I wondered if she'd been delivered in a box along with the rest of the uninspired furnishings.

"Hello. Ms. Draper?" Grayson asked, and flashed a charming smile.

"Ms. Draper's the owner," the woman said in a tone that mirrored none of Grayson's cheerfulness, whether it was fake or not. "I'm Ms. Gable. What can I do for you?"

"Oh. My mistake." Grayson smiled. "Forgive me. You have the air of ownership about you. An elegant pride, if you will."

The plump, frazzled woman sized Grayson up as if he were selling baby seal meat and she was head of Greenpeace. "Uh-huh. What do you want?"

Grayson smiled brightly and glanced over at me. "We have an appointment to tour the facilities. My sister Ginger and I are thinking of placing our granny here at Banner Hill."

"We only take men," Gable said bluntly.

Her red lips curled into a petty-tyrant smile. Mighty Casey was striking out. I stepped up to bat.

"Excuse me, Fred," I said, pushing Grayson aside.

He shot me a weird look. I knew why. For some reason, whenever I poured on the charm, it always came with a syrupy Southern accent. Don't ask me why.

I cleared my throat, moved a cheap vase of plastic flowers out of my face, and smiled sheepishly at Ms. Gable. "Yes. Well, Fred here would never admit it, but 'granny' is what our dear old granddad wants to be called nowadays. You know how it is. Dementia can be such an unpredictable thing."

Gable's face softened a notch. "Yes, it can. But at Banner Hill, we prefer veterans."

"Grandpa served in Vietnam, ma'am," I said. "By the way, I think it's super great that you want to honor those who've served our fine country."

"And their VA benefits guarantee payment," Grayson said.

I stepped on Grayson's foot, then leaned over the reception desk. "Yes, that's truly a blessing for everyone."

Gable eyed us both. "Now, this grandfather of yours. Is he ambulatory? This isn't a lockdown unit. We don't take wanderers."

I shook my head. "No. The poor thing can barely walk."

"He uses a cane," Grayson said.

Gable frowned.

"But mostly a wheelchair," I offered.

That cheered her up. Gable smiled and said, "Well, we do have a recent opening. Ms. Draper isn't here right now. Let me show you around."

"THIS WAY," GABLE SAID as she waddled down the facility's main corridor in shoes that appeared to have been constructed from road-killed marshmallows. The bleak hallway's sole decorative touches were metal grab bars and a smattering of cheap artwork in even cheaper frames.

Grayson and I trailed behind Gable like baby ducks. She stopped in front of a door with a small window in it.

"Have a look," she said, opening the door. "This is the rec room."

The room smelled of disinfectant, but was otherwise pleasant enough, given its overall clinical setting. On one side of the room, a couple of plastic-lined couches and lounge chairs had been grouped around a large-screen TV. On the other side, a half-dozen small tables were set up with checkers, chess, and other board games. In one corner, an old guy was passed out in a chair snoring, a book open on his lap.

Gable smiled. "One day, Mr. Green might just finish that book of his. He usually reads in his room, but he's taken to sitting in that chair since his roommate went mi—*ahem*—passed away three days ago."

"Oh," I said. "What happened?"

Gable looked at me funny. "He *died*. Follow me."

Gable turned and led us further down the hall to the kitchen to inspect the food preparation facilities.

"We're mighty proud of our food service here," she said, and opened a locked, metal door.

Inside, two rotund women in white scrubs and hairnets eyed us cautiously before giving us friendly, possibly even sincere smiles. I suddenly felt like a seventh grader standing in the cafeteria line staring at the lunchroom ladies, worrying that a double portion of French fries might give me more pimples.

"Very good," Grayson said to the pair, as if he were performing a military inspection. "Carry on, ladies."

"Wait," I said. I pointed at a metal tray. It was heaped with yellow clumps of glop dotted with suspicious red chunks—like a fake vomit omelet. "What's that?" I asked one of the women.

"Breakfast leftovers," she said. "Powdered scrambled eggs and Spam. You want some?"

"Oh. Sounds tasty," I said, with less enthusiasm than I'd meant to muster. "But I already ate."

"Why powdered eggs?" Grayson asked Gable.

Gable smirked as if she'd just told a private joke. "Like I said, most of the men we serve here are veterans. A majority have mental health issues. Most of the time, they think they're back in their military units. So we try to accommodate them by recreating G.I. rations. They eat 'em up, don't they, girls?"

The two women laughed. "Yes ma'am."

One woman with red curls peeking out of her chef's cap said, "Today's the first day in ages we've had any leftovers. Probably because of all the recent d—"

"*Ahem*," Gable growled forcefully, silencing the woman with a scathing look. "Ms. Frasier, I'll remind you that here at Banner Hill, we keep our clientele's business confidential."

Frasier looked puzzled. "But I didn't—"

Another glare from Gable sealed Frasier's lips for good.

"This way," Gable said to Grayson and me. "I'll show you what I mean about hearty appetites."

After taking another quick gander at the vomit omelet, I was skeptical. But when we stepped into the cafeteria, sure enough, the old guys inside were gumming their green Jell-O like there was no tomorrow.

"What unit you in?" one old man asked Grayson as we passed his table.

"Eighty-third," he said. "You?"

"Sixty, you piss-ant," he said, then shoveled another spoonful of gelatin into his toothless maw.

"See what I mean?" Gable said. "All they think about is war times. How about some coffee and cookies?"

My stomach gurgled. "Sounds delightful." I was starved. Grayson was so eager to get here that he hadn't even let us stop for donuts on the way.

Who in their right mind could forget about food?

We sat down at one of the worn, laminate-topped tables while Gable went to fetch coffee across the room.

"Spam. That could be significant," Grayson said under his breath.

"What do you mean?" I whispered.

Before he had a chance to reply, Gable returned with three cups of coffee and a plate stacked with vanilla sandwich cookies. She handed me a cup.

I took a sip. The coffee was so weak I almost longed for the crap at the Dilly Dally Motor Court.

Gable noticed my reaction. "Some of the men here drink coffee all day, so we water it down," she said.

"Ah," Grayson said.

I took a bite of cookie and could practically taste the expiration date. I tucked the rest of it into my napkin and tried to warn Grayson, but I wasn't quick enough. He popped a whole one into his mouth and nearly choked.

"So, Ms. Gable, what's your availability?" he asked, then proceeded to have a small coughing fit.

"Availability?" Gable asked.

Grayson took a slurp of coffee, swallowed hard, then glanced over at me. "Yes. Ginger and I'd like to bring gramps in for a tour, but we don't want to get his hopes up if there's no room at the inn."

"Tell you what," Gable said. "Fax me a copy of his military ID and monthly pension check, and I'll hold a space for him for twenty-four hours."

"That's mighty gracious of you," I said sweetly.

"It certainly is," Grayson said. "But I hope to return with him this afternoon, if that's amenable. He's quite anxious to find his new forever home."

"Certainly," Gable said. "Does four o'clock work for you?"

Grayson beamed. "Perfect."

"What's your grandfather's name?" Gable asked.

Before I could reply, Grayson blurted, "George Burns."

I closed my eyes so no one could see them roll.

Awesome, Grayson. I'm Ginger. You're Fred. Gramps is George Burns. Now all we need is Gracie and we've got our very own tragic variety show.

Chapter Fourteen

Back at the reception desk, we thanked Ms. Gable and promised to return with Grandpa Burns for an interview for possible admission to Banner Hill. As the exit door closed behind us, I grabbed Grayson by the arm.

"Geez, Grayson, I thought we were here to *find* missing war veterans, not to create more out of thin air!"

"Basic investigative tactic," Grayson said. "If we're going to track down the cryptid turning vets into Captain Crunch, we need to familiarize ourselves with the layout and players. Did you notice? None of the vets wore nametags."

"No. I didn't notice."

Grayson frowned. "That's going to make it harder to find Melvin Haplets." He motioned with his chin.

I turned to see the same three old smokers in wheelchairs who'd been staring at us when we'd walked in earlier that morning.

"Hello, fellows," I said. "Would one of you happen to be Melvin Haplets?"

They all exchanged glances with each other. "No. We don't associate with him," said the man in the middle.

"Why not?" I asked.

"He's a fuddy-duddy," the same spokesman said, initiating a round of dry, cough-like laughter from the trio of geezers.

"Yes," I said. "Nobody likes a fuddy-duddy." I turned to Grayson, my eyes pleading for direction. I was at a lost for what to say or do next.

Grayson grabbed me by the arm. "Have a nice day, gentlemen," he said, and tugged me down the sidewalk.

"Don't stir the pot on Melvin," he whispered. "It might make him the next target."

"Target?"

"Yes. Every night for the past three nights, a resident vet has gone MIA. I think we're going to need eyes on the place overnight if we're going to catch the illicit action."

"Illicit action?" I said. "Look at those guys. They can't even *walk* and *they're* the *cool* guys."

"Exactly, Drex. They're sitting ducks, and it looks like somebody's got a taste for Vietnamese gamecock."

"What?"

Grayson turned and walked briskly toward the RV. He only had three steps on me, but given his long legs, I had to sprint to catch up with him.

"What are you saying?" I asked, jogging to keep up. "That vampires prefer Asian cuisine?"

"No. And don't forget. Vampires are just one of the working theories at the moment. Did you know that Spam is a favorite food in Papua New Guinea?"

Wha??? Either I missed something or Grayson is insane.

"Grayson, what are you talking about?"

"*Spam*, Drex." Grayson stopped beside the RV.

"Spam?" I asked, leaning up against the door so he couldn't open it.

"Yes. The breakfast omelet they served had Spam in it," he said, using his fingers to put air quotes around the word Spam.

I shook my head. "Maybe I need some real coffee, Grayson, but I'm just not following you."

He cocked his head to one side. "In Papua New Guinea, the Korowai tribe believes it's necessary to kill and eat any person they believe to have been possessed by a khakua demon."

My face went slack. "Oh. Well, of course. How silly of me not to make the connection."

Grayson shrugged. "It happens." He reached for the handle to the driver's door. I slapped it away.

"Grayson, I was being facetious! What are you saying? That the spirit of a khakua arrived at Banner Hill in a Spam can?"

Grayson's eyebrow rose a notch. "Well, not exactly. But I have to say, that's an interesting theory. Did you ever see that movie about—"

"Grayson! Just tell me what *your* theory is, okay?"

"I thought I did already."

I shot him some side eye. "Humor me."

"Fine. Up until the 1970s, the Korowai still practiced cannibalism. Then they were introduced to Spam. They said it tasted like long pig."

"Long pig?"

"Yes. Human flesh. You see, Drex, Spam is the modern-day cannibal's equivalent to cold cuts. It's 'Man in a Can,' if you will."

My stomach flopped. "What?"

"Someone at Banner Hill enjoys the taste of human flesh."

I cringed. "You've got to be kidding!"

"Negatory."

"Okay. Say that's true. Why start killing vets? Why not just keep buying Spam?"

"Perhaps someone's got a hankering for the real thing. Or, maybe they're just trying to stretch the old food budget. You know, kill two old birds with one stone."

"That's crazy."

"Crazy like a khakua." Grayson grinned and opened the RV door. "So, let's go find us a gramps, shall we?"

"What? Where? At the Gramps-R-Us store?"

Grayson smiled. "If only. By the way, good save in there. Turning granny into grandpa. 'Dementia is an unpredictable thing.' I'm going to have to remember that one."

I climbed into the passenger seat. "It's true. My Aunt Betty had dementia. She used to put her socks in her soup."

Grayson's right eyebrow arched. "You don't say."

I sighed. "You know, the whole cannibalism thing aside, in cases like Aunt Betty's, I guess Banner Hill wouldn't be the worst place to spend the rest of your life."

Grayson shrugged. "Are you kidding? They've got no icky guy in there."

My nose crinkled. "Are you blind? No offense to those poor vets, but I saw plenty of icky guys in there."

Grayson shook his head and turned the key in the ignition. "No. *Ikigai*. It's a Japanese term. It means 'a reason to get up in the morning.' In Okinawa they live past a hundred because of ikigai."

I smirked. "Or, maybe with all the icky guys around, it just *seems* like a hundred years."

Grayson groaned, then looked past me through the passenger window. "Who's that?"

A man's muffled voice sounded to my right. "Hey, man. You guys really shouldn't park here."

I turned to see the wide chest and shoulders of a well-built black man in short-sleeved beige scrubs. He bent down until his head came into view. An open, friendly smile crowned his lips. Dreadlocks poked out from the beige bandana on his head.

I rolled down the window. "Excuse me?"

He poked a thumb over his shoulder. "The folks there ... across the street from Banner Hill. Well, let's just say this is a bad place to park. Tires have been known to ... you know ... *disappear*."

I followed the trajectory of the man's thumb over to the low-budget, Section Eight housing across the street from Banner Hill. The small, concrete hovels bore the unmistakable, dusty pallor of desperation.

Dirt yards. Faded paint. Dismal future.

"I lost a few tires myself," the man said, then laughed. "Then my whole car. Then my bike. Now I just take an Uber to work."

"You work here? At Banner Hill?" I asked.

"Yes. Just getting off shift."

"Hmm," Grayson said. "You need a lift?"

The man's face lit up. "Really? You sure?"

"Absolutely. I'm Nick Grayson. This is Bobbie Drex."

"I'm Stanley Johnson," the man said. "But I got to warn you, I live about ten miles from here."

"Climb in, Stanley," Grayson said. "Point us in the direction of the best taco stand in town, and your fare is paid in full."

I grinned and opened the door to let Stanley in, then crawled out of my seat and took a hunched-over position in the narrow passage leading to the main cabin of the RV.

"Tacos, huh?" Stanley said. "Well, let me tell you. You haven't lived until you've tried Topless Tacos."

My smile evaporated into a tight, white line.

Great. And here I'd thought I'd just left all the icky guys behind.

Chapter Fifteen

I kept my mouth shut and tried to be a grown-ass woman about the fact that I was going to a topless taco joint with two strange men, both of whom were—to my great irritation—attractive enough to keep my feelings about them seesawing in perpetual conflict.

Why is it handsome jerks seem to have that mysterious power over women? Or is it just me?

I'd relinquished my seat to Stanley, so I scooted back to the main cabin of the RV. I plopped onto the couch and conducted an extended test of how much pressure per square inch the enamel on my molars could take before cracking.

After a while, curiosity overpowered my anger. I leaned forward and craned my ear to listen in on the conversation Stanley and Grayson were having up in the front cab.

"How long have you worked at Banner Hill?" Grayson asked.

"Not long. Six weeks or so." Stanley's deep voice danced with the lyrical lilt of the Caribbean. "What brings you two to Banner Hill?"

"We're looking for a place to put gramps."

"*Your* daddy or the missus'?"

"What?" Grayson asked. "Oh. We're not married."

I sat up straight and scowled. Had Grayson sounded *relieved* we weren't married?

The nerve!

Stanley laughed. "Brother and sister, then?"

"Not a chance," Grayson said. "We're partners."

Not a chance? What's that *supposed to mean?*

"Uh-huh," Stanley said. "So, in other words, you two living in sin, huh?"

"No. Not in sin," Grayson quipped. "In *an RV*."

Stanley chuckled. "You're a funny guy, Grayson. I like you. This is a nice little rig you got, too. I had one kind of like it in Haiti."

"Haiti?" Grayson said. "Tough place."

"It can be."

"So, you're here on a green card?" Grayson asked.

"Sort of. Workin' on it, you know? Sometimes you got to pretend. Fake it till you make it, am I right?"

Grayson laughed.

"Hey man, do you mind if I slip out of these scrubs? I got a change of clothes in my duffle here."

"Not at all," Grayson said. "But it might be easier in the back."

"I heard that. Pretty tight up here."

Before I could scoot back on the couch, Stanley's head popped into the main cabin. My ears burned from being caught eavesdropping.

"Hey, sister. Just going to get into my civvies." Stanley held up his duffle bag.

"No problem," I said. "I'll just—"

Stanley flopped down on the couch beside me. I watched, open mouthed, as he wriggled out of his drawstring scrub pants and tugged them free over his white leather tennis shoes.

He stood. I gawked at his gorgeous glutes as he yanked his shirt off over his head, revealing bulging biceps and washboard abs that erased Grayson's six pack right out of my spinning noggin.

Stanley caught me staring and smiled shyly. "Oh. Sorry, Miss Drex. I hope you don't mind. I'm so used to—"

"No worries," I whispered, barely able to speak.

I knew it was rude, but I couldn't tear my eyes from the man's physique. I'd never seen a male specimen so suave he could actually rock an outfit of leopard-print underpants and white shoes and socks. Like a rabid pro-wrestling fan, not even one little part of me wanted to snicker at Jungle Jock.

"I'll be quick," Stanley said, and unzipped his duffle. He tugged out a pair of jeans and a red pullover sweater.

I watched in awe as his muscular legs, arms and chest disappeared underneath the denim and knit. Then, like some sexy cologne commercial, Stanley untied the beige bandana on his head and shook loose his dreadlocks so they could swing wild and free.

"Hand me those?" he said.

"Huh? Oh!" I unfroze, closed my drooling mouth, and handed Stanley the scrubs he'd tossed onto the couch.

"Thanks." He shot me that shy, sexy smile again.

As Stanley stuffed the scrubs into the duffle bag, something fell to the floor. I reached down and picked it up. It was a little leather bag tied with leather strapping—about the right size to hold a handful of pills, or maybe a nickel bag of pot.

"What's this?" I asked, handing it back to him.

"Oh, shit," he said. "Don't tell nobody, okay?"

"Tell who what?" I shot him a look I hoped was stern but still cool and sexy. "Are you doing drugs?"

Stanley's eyes widened. "No!" He tucked the little bag away in his jeans pocket. Then he glanced around and leaned over to whisper in my ear. "It's voodoo."

My left eyebrow raised an inch. "Voodoo?"

"Yeah. For protection."

My eyes grew wide. "Protection from *what?*"

Stanley glanced out the little window above the couch at the scenery whizzing by. He bit his lip and gave me a tight, close-lipped smile.

"Looks like we're almost there," he said. "I better go give your man Grayson some directions."

Then, before I could reply, Stanley and his duffle bag disappeared into the front of the RV.

Chapter Sixteen

"Turn here," Stanley's voice emanated from the front cab of the RV.

My fingers curled around the couch's armrest. A second later, I lurched sideways as Grayson hooked a hasty left. Once both of my butt cheeks were back on the couch, I turned and stood with my knees on the cushions. I glanced out the window above the couch. A sign for One Mile Stretch Road whizzed by.

A moment later, the RV came to a halt in front of a low-slung, concrete-block building. It was painted gunmetal gray. A dark-blue awning proclaiming TOPLESS TACOS hung over the front of the building like the Neanderthal brow-ridges of every caveman jerk who patronized the place.

I sneered.

So this is what a topless place looks like. Figures.

I clamped my jaw shut and stomped over to the side door of the RV. Stanley and Grayson were waiting for me in the parking lot. As I climbed out, Stanley shot me a tight-lipped smile. His eyes seemed to plead, "Let's keep this whole voodoo thing our little secret, okay?"

I scowled at him.

Why do all the good-looking guys have to be pervs?

Stanley flinched at my angry expression, then quickly recovered his smile. "You two are in for a treat," he said. "Follow me."

I prepared my women's rights speech in my head as he led us inside the building. But when I looked around, I was surprised to find that inside, the place actually looked like a legitimate restaurant.

I stared at the gleaming, red tabletops wondering where the dance poles were. The only tempting pictures on the walls featured empanadas and nachos. Not a scantily-clad bimbo in sight.

A cute, young woman in rather modest attire for a strip club came up to us carrying four menus.

Can't count to three, huh, honey?

"Sit anywhere you'd like," she said brightly. "I'll be right back to take care of you."

I bet you will.

I plopped down in a chair and glared at the menu like The Church Lady in an SNL skit. Then I read something that made me want to belt out a chorus of *Amazing Grace*.

"Oh, *look*, Grayson," I said cheerily. "TOPLESS stands for tomatoes, onions, peppers, lettuce, extra cheese, salsa and sour cream. Isn't that *clever?*" I shot him my best *stick that in your face and suck it* grin.

Grayson's wandering eyes settled on the menu. "Oh."

"What's good here," I asked my new best friend, Stanley.

He shot me the kind of tentative smile reserved for people with severe mood disorders. "Um ... the tofu tostadas are super yum."

"Hmm," Grayson grunted.

I smiled to myself. The disappointed look on Grayson's face would keep me grinning for at least the next three months.

AFTER TAKING A BITE of his Mahi taco, Grayson finally let go of his grudge and gave Topless Tacos the thumbs up. He washed down his mouthful with a sip of ginger beer and said, "Solid recommendation, Stanley. And, like I promised, lunch is on me."

Stanley let out a tinkling laugh. "Glad you like it, man."

The door to the restaurant opened, snuffing out Stanley's good humor like a paper match in a hurricane. Our new friend stared blankly at the man coming through the door.

It was a uniformed police officer.

The cop glanced our way and nodded at Stanley. "Johnson," the policeman said curtly, then headed to the cash register to pick up his take-out order.

I studied Stanley's face. The casual air about him was gone. In its place was a quiet, almost secretive determination. The best way to explain it was that Stanley had the look of a man who knew there was no such thing as a free lunch, but had decided to take his chances anyway—and lost.

The cop picked up his food and headed for the exit. He opened the door, then, when he was halfway out, said aloud to no one in particular, "Be careful of the company you keep." Then he disappeared out the door.

I glanced over at Grayson, wondering if the cop's remark had been meant as a joke, random advice, or a not-so-subtle warning. And who had he intended it for? Stanley? Grayson? Me?

"What's up with that?" Grayson asked Stanley.

"Officer Holbrook," Stanley said. "He's the cop who took down all my reports when my stuff got stolen outside of Banner Hill. I get the feeling he thinks I'm a liar."

"That's bull-crap," I said. "If he's not treating you right, why don't you report him?"

Stanley sighed. "Don't pay to stir up troubled waters when you got no piss-pot to bail your boat out with."

Geez. This guy mixes up metaphors worse than Grayson.

"I understand perfectly," Grayson said.

Of course you do.

I felt an eye roll coming on, but stopped it when Grayson locked his green eyes on mine.

"You can't look to the law for help when you're not exactly abiding it yourself, am I right Stanley?"

I shifted my gaze over to Stanley. He was nodding his dreadlocks. "Exactly, man."

Wait a minute. Is mixing metaphors an actual language? A kind of secret, male-to-male communication? If so, these two guys could be code-talkers.

"Well, you don't need to confess your sins to us," Grayson said to Stanley. "We operate outside normal parameters, ourselves."

Stanley's head cocked to one side. "Really?"

"Yeah," I said. "We're parano—"

Grayson kicked my shin. "We're paranoid about getting gramps into a good nursing home."

Stanley chewed on that information while I rubbed my shin. Finally, he said, "You look like good folks. Take my advice. Find another place for gramps. I wouldn't put my Pop Pop in Banner Hill. No way."

"Because of the *voodoo* problem?" I asked, my eyes darting to catch Grayson's reaction to my insider knowledge.

Stanley shot me a *what the hell are you talking about* look. Grayson followed suit.

I scowled. So much for winning one for the Gipper.

"Voodoo?" Grayson asked.

Stanley glanced around, then hunched his head down closer to his shoulders. "Something weird going down over there at the Banner, man."

"What do you mean, weird?" Grayson asked. "Have they been serving Spam more often?"

Stanley eyed Grayson like he was either a genius or a fool. I knew the look. I had it down pat myself.

"No. The men folk we been taking care of ...." Stanley sighed. "It's like something's sappin' the life juices out of 'em."

"So your voodoo charm isn't working?" I asked, keeping my eyes on Grayson. My partner stared at me as if I might be crazy.

So that's how it is? You're not gonna give me one ounce *of credit for knowing about the voodoo?*

"Voodoo charm?" Grayson asked, turning to Stanley. "Are you worried about the khakua?"

Stanley frowned. "No, man. Voodoo don't work like that. They called a plumber. The toilets were all fixed last week."

I would've laughed if it hadn't been for the tragic fact that less than an hour ago, I'd actually considered these guys to be among the most attractive and intelligent I'd come across in years.

Years!

Stanley pulled the tiny leather pouch from his pocket and showed it to Grayson.

Grayson eyed it skeptically. "So, what's the voodoo bag for?"

Stanley's eyes darted around the restaurant, then he leaned in across the table. "For the haint," he whispered.

Grayson's brow furrowed. "Who's 'the haint'?"

Stanley shot me an incredulous look. I shrugged and said, "He's from up north."

Grayson turned to me, a confused look on his face.

The man knows about a New Guinea khakua demon but not Southern haints? Ugh!

I groaned. "He means the place is *haunted,* Grayson."

Stanley licked his lips and rubbed the little leather bag between his thumb and forefinger. "She's right," he whispered. "There's some kind of spirit roaming the halls of Banner Hill, and it's out for blood."

Chapter Seventeen

"A malevolent spirit is loose at Banner Hill?" Grayson's green eyes lit up like twin traffic lights. "Tell me more."

Stanley glanced around, checking to see if anyone else was listening. Topless Tacos was empty except for us and another couple across the room. From the way they were shoveling nachos into their maws, I figured they couldn't hear us over the sound of crunching tortilla chips.

Stanley must've surmised the same. He leaned in over the table. His dark-brown eyes shifted from mine to Grayson's, then back again. "I seen her myself. That's why I gots me this protection amulet."

"What's inside it?" I asked, nodding at the little leather pouch.

"Don't know." Stanley shook his head. "If you look inside, you break faith. The voodoo spell won't work."

"Come on. That's bull," I said.

"Faith is the basis of *all* belief systems," Grayson said.

I opened my mouth to argue the point, then shut it. Maybe he was right.

"I probably don't need this thing, anyway," Stanley said, twirling the pouch by its leather string. "Old Mildred don't worry me too much. After all, it was her who gots me my job in the first place."

"Old Mildred hired you?" Grayson asked. "Are you referring to Ms. Draper or Ms. Gable?"

"Neither," I said. "Old Mildred's the haint, right Stanley?"

Stanley smiled at me. "That's right."

"So you're saying a spirit got you your job at Banner Hill?" Grayson asked.

"Round about, yeah." Stanley nodded. "Nina, a friend of mine, told me about the job opening at Banner Hill. She said they were looking for a *male* nurse, on account of Old Mildred."

"I don't follow you," Grayson said.

Stanley smiled slyly. "Old Mildred's a green-eyed devil, like you Grayson."

"Me? I'm no devil."

"He means she's the *jealous* sort," I said, translating for Grayson again. He might've been book smart, but Grayson didn't know his idioms or colloquialisms worth a crap.

"That's right," Stanley said. "Old Mildred's jealous as the day is long. She don't like no other women hangin' around. She done run off the last three women they hired at Banner Hill. That's why they took a chance on me. I was the only guy who applied."

"No way," Grayson said.

Stanley's eyebrow went up. "Look around for yourself. All the night nurses and orderlies there are men folk."

Huh. And here I thought that was because of the icky guy requirement.

"What about the manager, Ms. Gable?" Grayson asked.

"She don't work nights. Flies out of there at dusk like a bat out of hell."

"Have you actually *seen* Old Mildred?" I asked Stanley.

"Yeah. Seen her plain as I'm seeing you right now."

A shiver crawled up my spine. "It doesn't scare you—working with a ghost lurking around in the building? What if Old Mildred decides to take you next?"

Stanley studied me for a moment, then shrugged. "She won't. We got us an arrangement."

"What sort of arrangement?" Grayson asked.

"The Schultz, man."

Grayson nodded. "I see."

"The Schultz?" I asked.

"I know nothing, I see nothing," Grayson said. "Like that sergeant on *Hogan's Heroes*."

Somehow, I managed not to roll my eyes. "Oh. Right."

Stanley nodded. "I let Old Mildred do her thing, she lets me do mine. I set that right with her my first night on the job."

"How?" I asked. "What happened?"

Stanley glanced around the restaurant again. It was empty except for us and the trail of nacho crumbs that had fallen from the laps of the couple who'd just left.

"On my very first shift, I was walkin' down the hall in the middle of the night and felt something coming up behind me. I turned around and that's when I seen her. Old Mildred. She was all hunched over by the exit door, starin' at me."

"How do you know she was a spirit?" Grayson asked.

"She was all fuzzy-like," Stanley said. He raised his hands and spread them out before him like a fan. "She was surrounded in this dim, purplish light. I knew right then and there I had to choose."

"Choose whether she was a ghost or not?" I asked.

"No, man." Stanley shook his head. "Choose whether or not I wanted to keep my apartment. The rent was due in a week. I needed the paycheck. I decided on the spot to make my peace with Old Mildred."

Grayson leaned in closer. "How'd you do that?"

Stanley smiled slyly. "I give the old gal a compliment. She *is* a *woman*, after all."

Grayson's cheek dimpled. "What'd you say to her?"

Stanley grinned. "I said, 'Hey, you gots a nice glow about you.'"

Grayson nodded. "Well played."

Stanley picked up the tiny voodoo bag. "Yeah. But next morning, I went and got me this here amulet anyway. Women can be a tricky folk. It don't hurt to have a little something extra backing you up. You know what I mean?"

I nudged Stanley on the arm. "What did Mildred do when you complimented her?"

"She showed me her teeth. What she had left, anyway." Stanley chewed his lip. "Pretty sure it was a smile."

"Then what happened?" Grayson asked. "Did she dematerialize?"

"Nope. She turned around and headed the other way. That's when I seen the poor woman was a *jorobada*."

I nearly spewed my mouthful of iced tea. "A chupacabra?"

"No," Stanley said. "Jorobada. What you call it? A lump-back. You know. Like the whale."

"Humpback?" Grayson asked. "Did you see her flukes?"

"I think he means hunchback," I said.

"That's it!" Stanley said. "Hunchback."

"I see," Grayson said. "Tell me. Was Mildred more the *Quasimodo* type, or the *Igor* type?"

Stanley shot Grayson a sideways glance, then stared at me. I was powerless to help him. It was taking all the strength I had not to flee the scene myself.

"I get the feeling you two gots some strange business going on," Stanley said finally. "You ain't really here to put your old pop-pop in a home, are you?"

Grayson shook his head. "No. We're more interested in your friend Mildred."

Stanley's mouth twitched. "What you want with Old Mildred? She's a harmless old soul."

Grayson's eyebrow flat-lined. "I thought you said she was out for blood."

Stanley shrugged. "Well, it might be blood. I can't say for sure. The men's been disappearing. And Old Mildred's definitely looking for something. Could be they gots something to do with each other, or maybe not."

"Could Old Mildred be draining their vital juices?" Grayson asked.

Vital juices?

"All right," I said, clearing my throat. "Could we get serious here? Vets could be being kidnapped. We need to figure out who—or *what's*—responsible."

Stanley nodded. "Yeah. But how you gonna do that?"

"Via surreptitious surveillance, tracking, and evidence collection," Grayson said.

Translation: Lure them in Grayson's bedroom and collect samples of their scat.

"Hold up a minute," Stanley said, his back straightening. "Are you guys cops? FBI?"

"No," Grayson said. "Private investigators. We specialize in the unexplained."

"Unexplained?" Stanley asked.

"Yes, unexplained," I said sourly, shooting Grayson a smirk. "You know. Zombies. Vampires. Mothmen. That sort of thing."

Stanley's mouth fell open. "No shit."

"No shit," Grayson said, wagging his bushy eyebrows.

"Well, in that case, I got a story for you," Stanley said. "But you got to promise not to tell no police."

Chapter Eighteen

"Last night, I was minding my own business. You know, rearranging the supply closet," Stanley said, then crammed his mouth full of mango-tofu cheesecake.

"So, you were smoking a number," Grayson said, then slurped his coffee.

"Huh?" I grunted during the pregnant pause between the men's mouthfuls.

I was supposed to be typing notes on Grayson's laptop while he interviewed Stanley. But the two may as well have been man'splainin rocket science to a chimpanzee. Either that, or I was way less cool than I liked to think I was.

"How do you get 'smoking pot' out of 'rearranging the supply closet'?" I asked.

Grayson shot me a sideways glance, then locked eyes with Stanley. "Guess she's never worked retail."

Stanley laughed and gave me one of his shy, gleaming-white smiles. "Not much else to do at two in the mornin'."

Grayson nodded. "Go on."

Stanley licked cheesecake from his bottom lip. "Anyway, I just took my third toke when I started hearing voices."

"That must've been some good stuff," I said, trying to sound hip.

Grayson shut me down with a glance, then turned to Stanley. "Continue."

Stanley's eyebrows inched nearer to each other. "That's when I overheard two people talking out in the hall. Somebody said, '*We need another one.*'"

"Another what?" I asked.

Grayson locked eyes with me and shook his head. I scowled and looked down at the keyboard.

"Go on," he said to Stanley. "What did they say next?"

Stanley chewed his lip. "Something like, 'I can't take another one so soon. It'd be too suspicious.'"

"Were the voices men or women?" Grayson asked.

Stanley frowned. "Couldn't say for sure. It was mostly whispering."

Grayson nodded. "What else?"

Stanley sighed. "I slipped my roach back in my pocket and cracked the door open. You know, to get a peek—"

"Wait," I said. "Don't they drug test you guys?"

Stanley shrugged. "Sure. But grass don't count no more. If it did, they couldn't find nobody to work nowhere."

"Go on," Grayson said. "You were opening the door."

"Oh, yeah." Stanley exhaled. "But first, I waited until the smoke cleared—"

"Nice pun," I said.

"Pun?" Stanley asked.

Grayson stared me down, then ran a finger across his throat. I shut the hell up.

"What did you see?" Grayson asked.

"I thought I saw the shadow of Old Mildred on the wall, man. But then that damned roach started burning a hole my leg. Thought it was out."

I stopped typing and looked up at Grayson. He chewed his lip, then said, "Anything else?"

Stanley shook his head. Then, suddenly, he sat up straight in his chair. "Wait. I just remembered. I heard this strange sound. *Scree. Scree.* You know, like a squeaky wheel."

Grayson rubbed his chin. "Hmmm. A squeaky wheel gathers no moss."

Stanley nodded slowly. "*Exactly*, man."

I typed the words, *Really, God?* then backspaced over them.

"So then what happened?" Grayson asked.

"I snuck down the hall, following that freaky sound, man. Then I heard another noise. Sounded like the click the metal bars on the exit doors make. I peeked around the corner, but wasn't nobody there. Only an empty wheelchair sitting beside the glass doors."

"Hmm," Grayson said. "Is that unusual?"

"Kind of. Most guys at Banner Hill don't go nowhere without their chairs."

"Did you see anyone milling around outside? Staff members? Strangers?"

"No. But it was dark, so I didn't want to open the door, you know? But the wheelchair belonged to Charlie Perkins in 3F."

"How'd you know it was Charlie's chair?" Grayson asked.

"Because of that weird sound it made. I think one of the bearings is froze up on it."

Grayson nodded. "Proceed."

"Well, I wheeled Charlie's chair back to his room to check on him. He was gone. Like the others. Just vanished."

"Did you tell anyone?" I asked.

Stanley shook his head. "No. Not right away. I took the chair back to the exit doors. I figured I'd wait a bit. See if Charlie had just slipped out for a smoke or something."

My nose crinkled. "How could Charlie leave if he didn't have his wheelchair?"

"Not everybody in a wheelchair can't walk," Stanley said. "Some's just pure lazybones."

"Did you see anything else suspicious that night?" Grayson asked.

Stanley nodded. "Yeah. One thing."

My fingers poised with anticipation over the laptop keyboard.

"What?" Grayson asked.

Stanley chewed his lip thoughtfully. "Old man Windham's mole on his left cheek. I think that thing's turning color, you know?"

My fingers went limp.

"Did you report the incident the following morning?" Grayson asked.

Stanley shook his head. "No. I thought I'd monitor it for changes, first. See if it gets any bigger."

A tendon appeared in Grayson's neck. "I meant the disappearance of Charlie Perkins."

Stanley grimaced. "No way, man. You know how it is. Whoever smelt it dealt it. Am I right?"

Grayson sighed. "The law of the land."

My brow furrowed. "What?"

Grayson stared at me as if I were clueless, which, at that moment, I totally was.

"People who report crimes to the police often end up on the top of the suspect list," Grayson said.

"Exactly." Stanley bobbed his headful of dreadlocks. "That's why you got to promise you never heard any of this from *me*, okay?"

"If you're innocent, what does it matter?" I asked.

"Can't take the chance, man. I can't go back to Haiti."

My eyes grew wide. "Why? Are you a fugitive?"

Stanley's brown eyes stared at me pleadingly. "No, man. I just can't stand the sound of steel drums no more."

"Totally understandable," Grayson said, nodding thoughtfully. "Besides the abandoned wheelchair, did you see any strange lights, odd footprints, or whatnot?"

Stanley's left eyebrow rose. "You know, now that you mention it, I saw a strange, purple glow outside the door. The same kind I seen around Old Mildred."

"Interesting," Grayson said.

"Hold up," Stanley said. His eyes doubled in size. "You don't think these guys are gettin' beamed up by purple aliens or something, do you?"

Grayson pursed his lips. "Well, Stanley, that's what we're here to find out. So, any chance you know where we could rent a grandpa for the night?"

"You serious?" Stanley eyed Grayson and me. "What kind a kink you two into, man?"

"No kink," Grayson said. "We need gramps for bait."

Chapter Nineteen

"So, exactly how do you spell Balsijet?" Grayson asked the derelict gumming grits across the booth from us at a local diner called, quite aptly, Johnny Grits.

About a half an hour ago, we'd dropped Stanley off at his apartment. Then, following our new operative's advice, we'd headed straight for the nearest plasma donation center in search of "grandpa bait" for our Banner Hill stakeout scheme.

After sizing up the unseemly selection of pale, toothless, ne'er-do-wells milling about the place, Grayson had lured an old man into his RV with a Jim Beam miniature and the promise of "more where that came from, mister."

I, in turn, had been assigned the lovely task of keeping gramps from escaping out the back of the RV while Grayson drove around searching for a good spot to conduct an interview to ascertain the old guy's mental capacity for the job.

Under my watch, the nearly toothless geezer had sat on the couch across from the banquette and downed three miniature whiskeys in under three minutes.

I was down to the last one and about to panic when Grayson pulled into a parking spot. Instead of handing the tiny whiskey bottle to guzzling Gus, I'd pocketed it. I'd had a sneaking suspicion I was going to need it myself.

With phase one of our scheme complete—procure "old guy"—we'd moved on to phase two. This involved getting "old guy" inside Johnny Grits and sitting upright in a booth without him puking on my shoes or feeling me up. Mission accomplished, phase three had commenced—interview and assess "old guy" to see if he was fit for duty.

We'd ordered breakfast for our new companion, and a bottomless pot of coffee for ourselves. Thankfully, the heavenly aroma of dark-roasted java was masking most of the un-heavenly aroma emanating from our new dining companion.

Wedged in the booth beside me, Grayson was attempting to elicit enough information out of the half-coherent old goat to fill in the blanks on the admissions paperwork for Banner Hill. So far, so good, as we'd yet been asked to leave the premises, despite the fact that the old guy was gassier than the Hindenburg.

"What?" the old man yammered, slinging a mouthful of hominy grits back onto his plateful of congealing fried eggs.

"How do you spell your last name, Mr. Ballsijet?" Grayson repeated.

While Grayson wheedled the details out of gasman, I was to fill out the application and try to keep the grease stains off the paperwork. Easier said than done when the interviewee was a toothless stutterer with a mouthful of grits.

"B-A-L-L-S-ijet," the old man slobbered.

"What was that last part again?" Grayson asked.

Hunched over, covering the admissions application with my arm like the class nerd during a pop quiz, the answer suddenly came to me. I looked up and smirked.

"I got it, Grayson."

B-A-L-L-S, idiot.

"Do you have any identification on you, Mr. Balls?" I asked with utmost cordiality.

Balls grinned, proudly displaying his one remaining tooth. "Right 'cheer." He reached into the breast pocket of his threadbare Hawaiian shirt and produced a pink wallet covered in tiny unicorns jumping over rainbows.

Right. As if this isn't surreal enough already.

Unicorn man opened a flap in his wallet and handed me a laminated card with his picture on it. It was the kind of ID card Florida required of residents in order to claim Social Security checks, food stamps, and/or avoid being picked up for vagrancy. Based on the wear around the edges, Mr. Balls had put the card to good use on all counts.

"Albert Balls," I read aloud, then glanced around for some hand sanitizer.

"That's me," Balls said, and stuck a boney thumb at his boney chest.

"Were you ever in the military, Mr. Balls?" Grayson asked.

"Yep. Army. Gulf War."

Grayson's left eyebrow formed an angular arch. "Pardon me, but you look rather old to have participated in that particular skirmish."

"According to his ID, he's only forty-nine," I said.

"Hmm," Grayson said. "So, Mr. Balls, what precipitated your accelerated physical deterioration? Radioactive fallout?"

"Huh?" Balls' eyes narrowed. "This ain't another one a them government experiment gigs, is it?"

"No, sir," I said cheerfully. "We simply want you to spend the night somewhere and report back to us what happened."

Balls eyed me suspiciously. "I ain't fallin' for that one again."

"What do you mean?" Grayson asked.

I kicked him under the table. "This is nothing like the last time," I said, smiling sweetly at Balls. "I think you'll like this gig. It comes with free Jell-O and Netflix."

"Humph," Balls said, licking grits from his livery lips. "What flavor Jell-O?"

Chapter Twenty

Grayson had been gone so long our waitress had left—without even saying goodbye. The woman who took over her shift was giving me and Mr. Balls the evil eye for the umpteenth time.

I could barely blame her.

Not only had we gone through over a gallon of free coffee refills, the body odor emanating from Balls had caused a no-fly zone that now encompassed the poor waitress's entire combat station. Every customer she tried to seat within twenty feet of us had waived a white napkin of surrender and fled.

I, however, had no such option. I'd been assigned KBFE duty—Keep Balls From Escaping—until Grayson got back.

I drummed my nails on the table and watched a glistening string of drool drip from Balls' lips onto his plate.

Come on, Grayson. How long does it take to find a place to fax a damned application?

My pinkie landed in something gooey. I glanced down.

Grits shrapnel. *Ugh.*

I reached for a napkin and cringed in pity for our replacement waitress. Our table looked like a herd of grits-shitting mole-rats had plowed through it after a drunken orgy in a mud pit.

I glanced around, then slunk lower into the booth. What else could I do? I couldn't take Balls out to the parking lot. That would've required me waking him up. As it currently stood, Balls was unconscious, face-down in a slice of apple pie á la mode. Monitoring his breathing seemed a hell of a lot easier than holding him hostage—or, heaven forbid—carrying on a conversation with him.

I shot the Johnny Grits waitress a sympathetic smile and waved a twenty-dollar bill at her. She took a deep breath and sidled over to the booth.

"He ain't dead, is he?" she asked, pocketing the twenty.

I glanced at Balls. He made a few more bubbles in his melted ice cream.

"Sorry about all this," I said. "Poor gramps is on his last legs." I glanced at her nametag. "We're waiting on the paperwork to get him into a nursing home, Wanda."

"Oh," Wanda said, trying not to inhale. "How much longer you gonna be here? I think my boss is getting ready to call the cops."

She nodded to her left. I glanced over at a red-faced man in a dirty apron. He was glaring at me as if I'd brought a herd of drunken, grits-shitting mole-rats into his fine establishment.

"I ... uh ...," I stuttered. Then I caught sight of Grayson coming through the front door. I nearly fainted with relief. "Oh! Wait! Here's my brother now!"

Grayson came strolling up to the booth in his all-black attire. He tipped his fedora at Wanda and me.

"He ain't dead yet," Wanda said.

"Dead?" Grayson asked.

Wanda nodded. "Ain't you the undertaker?"

"I assure you, Miss, I'm not taking anyone 'under' any time soon." Grayson flopped into the booth. "Could you warm up my coffee, please?"

Wanda scowled and wandered off behind the waitress station. I hoped for Grayson's sake she didn't keep a stash of arsenic on hand.

"Good news. Ms. Gable approved the paperwork I faxed over," Grayson said, wagging his bushy eyebrows at me. "Balls' admission is just pending an on-site interview. Our appointment's in an hour."

"An hour?" I glanced over at Balls. "He's gonna need a shower and clean clothes first."

Grayson sniffed the air. "Maybe we should rent a pressure washer."

"Your coffee, sir," Wanda said. She set the mug on the table in front of him and lingered there a moment. I thought I saw her lips curl slightly before she turned and swaggered away.

I chewed my lip. As a veteran of "the restaurant wars" myself, I'd have bet a solid hundred Grayson's java contained a side of "special sauce."

As Grayson's fingers curled around his coffee mug, I debated whether to warn him of his possible imminent demise via passive aggression. But then again, the guy was being pretty lackadaisical considering we now had less than an hour to get Balls prepped and ready for our mission.

"We're gonna need clean clothes for Balls," I repeated. "Walmart trip?"

Grayson raised the mug to his lips, then set it back down without taking a sip. He studied Balls for a moment. "No. In his state, Walmart might prove to be too much stimulus. Could incite a panic attack."

Grayson had a point. The Walmart in New Port Richey was, after all, a supercenter.

"Where we gonna find him a new outfit, then?" I asked.

Grayson picked up his coffee mug again. "Salvation Army donation box."

I frowned. For a beggar, Balls had turned out to be quite the little chooser. Before he'd fallen face first in it, he'd insisted on *two* scoops of ice cream with his apple pie á la mode.

"Balls might not go for hand-me-down clothes," I said.

Grayson laughed. "Believe me, he's not that particular. When you were in the ladies room earlier, he ate a dead fly on a dollar dare."

Chapter Twenty-One

"Whew!" Grayson said, emerging from the tiny bathroom in the RV. "I've got to hand it to Mr. Balls. He certainly lives up to his name."

I gagged on the red Tootsie Pop in my mouth. "For the love of God, please don't elaborate."

Balls stepped out of the bathroom wearing nothing but Smurf underpants and a toothless grin. I looked down. Pappa Smurf appeared to have a bad case of the mumps. I died a little inside.

"Whelp, there she went," Balls said, and held up his hand.

Still cringing from my Papa Smurf sighting, an overwhelming force I couldn't understand made me open one eye. There, between Balls' thumb and forefinger, he held what appeared to be an un-popped kernel of corn.

"My last tooth," he said, displaying it as proudly as if he'd just found a gold nugget.

"That'll certainly cut down on the dental bills," Grayson said, then looked my way. "Your turn now, cadet. Get Mr. Balls dressed for his debut."

"Me?" I cringed. "Why *me?*"

"Because *I* just gave him a bath."

"So? Isn't that why you get paid the big bucks?"

"Yes. And that's why I get to make the executive decisions, too. Now, if you want to earn your P.I. merit badge, I suggest you get busy, girl scout."

I WIPED THE SWEAT FROM my brow, my hand trembling from exhaustion. Getting old man Balls dressed had been a feat akin to trying to cram a feral cat inside a garbage bag full of yapping Chihuahuas. *And* I'd had to do it while Grayson drove the RV like a bat out of hell.

"Good job, cadet," Grayson said as I flopped into the passenger seat next to him.

"How much longer to Banner Hill?" I asked.

"Almost there. How'd you manage it?"

"Please," I said, staring blankly at the windshield. "Just let the memory fade."

I reached into my pocket and pulled out the tiny Jim Beam bottle I'd stashed away earlier. I twisted off the cap and guzzled it down.

MY THROAT HAD ALMOST stopped burning when I heard a grunting sound coming from the back of the RV.

Grayson shot me a look. "What's up with Balls?"

I swiveled in my chair and leaned forward, trying to catch a glimpse of Balls without having to get up. He was lying on the sofa, sucking down a tiny bottle of whiskey like a baby goat. I stared at the empty miniature in my hand.

Dear God. That could be me *in twenty years.*

Horror hackled the hairs on the back of my neck. "Why do you buy booze in miniatures?" I asked Grayson angrily. "They cost a hell of a lot more than buying it by the quart."

Grayson shrugged. "I like the tiny little bottles. They're cute. And they're just the right size to mix vitamin water for Gizzard."

"Hey, what's with the lizard?" Balls' voice bellowed from behind us.

"Gizzard isn't a lizard," Grayson yelled back. He hit the brakes. I looked up and realized we'd arrived at Banner Hill.

As Grayson maneuvered the RV into a parking space along the street in front of the nursing home, he said, "Technically, Mr. Balls, Gizzard is an anole."

"Aww. Don't be talking trash about this here poor lizard," Balls yelled back. "She ain't so assholey."

"Not assholey," Grayson said. He cut the ignition. "Anole. *Anolis carolinensis*, to be precise."

I unbuckled my seatbelt. The whiskey had me feeling loose and sassy. I glanced over at Grayson. "You and your stupid phylum fixation. Lizard. Anole. What's the difference?"

"You're kidding," Grayson said, looking somewhat aghast as he stood and pocketed the keys. "A lizard is a reptile of the squamata order."

I scowled.

I'd like to squamata your *order.*

Instead, I hauled my butt out of the chair and followed Grayson into the main cabin of the RV.

"Anoles are part of the iguana family," Grayson said, picking up the terrarium from the banquette table.

"You don't say," Balls said, then stuck his tongue inside one of the empty whiskey bottles littering the sofa around him like a hobo nest.

Due to the slim pickings available at the Salvation Army drop box, Balls was dressed in a hot-pink Backstreet Boys T-shirt, white size-zero girls' jeans, black-and-white checked sneakers, and Gizzard-green socks.

Grayson studied him for a moment, then turned to me and whispered, "I don't think even an army could salvage that outfit. Let's hope Ms. Gable is colorblind, or our mission is doomed."

Balls half-rolled himself off the couch and stumbled toward us. He swayed gently up to the terrarium.

"Where we at, little lizard boy?" he asked Gizzard. His breath steamed up the glass.

"Like I said, Gizzard is a green *anole*," Grayson said, turning sideways to buffer the terrarium from Balls' deadly breath zone. "And she's female. You can spot the males by their brightly colored dewlaps."

I sighed audibly. Grayson was on another of his useless-fact tirades, and, as usual, at the worst possible moment.

Grayson, if you had a dewlap, I'd sooo be slapping it until it was brightly colored.

"Anoles belong to the chameleon family," Grayson went on, tucking the terrarium under his arm and safely out of Balls' reach. "This lucky girl can change color at will, disappearing into the background to avoid detection."

I glanced at Balls, then Grayson. Suddenly, I found myself jealous of a five-inch long, mealy worm-eating varmint.

Disappearing would come in sooo handy right now ....

"Whatever," Balls said, then peeked out the tiny window above the sofa. "Hey. Why'd we stop here?"

"For your assignment," Grayson said. He handed Balls a twenty-dollar bill. "Get us what we need and there's more where that came from, mister."

"Humph," Balls grunted, staring at the twenty.

"Stay right here for a moment," Grayson said. "I just need to get something from the glove compartment." Grayson turned and discretely nudged me on the shoulder. "Follow me," he whispered under his breath.

I trailed Grayson back into the front cab of the RV, hoping by some miracle he was going to tell me he was calling the whole thing off. Instead, he reached into the glove compartment and pulled out a black writing pen.

"See this?" he said.

"A pen?" I asked. "What're you gonna have Balls do? Hand out autographs?"

Grayson shot me a look. "It's a *spy* pen, Drex. Once activated, this little baby can deliver up to four hours of uninterrupted video and audio."

"Oh." I crinkled my nose at the innocuous looking writing instrument, then made a mental note to never accept another free pen from anybody. Ever. Again.

"Hopefully, this will catch some of the action going on in the nursing home overnight," Grayson said.

I cringed. "Like what? Bedpan races? Or Balls scratching his, you know—"

"That's a calculated a risk we have to take," Grayson said. "However, now that you mention it, to minimize that possibility I'm going to tuck the pen inside Balls' front pocket and aim it outward, like this."

He stuck the pen in his own pocket to demonstrate. "Now you do it to Balls."

We went back into the cabin. I stuck the pen in the pocket of Ball's pink Backstreet Boys T-shirt.

"What's this?" Balls asked, looking down at his shirt.

"A popular boy band," I said, hoping to deflect his attention from the pen.

"A monitoring device," Grayson said, negating my attempt at stealth. "So you can—"

"*Can*," Balls said, cutting him off. "I gotta go to the *can*."

"Right," Grayson said. "It's just right there."

We both stared at Balls.

"A little privacy, please," the old man said.

"Huh?" Grayson grunted.

I grabbed Grayson's arm. "I know exactly how you feel, Mr. Balls. Come on, Grayson. We'll be up front in the driver's cab."

"OUR APPOINTMENT'S IN five minutes," Grayson said, checking the time on his cellphone. "Think he'll be a while?"

"Like *I* would know?"

Grayson rolled down the driver's side window and shrugged. "Just in case, you know."

I knew. And I didn't want to think about it.

We sat in our seats and twiddled our thumbs. A few minutes later, from the back of the RV, a door slammed so hard the whole motorhome shook.

"Mr. Balls?" Grayson called out. "Are you okay?"

Suddenly, something flew through the driver's side window, hitting Grayson square on the side of his head. As it fell to his lap, I realized it was a wadded up twenty-dollar bill.

"I ain't crazy, you know!" Balls yelled.

"What?" I scrambled out of my seat and leaned across Grayson, craning for a view out the driver's side window.

Balls was standing in the parking lot about twenty feet away, hopping from foot to foot in his checkered slip-on tennis shoes. Suddenly, he began to belt out a loose, sing-song rap.

"You can put me in a war zone. You can put me in a disaster zone. Hell, you can put me in a cyclone! But ain't *nobody* puttin' me in no *nursing home!*"

"Wait!" Grayson yelled.

But, apparently, Balls wasn't in the mood for following orders. He took off in his tight white jeans and pink top like a love-struck teenybopper who'd just spotted Jonathan Knight.

"Crap," Grayson said. "There goes fifty-nine bucks for the spy pen."

"Sorry," I said, climbing off him and handing him the wadded-up twenty.

Grayson looked me up and down. "Well, cadet. Looks like it's time for plan B."

Chapter Twenty-Two

"Plan B?" I asked.

The words left a taste in my mouth worse than pure evil had.

"Yes," Grayson said. "Congratulations. The Balls is in your court."

I sighed. "Grayson, the expression is, 'The *ball* is in my court.'"

"No. *Balls.*" Grayson clapped a hand on my shoulder. "As in, *you're* the new Balls."

My stomach dropped four inches. "What?! But .... I *can't!*"

Grayson raised an eyebrow. "Why not?"

"Well, I ... I'm *a woman*, for one thing!"

Grayson snatched the auburn wig off my head. "Could've fooled me."

I ran my hand across the red fuzz growing back from my hospital buzz cut. My mind raced like a rabid squirrel, trying to chase down another excuse.

"What about these?" I said, sticking out my chest. "Balls doesn't have boobs."

Grayson's lips twisted into a sadistic grin. "You're forgetting, cadet. You *yourself* told Gable that our dear old grandpa wanted to be a *granny*. Who says he hasn't had a bit of reconstructive surgery?"

My chest fell. "But ... but ...."

Grayson smiled. "Your quick thinking saved the day with that one."

I scowled. "Saved *your* day, maybe."

"But this is your reward," Grayson said.

"*Reward?* Posing as a geriatric tranny-granny? Come on, Grayson. You can't be serious!"

"Think of it this way," he said. "Now's your big chance, Drex. You get to go *undercover*. This is *real*, honest-to-God P.I. training."

My shoulders slumped.

Crap.

I glanced down at the discarded Salvation Army clothes piled up in the corner like the aftermath of a hobo three-way. I groaned. I knew full well my butt would never fit in any of those pants.

I launched into my own plan B—Begging.

"Can't we find someone else?" I whined.

"There's no time." Grayson glanced at his cellphone. "Our meeting with Gable is in three minutes."

I chewed my lip. "Can't we reschedule?"

"And lose another night? No." Grayson shook his head. "Who knows how many vets' lives could be at stake here?"

"But what about the surveillance pen? Balls ran off with it!"

Grayson grinned. "No worries on that count. I've got a whole case of them."

I sighed and watched my last hope fly out the RV window like Balls' golden tooth. I glared at Grayson. "You can't remember to buy toilet paper, but you've got a whole case of spy pens?"

Grayson shrugged. "Different folks have different priorities." He handed me a pair of purple leotards. "Now, how about trying these on for size?"

Chapter Twenty-Three

"It's shooow-time," Grayson announced as he wrestled the folding wheelchair out of the RV and onto the street in front of Banner Hill. "Are you nervous about your first stakeout?"

I was. But I felt more angry than nervous. I glared at the wheelchair, wanting to kick myself. It'd been my idea to take the damned thing in the first place. I'd spotted it abandoned behind some bushes by the Salvation Army collection box where we'd filched the clothes for Balls.

Grayson unfolded the wheelchair and patted the seat. "You ready, Grampa Drex?"

I scowled and plopped my butt down in the chair. "Just push me, already," I demanded, and stuck a Tootsie Pop in my mouth.

Grayson heaved the chair, grunting from the effort. "Get out. Let me get the wheels up over the curb first."

"Nope." I crossed my arms and smiled. "Not a chance."

"How am I supposed to get you onto the sidewalk?"

"You're the investigative genius. Figure it out."

Grayson tugged until I thought he might blow a gasket. Still, I didn't budge.

I might've been more obliging if I'd had on a decent outfit. But as it stood, there was no way I was going to stand up and be seen in public dressed in smiley-face boxer shorts and purple leotards. Not in this lifetime.

"You wanted me on this stakeout, you gotta pull your weight," I said.

"I am," Grayson argued, tugging at the wheelchair. "I just wasn't expecting to have to pull *yours*, too."

He yanked the chair a final time. One wheel went up onto the curb. The chair skittered sideways, nearly dumping me out on my head.

"Careful!" someone yelled from across the parking lot. "You need a hand?"

"No!" Grayson called back. "It's all under control now."

Yeah, right.

"Geez, Grayson, I almost ate a dirt sandwich," I grumbled as he maneuvered the wheelchair onto the walkway. As he wheeled me toward the nursing home entrance, I checked my cellphone. "We're late for our appointment."

Grayson leaned over and whispered into my ear. "Give me your cellphone."

The hair on the back of my neck pricked up. "*No way* am I going in there without this, Grayson. What if somebody goes mental in there? How am I gonna call for help?"

"That's why they have those little call buttons by the beds," he whispered. "Now hand it over."

"Not happening." I tucked my cellphone into my leotard.

Grayson glanced around and sighed. "Fine."

"Fine," I hissed back, and punched the big red button marked *For Handicapped Access* with my fist.

The double glass doors slid open automatically. Grayson shoved the wheelchair over the threshold.

"Take it easy with the merchandise," I grumbled. Then I spotted Gable and lowered my voice an octave. "There she is."

I nodded toward the reception desk, where a smooth, helmet of hair was rising like a brown moon from behind the laminate countertop. It was quickly followed by Ms. Gable's glowering face and stout torso.

"You're five minutes late," she barked when she spotted us. "I just put your paperwork in the trash."

"Oh! So sorry about that," Grayson said, pouring on the charm. "Gramps was so excited, he couldn't decide what to wear. See?"

Gable looked at me and flinched.

"By the way, may I say you're looking lovely today?" Grayson added.

Gable didn't look too convinced. She gave me the once-over and said, "*That's* your grandfather?"

"Yes." Grayson reached down and adjusted the collar on the black button-down shirt I'd stolen from his closet after he tried to get me to wear a Looney Tunes hoodie. There was no way that was happening. It was too on the mark.

"Try to suck in your boobs," he whispered.

"What?" Gable asked.

Grayson whipped around to face her. "I told gramps he shouldn't suck those things."

"Agreed," Gable said. "Nasty habit. Choking hazard."

Grayson shot me a look. "I keep telling him that."

"Where's your sister?" Gable asked.

"She's um ... indisposed," Grayson said.

"Indisposed?"

"You know. Getting a high colonic. She ate a bad burrito. Her hemorrhoid cushion blew out and—"

I kicked Grayson's knee out. He nearly fell to the floor. He turned and shot me *what was that for* glare.

"Gramps gets feisty when he doesn't get his Geritol." Grayson held out his hand. "Hand over the lollipop."

I plucked the Tootsie Pop from my mouth and plopped the sticky sucker end into Grayson's palm.

Gable's eyes narrowed in her plump cheeks. "The paperwork you faxed over is for Albert Balls. I thought your grandfather's name was George Burns."

"Uh ... you mean *Georgie* Burns," Grayson said, spinning around to face her. "That's his ... I mean *her* stage name." Grayson sidled up to the reception counter and whispered, "Remember? We told you about his little ... *transition*."

Gable scowled. "I remember."

Grayson grinned like a used insurance salesman. "So, you see, the thing is, now he—I mean *she*—won't answer to anything but Georgie."

Gable eyed me like I was a fake freak-show exhibit—The Person with No Discernable Reason to Live.

"Humph," Gable grunted. She skirted around the reception desk and addressed me. "Albert?"

I didn't react.

"George?" she asked as she reached my wheelchair.

I stuck my nose in the air.

"Georgie?" she said.

I glanced up at her and smiled. "Hi."

Gable frowned. "It says on your application he's got no teeth."

"Of course," Grayson said. "Those are dentures."

Gable nodded in admiration. "Huh. Pretty nice set." She turned to Grayson. "But they'll have to come out before bedtime."

Grayson nodded. "No problem."

No problem? I see a problem!

"He ... I mean *she* won't put up a fuss?" Gable asked.

"Georgie? No. No fuss at all. Right, Georgie?"

I glared at him.

"If she ever *does* get upset, just do this." Grayson reached over and snatched off my ball cap. Then, with the palm of his hand, he rubbed the red fuzz growing in on my head. He locked eyes with me. "See? She *really likes it* when you do that."

I forced a smile, and Grayson stopped. But when he pulled his hand away, I snapped at it like a rabid Pekinese.

Gable gasped. "She's a biter?"

"Only at me," he said. "Otherwise, Georgie's quite tame, aren't you, sweetie?"

I nodded and smiled sweetly.

Gable's face softened a notch. She went back to the reception desk and did an encore of her brown sunset impersonation. When she re-arose, she had our application in her hand.

She studied it for a moment, then looked over at me. "Remarkable family resemblance," she said. She glanced over at Grayson. "You look just like your grandpa."

I heard another gasp. I wasn't sure if it was from me or Grayson.

Gable picked up a big rubber stamp and pounded the application with a resounding thud.

"Okay, Georgie," she said, smiling at me. "Welcome to Banner Hill. You're just in time for dinner."

My mouth fell open. It was only 4:30.

"What's on the menu?" Grayson asked.

"A Friday-night favorite," Gable said.

"Fish and chips?" I asked.

"Nope," Gable said. "Liver and onions!"

Chapter Twenty-Four

"I gotta say, for nursing home fare, the food wasn't half bad," Grayson said as he wheeled me toward my room.

"It wasn't *half* bad, Grayson. It was *all* bad," I hissed.

The main hallway now reeked of liver and onions, making me nostalgic for the homey smell of disinfectant and stale urine.

"Come on, Georgie, where's your sense of adventure?" Grayson asked as he shoved me down the hallway, jockeying for position along with the other wheelchair-bound residents.

What is this? A high-stakes race to see who can make it to the toilet in time?

"Adventure?" I asked.

"Enjoying local cuisine is an important part of the experience," he said.

I scowled. "You've got to be kidding. The only thing worse than liver and onions is chicken potpie."

"Potpie?" a frail voice said beside me.

I glanced to my right and caught a glimpse of a thin, black woman pushing a pasty old man slumped into a wheelchair.

"Don't be silly, Melvin," the woman in scrubs said. "You just ate. But don't worry. Tomorrow's Saturday. You'll have potpie for dinner then."

I groaned. Could this get any worse?

Then, as if to prove it could, Grayson leaned down and whispered in my ear. "That must be Melvin Haplets. You know. The grandfather of the guy who called in the reports. I want to talk to him."

Before I could protest, Grayson spoke up cheerily. "Melvin, do you mind if we visit for a few minutes? I want to introduce you to my grandpa. He needs to make new friends. It's his first night here."

The nurse smiled. "Of course. Melvin loves company, don't you Melvin?"

The old man stared up at her blankly from beneath his massive, snow-white comb-over.

She turned her head and shot me a kindly smile. "What room are you in—?"

"Georgie," Grayson said. "Room 3F."

"Perfect. It's just across the hall from Melvin in 4F." She put a hand on Melvin's shoulder. "How about I get you settled in your chair and you can have a nice chat with Georgie?"

Melvin drooled.

"That looks like a yes," she said, beaming at us. "I'm nurse Nina. Follow me."

Nina settled Melvin into a brown, plastic-lined Barcalounger, then aimed him at the TV mounted high on the wall.

"I've got your channel all set," she said to Melvin, and switched on the TV. Suddenly, we were blasted with five million decibels of static.

"Oops," Nina said, lowering the volume. "I better get going. My shift ends in an hour. I've still got rounds to make." She handed the half-comatose old man the remote. "Bye, Melvin. Have a good evening."

Melvin drooled and stared blankly ahead as she exited the door.

I elbowed Grayson in the stomach through the vinyl back of my wheelchair. "The guy's a turnip. We're not gonna get any information out of him."

"You're right," Grayson conceded. He shot Melvin a quick nod. "Enjoy your evening, sir."

As Grayson began a three-point turn to get us out of Melvin's room, the volume on the TV began to rise. Barely audible above it, someone said, "What kind of information youse guys lookin' for?"

Grayson stopped mid-turn. We both turned and stared at Melvin. He was still drooling, but his eyes had taken on a slightly more focused, semi-coherent glow.

"Khakua demon possession," Grayson whispered. "I knew it!"

"What?" I said, squirming in my chair. "That accent doesn't sound like New Guinea to me."

"Hush. Stay still." Grayson held me down by my shoulders. "The khakua has him in a psychic trance."

Grayson spoke directly to Melvin. "Great spirit of the Khakua, what is your purpose here?"

Melvin stared at us blankly.

"We mean you no harm," Grayson continued. "We're here to save you and your friends."

Suddenly, Melvin's eyes began to dart around wildly. I gripped the arms of my wheelchair and watched in horror as Melvin's hand reached out ... and grabbed a tissue from a box by his armchair.

Slowly, Melvin wiped drool from his chin, then locked eyes with Grayson. His mouth opened. Words began to form on his lips ....

"Listen, Bozo. My grandson send you, or what?"

I nearly fell out of my chair—not over Melvin's human veggie act, but from his Brooklyn wise-guy accent.

"As far as you know, yes," Grayson said, not missing a beat. "What's with the miraculous recovery from senility?"

Melvin sighed and rolled his eyes. "It's a ruse."

"A ruse?" I asked. "Why?"

Melvin shrugged. "I used to be an accountant. Everybody's always asking me for tax advice. If you're not careful, the idiots in here will talk your ears off. What do I care about their stupid reverse mortgages or their hippie-dippie grandkids' trust funds?"

"Perfectly understandable," Grayson said. "And, might I add, well played."

Melvin offered up half a smile. "Thanks. So what's *your* scam?"

"Scam?" Grayson asked, taken aback.

Melvin eyed me up and down. "I may be old, but I still know a *broad* when I see one."

"And I know an *antique* when *I* see one," I quipped.

"Grandpa Georgie has gender identity issues," Grayson said.

"Yeah." Melvin smirked. "Whatever. But lemme tell you, sonny, if you care about your dear old 'gramps' there, you won't leave her here overnight."

"Why not?" I asked, beating Grayson to the punch.

"Sounds like you already *know* why," Melvin said.

Grayson nodded. "The missing vets, yes. But we only know part of the story. We need you to fill us in." He sidled up to Melvin and clicked the black spy pen in his hand. "Tell us about the suspicious activities you've witnessed."

"Okay." Melvin glanced around, cleared his throat, then leaned in and whispered into the pen, "That was the *third* time this week they've served liver and onions."

Grayson's face fell like a drop-kicked soufflé. He clicked the pen again. "Well, thanks very much for the intel, Mel."

"No," Melvin said, grabbing him by the arm. "You don't get it. The Army always fed us liver to strengthen our blood. You know. So we could donate to the wounded."

"The guy's delusional," I whispered to Grayson. "He thinks he's still in the army." I gave Melvin a sappy smile. "We're at a *nursing home*, Melvin."

Melvin shot me a sour look. "No shit, Sherlocksky. But I know a battle zone when I'm knee deep in one."

Grayson chewed his lip. "What do you mean? Facilities like this are supposed to be the safest place for seniors such as yourself."

"Oh yeah? Tell that to Charlie," Melvin said. "Or Harry and Larry. Guys are disappearing around here faster than the stale cookies at teatime."

"Charlie Perkins?" Grayson asked.

Melvin glanced around, then upped the volume on the TV. "Yeah. He's the latest. He disappeared from 3F last night."

I grimaced. "*My* room?"

"What do you know about it?" Grayson asked.

Melvin hunkered down and turned up the volume on the TV even higher. He chewed his lip for a moment, then said, "All this past week, Charlie and the other guys kept disappearing for a couple of hours after breakfast. When they came back, they were all pale and weak, like somebody'd nearly sucked the life out of 'em."

"Maybe it was the liver and onions," I said.

"Or maybe *they* were the liver and onions." Melvin said.

"Huh?" I asked.

Melvin's eyes shone like a mafia madman's. "Don't you see? They *feed* our blood, then they *feed* on us!"

"Spam," Grayson said absently.

"What?" My eyes darted from Charlie to Grayson and back again. "Are you saying Charlie was *eaten?*"

Worst liver and onions EVER!

Melvin nodded. "Yeah, that's *exactly* what I'm saying. It's the only thing that makes any sense. They did something to Charlie and the other guys for a couple of days, then took them away for good in the middle of the night."

"What do you think 'they' did to the men during the days before they disappeared?" Grayson asked.

Melvin scowled. "Season 'em with A-1 Sauce? Sprinkle 'em with meat tenderizer? How the hell should *I* know?"

"Okay," Grayson said. "Do you recall exactly when Charlie disappeared last night?"

"Yeah. I'd just switched off *America's Got Talent*. That's when I heard his wheelchair squeaking down the hall in the middle of the night."

"Did you note the time?" Grayson asked.

"No. But it had to be nearly nine o'clock."

"That's the middle of the night?" I asked.

Melvin made a sour face. "It is around here, dick-chick."

Grayson nodded. "Did you *see* Charlie?"

"Naw."

"Then how did you know it was him?"

Melvin sighed. "Listen, bub. I was a mechanic in the Army. I used to be able to tell a Ford engine from a Chevy half-drunk and blindfolded at a hundred paces. It was Charlie's wheelchair all right. I could tell by the squeak of its wheels."

"Right," Grayson said. "Was Charlie alone? Did you hear any voices?"

"No. Just his wheelchair squeaking. Then he didn't show up for breakfast this morning."

"What do you think happened?" Grayson asked.

Melvin turned up the volume on the TV so high I thought his Miracle Ear might explode. "Aren't you listening? They *took* him." His fist pounded the arm of his Barcalounger. "The bastards sucked the blood out of Charlie, marinated him in mustard sauce, then served him for dinner!"

I blanched in horror and disgust.

Melvin leaned over toward me. "A little tip, Missy. Whatever you do, don't eat the potpie."

I shot Grayson a pleading look and mouthed the words, "Can we go now?"

Grayson cleared his throat. "Melvin, the nights that the other men disappeared. Were the circumstances similar?"

"Identical," Melvin said. "That's why I got me this." He reached over and opened a drawer on the nightstand.

I gripped the wheels on my chair, in case Melvin was packing a machete and I needed to burn rubber. I glanced over at Grayson. He was reaching for his Glock.

"Never go to bed without it," Melvin said, and pulled out a whole head of raw garlic. He peeled off a clove and popped it into his mouth.

"Garlic?" I asked.

"Yep," Melvin said between gnashing his dentures. "They don't cook with garlic around here. Say it gives the old guys the farts."

"And it keeps the vampires away," I deadpanned.

"That's just a myth," Grayson said.

"The garlic farts or the vampires?" I quipped sourly.

"Better to have garlic breath than end up a garlic pot roast!" Melvin said. He leaned forward and grabbed my arm. I nearly jumped out of my wheelchair. "You know what? If you like, you can call me Shrimpy."

I grimaced. "Uh ... no thanks."

"You got some nice choppers there," Melvin said, staring at my teeth. "Better hold on to 'em tight."

I cringed and yanked my arm away. "Why?"

"They ought to call this place Scammer Hill," Melvin said. "It's crawling with kleptomaniacs." He glanced up at the TV. "Listen, you two better get out of here, on the double."

"Before they get suspicious?" I asked.

"No. Before my TV show comes on."

"Matlock?" Grayson asked.

Melvin shook his head. "No. It's time for Hannibal."

Chapter Twenty-Five

"What do you think—vampires, cannibals or khakua?" Grayson asked as he wheeled me to my room across the hall from Brooklyn Mel.

"Dementia," I answered. "Melvin got all those crazy ideas from watching reruns of Hannibal Lecter."

"I disagree. Hannibal never drained his victims of blood. At least, not over a prolonged period of days."

"*That's* your problem with this?" I asked, shaking my head. "Grayson, I'm telling you, nobody's getting killed by vampires around here. And nobody's being served up for dinner, either. They're all merely the delusions of a lonely old man."

"But the *disappearances* aren't a delusion," Grayson argued, wheeling me into my room. "How do you explain the missing men?"

I got up out of the wheelchair and closed the door to my room. "Here's a concept. Maybe they all *died of old age.*"

Grayson frowned skeptically. "But why hide it?"

"Duh! Maybe the staff here didn't want to upset the other residents?"

Grayson laughed. "That's what I like about you, Drex. I can always count on you to come up with some ridiculous alternative solution."

"Wha—" I threw my hands in the air. "Wow. Look at the time. I better get ready for bed. It's almost six thirty. Surely visiting hours are over, aren't they?"

I glared at my unwanted houseguest as I unbuttoned the black shirt I'd stolen from his closet. Underneath, I was wearing a Dead Head T-shirt so tight it doubled as a corset and a bra. I untucked the T-Shirt from my purple leotard and smiley boxer shorts, and looked around for the duffle bag with my stuff in it.

Suddenly, the door to my room popped open. A familiar face surrounded by dreadlocks poked in.

"How's our new resident settling in?" Stanley asked, and shot Grayson a wink. Then he glanced over at me. His eyes doubled in size. "What are *you* doing here?"

"Balls flew the coop," Grayson said.

"And I'm plan B," I said.

"Geez!" Stanley stepped inside and closed the door behind him. "Are you serious?"

"Afraid so," I said.

Stanley eyed me up and down. "You can't wear that to bed. Let me get you a gown."

"A nightgown?" I said. "I'm trying to look like a *man*, remember?"

"I meant a *hospital* gown." Stanley stepped out into the hallway and returned pushing a small laundry cart. "I've got a fresh one here somewhere." He fished around in a pile of folded clothes. "Aha. Here we go." He handed me a mint-green gown that tied in the back.

I scowled. "My favorite designer. Louis Butt-out."

Grayson helped himself to a white lab coat from the cart and stuffed it into the duffle bag containing my "personal effects."

"I did *not* just see that," Stanley said.

"What do you want with the lab coat?" I asked Grayson.

"I plan to conduct a review of the missing guys' charts tonight," he said. "How about a little help, Stanley?"

Stanley closed his eyes and stuck his fingers in his ears. "I see nothing. I know nothing." He opened one eye and shook his head at Grayson. "Sorry, man. That's all the help I can give you."

Grayson clapped a hand on Stanley's back. "All I'm asking for is a little night watchman service. Keep an eye out while I peruse some files. Easy-peasey."

Stanley shook his head so hard his dreadlocks began to sway. "No way, man. I need this job."

"Fair enough," Grayson said. "Thanks for the doctor duds."

"You didn't get those from me," Stanley said, checking off something on a clipboard.

I picked up the glass of water by my bedside and held it up to the light. "This water looks bluish. Is it safe to drink?"

"That isn't for drinking," Stanley said. "It's for your teeth."

"My teeth?" I asked.

"Yeah. The ones that go into the glass."

My nose crinkled. "Oh. But I don't have dentures."

"You don't?" Stanley glanced down at the clipboard, then back at me. "According to this, you better get some quick. Before the count comes."

"Count?" Grayson asked. "As in ... *Dracula?*"

Stanley shot him a look. "No. As in *bed* count. It's lights out, dentures out at seven-fifteen, sharp."

"Sharp," Grayson said, nodding slyly. "Is that some kind of code?"

Stanley eyed Grayson. "Code?"

"For vampires. Sharp teeth and whatnot."

I shot Stanley an apologetic look. "Anything else I should know before we call it a night, Stanley?"

"Yeah. Don't listen to Melvin across the hall. He's crazy."

I smirked. "Ditto for Grayson."

AT FIVE MINUTES PAST seven, Grayson waltzed back into my room and tossed a small brown bag on my lap.

"What's this?" I asked, sitting up in my bed. The crunch of the plastic liner on the mattress made me cringe with disgust.

"It's your get-out-of-the-dentist-free card," he quipped.

I opened the bag and pulled out a pair of cheap, plastic vampire teeth. "What the?"

He shrugged. "Best I could do on short notice. Walmart doesn't sell choppers off the shelf."

As I plopped the fanged dentures into the glass of blue water on the nightstand, the door opened. An orderly I hadn't seen before glanced first at me, then at the teeth in the glass. He scribbled something on a clipboard and said, "Visiting hours are over in ten minutes. You need a bedpan, Georgie?"

"No. sir."

"Very good." The orderly disappeared, closing the door behind him. Grayson pulled a black pen from his jacket pocket.

"Here's your granny cam," he said, and hooked it to the sleeve of my thin, cotton gown. "Just tap here to start recording."

"Okay. When should I activate it?"

"Whenever you see something suspicious. Or you feel like you're going to pass out. Whichever comes first."

"Pass out? Why would I ...? Never mind."

"You gonna eat that pudding?" Grayson asked, nodding at a plastic container sweating condensation on my nightstand tray.

"Maybe."

"I was thinking it could be porphyria."

I crinkled my nose at the container. "I thought it was tapioca."

"I meant what's going on here," Grayson said. "Porphyria's a blood disorder, Drex. One of the treatments for it used to be the drinking of human blood."

There goes my appetite.

I handed Grayson my pudding cup. He peeled off the top and dug into it with a plastic spoon. "Mmm."

"Eat fast and then beat it," I said, folding my arms across my chest. "You've got one minute, then I'm pressing my alarm button."

Chapter Twenty-Six

At exactly 7:15 p.m., I saw the hall lights blink out through the crack under the door. I stretched out in my nursing home bed and yawned. After two weeks of sleeping in either sleazy hotels or the lumpy sofa in Grayson's RV, I felt like I'd won a free night in P. Diddy's retirement crib.

I was living large with my own full-sized bed, full-sized TV, and full-sized bathroom—one that, by the way, would *not* come with Grayson screeching *Bat Out of Hell* at the top of his lungs tomorrow morning at the crack of dawn.

Yeah. A girl could get used to this ....

I clicked off the lamp beside my bed and snuggled under the sheets. In the eerie green glow of the bathroom nightlight, I giggled like a naughty teenager as I fished around in the covers for my contraband cellphone. I pressed speed dial and called the only person I knew who wouldn't ask too many questions—or be freaked out by my answers.

"Hey, Beth-Ann," I whispered to my geeky, Goth girlfriend back home in Point Paradise.

"Bobbie. You're still alive," she deadpanned. "I was beginning to wonder."

"Yeah. Still got all my fingers and toes. How's the beauty-shop biz?"

"Slow. All the old ladies are saving up their cash for next week."

"Next week? Somebody's funeral?"

"No. Thanksgiving. It's the calm before the wash-n-set storm. Come next Tuesday, I'll be a madwoman, curling and teasing every old biddy's silver-blue do from Waldo to Fairbanks."

I snorted. "Why in the world do they bother?"

"I dunno. I guess they all wanna look better than their relatives. Or, at least better than the stuffed turkey they're sitting next to."

I grinned. "Speaking of turkeys, have you heard from my cousin Earl lately?"

"No. Why?"

"I was just wondering. You think he's actually trying to run the auto shop, or is he letting our family business fall to pieces?"

"I thought that already happened years ago."

I winced. "Ha ha."

"Listen. If you want, I can drive by the garage and snoop around. Tell Earl I've got transmission trouble or something."

"No." I sighed. "You're busy. Let's save that idea for a future emergency. Right now, I've got a different one on my hands."

"Don't tell me. You're pregnant!"

"Geez! No!"

"Sorry," Beth-Ann said. "At least tell me you've gone to bed with Grayson by now. I need some juicy gossip, stat."

"I'm in bed. But not with Grayson."

"Ooo la la! With who, then?"

"Not *who*. *Where*. I'm doing my first private eye stakeout!"

"Where? In a brothel?"

My nose crinkled. "No. A nursing home."

"Nursing home?" Beth-Ann laughed. "Why? Somebody steal gramps' Geritol?"

"No. They stole gramps himself."

"What?"

"I'm not kidding. People keep disappearing from here."

"New Port Richey? Of course they do, Bobbie. Anybody with brain cells and bus fare."

"I'm serious, Beth-Ann. Grayson thinks something really odd is going on."

"So do I. Why haven't you two hooked up yet?"

I shook my head. "Good grief, girl. Is that all you think about?"

"That and hair dryers."

I blew out a breath. "Look at us. Just like old times. Friday night and neither one of us has a date."

Beth-Ann laughed. "Sad, but true. At least your odds are better than mine."

"How so?"

"You're surrounded by beds full of men."

"Yeah. All old enough to have voted for Barney Rubble for president."

Beth-Ann giggled. "We *are* a pair, aren't we? I got stuck with all the old ladies. You got stuck with all the old men."

"Yeah. Lucky us."

"Eeew."

"What?" I asked.

"I just had a thought."

"About what?"

"Watch yourself, Bobbie. Old men can still get it up, you know."

"Eeew."

"Exactly. Hey! You know how you can tell which ones still can?"

I grimaced. "No."

"Depends."

"Depends?"

"Yeah," Beth-Ann said. "Depends on the bulge in their pants—if it's in the front or the back."

Chapter Twenty-Seven

Brooklyn Mel was in my room.

He was dancing around in a diaper.

It was bulging on the least favorable side.

"Rock and roll is the Devil's music," he said, then pirouetted toward a bookshelf like Doris Day on speed. "I prefer easy listening, myself."

He flipped the switch on a portable radio. Michael Franks' Popsicle Toes *began to play. He sidled over to my bed and slipped a cold hand under my covers. He grabbed ahold of my left foot and lifted it toward his open mouth.*

He wasn't wearing his dentures.

"Stop!" I yelled. I reared back my leg, preparing to kick Mel and his denture-less mug all the way to Denver.

Suddenly, Quasimodo burst into the room and bonked Melvin over the head with a bedpan.

I closed my eyes and hoped against hope that the pan was empty ....

I AWOKE WITH A SNORT, twisted up in the sheets like a pretzel. My naked butt was hanging off the left side of the bed.

The door cracked open. I squirmed to cover myself.

"Sleep well?" Stanley asked, poking his head in the door. "I just thought I'd check in on you before breakfast."

I jerked the covers over my derriere. "What time is it?"

"Five-twenty."

"A.m. or p.m.?"

Stanley grinned. "So, I take it you slept well."

"I was out like a broken taillight." I sat up in bed. "Do they put drugs in the water around here or what?"

Stanley shrugged. "Don't ask, don't tell. That's my policy."

"Right. I forgot."

"So, you're okay?"

"Yes. No body parts missing. Thanks for checking. Have you seen Grayson?"

"Not this morning. But breakfast is at six. Invite him, if you want. I'll come back and wheel you down."

"That'd be great. Thanks."

Stanley left without mentioning my embarrassing Southern exposure. I laid back in bed and counted my blessings. At least it hadn't been my smartass cousin who'd seen me. Mercifully, Earl didn't know anything about this stakeout. And he never would. I'd sworn Beth-Ann to secrecy over the phone last night.

I sucked in a deep breath and sighed. Then I stretched out on the bed like a stray cat on vacation. I hadn't slept this well since the time I drank eight margaritas and slashed all four tires on my cheating boyfriend Blanders' moving van.

Ahh. Precious memories ....

AS PROMISED, STANLEY returned to fetch me for breakfast. As he pushed my wheelchair around the corner and into the breakfast room, I nearly gasped. I'd expected Grayson. The other hairy, ape-like creature sitting beside him, not so much.

"What are you doing here?" I hissed.

"Hiya, Cuz," Earl said, swiping his shaggy black bangs from his eyes. "You didn't think I was gonna miss *this* did you?"

I shot Grayson a look that could've curdled the milk inside a Billy goat. He shrugged. "With you indisposed, I needed the backup."

Earl snickered at me in my wheelchair. "You got a bedpan under there, Bobbie?"

I sneered. "If I did, I'd have already beaned you upside the head with it."

"Well," Stanley said, "I'll leave you to your happy family reunion. I've got to go get Melvin, anyway."

As he turned to go, the skinny nurse from yesterday came running into the breakfast room.

"Stanley!" she gasped, nearly out of breath.

"What's wrong, Nina?"

Nina saw us staring, and lowered her voice. "I ... I just came from Melvin's room. He's not there. No one's seen him this morning!"

Chapter Twenty-Eight

After sampling a spoonful of slimy porridge from his Banner Hill breakfast tray, Grayson had suggested we dine out. I'd darn-near left skid-marks on the terrazzo burning rubber with my wheelchair.

We were back at Johnny Grits, but I wasn't worried about getting thrown out, this time. Disguised as an old man in a wheelchair, I figured no one would recognize me without my sidekick, Balls. As for Grayson? He was on his own.

"So another poor old geezer flew over the cuckoo's nest?" Earl mumbled through a mouthful of bacon. "What's that make? Four now?"

"Yes," I said, eyeing Grayson sullenly. "How could you leave me in that place alone last night? *I* could've been the one who ended up buying it!"

"Buying what?" Earl asked. "I thought they didn't allow no solicitors."

Grayson eyed the tendons poking from my neck. "I had your back," he said to me. "I was camped out in the RV in the parking lot the entire night. All you had to do was ring me."

"Right," I said sourly. "And just how did you plan on getting in?"

"Stanley."

I slunk back in the booth. "Oh."

"That dude who wheeled you in for breakfast?" Earl asked. He wagged his eyebrows at me and laughed. "He your new boyfriend, Bobbie?"

I shot my annoying cousin my best evil grin. "I've got a scalding cup of coffee here, Earl, and I'm not afraid to use it."

Earl shrunk back in his seat. "Feisty this mornin', ain't ya."

Grayson took a bite of hash browns. "Let me see your pen, Drex."

Crap.

"I uh...I forgot to activate it last night."

Grayson eyed me blankly for a moment as he chewed his hash browns. He swallowed. "Did you see anything unusual last night?"

I winced. "Do dreams count?"

Grayson perked up. "Absolutely."

"I ...." I glanced over at my cousin, then leaned in and whispered something into Grayson's ear.

"What? I can't hear you," he said.

I scowled. "I said, I dreamed Melvin was dancing around in a diaper. Then he tried to suck my toes."

Earl laughed so hard he blew coffee through his nose.

I glared at him. "If you need the Heimlich, don't come crawling to me."

"Did you take a shower this morning?" Grayson asked.

I surreptitiously tried to smell my armpit. "No. Why?"

"Good. I need to swab your toes for saliva."

Earl hooted so loudly the waitress came running over.

"Is everything all right?" she asked, her eyes as big as the poached eggs she was carrying.

"Sorry 'bout that," Earl said, sopping up coffee with his toast. "Looks like I'm gonna need me some extra napkins."

I closed my eyes and smiled, secure in the knowledge that if I survived this moment, there was *no way* my life could ever get any worse. I opened my eyes. Grayson was holding a Q-tip in my face.

Well, there went that pipe dream.

"Can the swabbing wait until after breakfast?" I asked.

Grayson shrugged. "Sure. I guess so." He put away the baggie of cotton swabs.

While Earl was busy dabbing at his head-to-lap coffee stains with the extra napkins dumped off by the waitress, I leaned across thc table and spoke to Grayson through gritted teeth.

"I still don't see why you had to tell Earl about our case."

"Like I said, I needed the backup." Grayson stirred a pinch of salt into his coffee refill. "And when I found out he was already in town, well, how could I resist?"

"Already in town?" I turned and scowled at my soggy, flannel-shirted cousin. "Are you *stalking* me, Earl?"

He laughed. "You *wish*, Cuz. I'm in town for the revival."

"The revival of what?" I asked. "Your dead brain cells? Too late for that."

"Faith," Earl said reverently, then patted his coffee-stained chin demurely with a paper napkin. "You remember the Baptist Evangelical Resurrection Path Seekers, don't ya, Bobbie?"

My nose crinkled "The *who?*"

"The BERPS," Earl said. "They came through Point Paradise about ten years back?"

I stared at him blankly. "I got nothin'."

Earl cocked his head at me as if I were a five-legged frog. "Come on, now. Reverend Bertie? He performed that miracle, remember? He healed that boil on Artie's butt."

I grimaced at the unearthing of a memory I'd worked hard to bury. "Oh, yeah."

"That doesn't sound like much of a miracle to me," Grayson said.

"Well, you didn't see the boil," Earl said.

I sighed. "Or the butt."

"Hmm," Grayson said. "Why is it I've never heard of these BERPS?"

"Luck?" I said.

"Oh, man! Mr. G, you're in for a treat!" Earl grinned and slapped Grayson on the back. "Nothing beats The Bertie in action! I'd bet good money that feller could even raise the dead!"

"Hmm," Grayson said. "If so, Bertie may be just the guy we're looking for."

Chapter Twenty-Nine

"*Melvin was dancing around in a diaper. Then he tried to suck my toes.*"

My mouth fell open. I'd just heard my own voice—but I hadn't uttered a word. I scooted my wheelchair up toward the front of the RV.

"What's going on up there?" I asked.

No one answered.

Confined to my role as a wheelchair-bound vet, I'd been relegated to the back of the RV. I'd rolled the wheelchair up to the narrow passage leading to the front cab, but it was too wide to fit through.

I banged the wheels against the walls a few times, then I remembered that I could walk. I got up out of the wheelchair and poked my head into the driver's cab. Grayson was driving. Earl was in the passenger seat, fiddling with Grayson's laptop.

"Hey, Bobbie!" Earl said. He grinned at me and started dancing a jig with his upper torso, working the black spy pen like a majorette's baton. "Waahoo! It worked!"

"What worked?" I grumbled.

"This here spy pen! Looky here!"

Earl pushed a couple of keys on Grayson's laptop. A video of me came on the screen.

I flinched. I recognized the booth at Johnny Grits, but not the close-up shot of the face on the screen. Whoever it was looked like Lucille Ball trapped in a lice-infested internment camp.

My mouth fell open as I watched my face filled the screen like a hostage selfie. Then my video image said, "*Melvin was dancing around in a diaper. Then he tried to suck my toes.*"

Earl had struck blackmail gold.

"Ha Ha! Got you good, Bobbie!" my cousin said, twirling the spy pen between his huge fingers. "Boy howdy, I want me one of these babies!"

I snatched the pen away from him. "Grayson's got a whole case full of 'em. If he gives you one, will you go away?" I glared over at Grayson. His eyes were on the road, but his cheek was dimpled.

Jerk!

"Well now, that ain't very charitable of you," Earl said, "seeing as how I come all this way to help you out."

"You came to see Reverend Reflux," I said.

"Bertie and the BERPS," Earl corrected haughtily.

"Whatever!"

"I'm pulling over to get gas," Grayson said. "Drex, go sit on the couch and take your shoes off."

"Yeah. Cool your heels," Earl said. "Good idea, Mr. G."

"What?" I hissed.

"I'm not taking sides," Grayson said. "Actually, Earl just reminded me that I forgot to swab your toes."

"It was just a *dream*," I said.

Grayson maneuvered the RV onto an exit ramp. "You never know. The khakua is a tricky demon."

"That's right," Earl said. "Why you think they sell so much Ex-Lax?"

Something inside me gave up. I surrendered, blew out a huge sigh, and went back and flopped onto the couch.

GRAYSON FINISHED SWABBING my toes, then dropped the Q-tip into a vial. "If it tests positive for saliva, I'm going to need samples to compare it with," he said as I inched my feet back into my cheap, black, nursing-home issue slippers. "Next time you're in the cafeteria, I want you to swab the cups and glasses. I'll also need samples from the staff."

I shot Grayson a look. "I've got a better idea. Why don't *you* play gramps tonight and swab people yourself?"

He grinned. "I would, but Gable would recognize me."

I grinned back. "It's *Saturday*. She doesn't work weekends."

"Hmm." Grayson chewed his bottom lip. "That gives me an idea."

I groaned. *Not another one.*

"Let's all go to the plasma center. See if we can spot Balls."

"Pardon me, Mr. G," Earl said, chewing his lip. "But ain't that illegal?"

My eyes rolled involuntarily. "Balls is the name of the guy who was supposed to be spying for us last night."

"Oh," Earl said. "How would we spot him?"

I deferred to Grayson.

He looked to his left and said, "Well, for one thing, the guy's especially well-endowed."

"WHY DID THIS BALLS feller run away in the first place?" Earl asked as we drove toward the plasma center after the gas-up and swab-down.

Because he has even more brains than he's got balls.

"Some people just can't be caged," Grayson waxed philosophically.

"Ain't that illegal?" Earl asked.

I closed my eyes and laid back on the couch.

Apparently, I've died and am now in some kind of psychotic purgatory. It's the only thing that makes any sense.

"Here we are," Grayson said, pulling up to the curb. He slammed on the brakes. I nearly fell off the sofa.

"There he is!" Grayson yelled.

"Balls?" I called back.

"Yes," Grayson said. "I'd know those Smurf underpants anywhere!"

Yep. Psychotic purgatory it is.

"He's taking off," Grayson said, bursting into the main cabin. "Let's go. We've got to catch him!"

"Sorry," I said, lying back on the couch. "I can't run in these stupid nursing home slippers."

Grayson eyed the black, plastic shoes. "Okay, Earl. It looks like it's you and me, bud."

Earl nodded. "You can count on me, Mr. G."

The two scrambled out the side door. As it slammed behind them, I laid back on the couch and smirked.

Two boobs against four balls.

May the odds be ever in my favor.

Chapter Thirty

I was up in the front cab, contemplating stealing the RV and never looking back, when I spied Earl and Grayson stumbling around the corner of the plasma center. Each was holding tight to the arm of some naked guy who was squirming like a dog about to get dunked in a vat of flea dip.

I leaned closer to the windshield for a better look. The guy wasn't naked. He had on Smurf underwear. As my eyes moved upward to scan his face, I realized it wasn't Balls. I poked my head out window.

"Let him go," I yelled. "That's not Balls."

"You sure?" Earl hollered. "How can you tell?"

I blew out a sigh, hoping to erase the image of Papa Smurf seared into my brain. "Believe me. A woman knows these things."

"I know he's not Balls," Grayson said, wrestling with the guy's arm like it was a python. "But he's got on his underwear. I detained him for questioning, and I need you to take down his testimony."

Lucky me.

"I demand that you unhand me at once," the man said. For being dressed solely in boy-sized Smurf underpants, the guy managed to pull off a fairly dignified huff.

"Where'd you get the Underoos?" Grayson asked.

The man bucked like an angry burro. "I found them by the trash cans over there."

"He was carrying this," Grayson said, and handed me Balls' pink unicorn wallet.

Crap! Where's the Purell?

"Where'd you get the wallet?" I asked, holding it between the pinch of my thumb and forefinger.

He shrugged and shot me a sullen stare. "Came with the underpants."

I grimaced, totally jonesing for some industrial-strength santizer. "What happened to the rest of your clothes?"

The guy stopped squirming. "Look, I didn't know she was a cop, okay?"

"Who?" I asked.

"Right," he said sourly. "Just read me my Mirandas and get it over with."

A speck of his spittle landed on my forearm. I wanted to jump into a vat of bleach. "Look, perv, we're not after *you*. We're after the guy who was wearing those Smurfs before you. Do you know him?"

"No."

"Did you see him drop them?"

His nose crinkled. "No way. I don't swing that way."

"Well, did you—"

"You ask a lot of questions for a man with boobs," he said, shooting me a cocky stare.

My neck muscles tightened. I held up the spy pen I'd swiped back from Earl. "Look. You didn't happen to see a pen like this one, did you?"

"Well, yeah," he said.

I nearly fell over. "Uh ... okay. Hand it over."

"I don't have it."

"Why not?" Grayson asked.

The guy shrugged. "I didn't want it."

Earl gulped like an unclogging drain. "You didn't *want* it?"

The guy scowled. "What for? It's not like I need to write a rent check to Rockefeller." He nodded his greasy head to the left. "It's over there. By the garbage cans."

Earl let go of the guy's arm and sprinted toward the trash bins.

"Where is everybody?" Grayson asked captain underpants. "The plasma center's usually swarming with people."

He shrugged. "Down at the revival, I guess. Some guy came up in a van and announced they had free food over there. I was nearly trampled in the stampede."

"BERPS?" I asked.

"Sorry," he said. "Mushrooms always give me gas."

"Found it!" Earl hollered from behind me.

Grayson and I turned to look. Captain underpants seized the opportunity to escape. He jerked free of Grayson's grasp and ran for it.

"Dang! Should I chase him down?" Earl hollered.

"No. Let him go," Grayson said. He took the pen from Earl and slapped him on the back. "Good job."

"Huh," Grayson said, studying the spy pen.

"What?" I asked.

"It appears to have been activated. It could contain valuable information."

I sneered. "Or E.coli."

Grayson stuck the pen in his shirt pocket. "I think this calls for a celebration, team! How about some topless tacos?"

Earl looked at him sideways. "Sorry, Mr. G. But ain't that illegal?"

Chapter Thirty-One

While Earl and I munched on topless tacos, Grayson pulled Balls' spy pen in half, revealing the USB stick hidden inside. He stuck it into a port on his laptop and, after wiping his fingers with a wet-nap, grabbed a tortilla chip, crammed it into his mouth, and punched a few keys.

The computer screen blinked to life. "Showtime," Grayson said, wagging his eyebrows like Groucho Marx.

Earl and I scooted our chairs around the table for a better view of the video. But we needn't have. The audio crackled with static, and the video remained totally black.

"Maybe he was wearing an eye mask," Earl said.

Grayson and I exchanged glances, then looked back at the screen. "The pen must've been inside Balls' pocket," Grayson said.

"I *hope* it was his pocket," I said, then took another bite of taco before I lost my appetite.

"Come on, I'll give you a dollar for it," Balls' voice suddenly emanated from the laptop speakers.

I paused mid-bite. We all leaned closer to the screen.

"You ain't got no dollar," a woman's voice said.

"Do, too."

Grayson paused the video and whispered, "I bet that's the dollar I gave Balls for eating a dead fly."

Earl's nose crinkled. "Ain't that illeg—"

I slapped my hand over Earl's mouth. "Shhh!"

Grayson tapped a button to resume the video, which continued on in pitch blackness.

"See here?" Balls' voice asked.

"Huh. Where'd you get the condom?" the woman asked.

"Came with the wallet."

"All right. Have a swig."

A *glug-glug* sound—like a bottle being poured down a drain—emanated from the speaker.

"Hey! That's more than a swig!" the woman screeched.

Balls grunted, then the sound of him panting hard and heavy filled the speakers.

"Gross. What's he doing now?" I asked, not wanting to know.

"Running, I think," Grayson said.

"Ungh! Ow!" Balls grunted.

"That would be him falling down," Grayson said.

"No!" Balls screamed.

Suddenly, a video image blinked onto the screen. It was a side view of one of Balls' checkered tennis shoes, his foot still in it.

"He must've dropped the pen," Grayson whispered.

"Or it fell out of his pants," Earl said.

A weird, helicopter-like whooshing sound overtook the audio. Leaves and garbage lifted up and began swirling around Balls' feet. A strange, purple glow shone on the white squares of his tennis shoes.

"This is your last chance," an unearthly voice said in a strange accent.

"Romanian?" Grayson asked.

"No thanks," Earl said.

Suddenly, Balls' checkered sneaker pivoted on its heel. He was turning, possibly to flee. The pen must've rolled slightly, as a brief image of Balls' terrified face flashed onto the screen. Then everything blinked out to black. Both the video and audio cut out.

"Crap," Grayson said. "He must've stepped on the pen and turned it off."

I glanced over at my cousin. His eyes were the size of globe grapes.

"What just happened?" Earl whispered. "Did outer space critters get Balls?"

"Inconclusive," Grayson said. He sat back in his chair and rubbed his chin. "Stanley mentioned that Old Mildred emitted a purple glow. He also said he saw a strange purple light outside the nursing home the night Charlie Perkins disappeared."

"And now, here the lights are again," I said.

Earl grabbed my arm. "You think it could be an attack of the Purple People Eaters?"

I jerked my arm free. "Get serious!"

"What?" Earl balked. "They're *real*, Bobbie. They made a song about 'em and everything."

I looked to Grayson for support. To my surprise, he appeared to be mulling the idea over.

Great.

I shot him a dirty look.

"What?" Grayson asked. "Many folk legends and ballads are based on real events."

Earl smirked. "Told ya so, Cuz."

I lifted my butt cheeks one at a time and sat on my hands. It was the only way I could stop myself from slapping someone.

Chapter Thirty-Two

Grayson was deep in thought as he drove us back to Banner Hill. I was in the passenger seat beside him, fake disability be damned. I'd called shotgun right before we left Topless Tacos, and now Earl was in the back cabin, trying his best to pop a wheelie in my wheelchair without landing on his fat head.

I tapped Grayson on the shoulder. "What else could cause a purple glow?" I half-whispered, hoping Earl wouldn't overhear.

"Ionizing radiation, for one," Grayson said.

I flinched. "Radiation?"

Grayson nodded. "Radium, in particular. Sufficient quantities of radioactive radium or polonium can create an eerie purple glow, if the conditions are right."

"What kind of conditions are necessary?"

"Well, being at sea level, for one."

"Okay. We've got that one covered. What else?"

"A critical accident in a particle accelerator."

My gut slumped. "You mean like a nuclear meltdown?"

"Precisely."

I ground my teeth in frustration. Still, an atomic explosion seemed more plausible than Purple People Eaters. "Crystal River nuclear plant is only fifty miles from here."

"Hmm." Grayson shifted his eyes from the road toward me. "Any reports of recent mushroom cloud activity in the area?"

I returned his stare, dead on. "No. I think we'd have heard something about it on the radio or something."

"Humph. Too bad." Grayson turned back to face the road. "That would've explained the sudden wind gust quite nicely."

We drove along US 19 for a few minutes in silence, taking in the sights of the city—mainly factory-outlet carpet stores and used automobile sales lots.

"Wait," Grayson said. "There *is* another possibility."

I tore my eyes from a late-model Buick with a windshield sticker marked down to $649.99. "What?"

Grayson hesitated. "Nah. You'll think it's silly."

I glanced back at Earl sitting in my wheelchair making gorilla faces into a hand mirror. "Try me."

"Well, certain types of mushrooms glow with purple bioluminescence."

I smirked. "Before or *after* you eat them?"

Grayson's cheek dimpled. "Take the order Agaricales. It's indigenous to temperate and tropical climates, and includes over seventy-five species of bioluminescent fungi."

"What are y'all talkin' about?" Earl asked, poking his shaggy skunk-ape head into the cab.

"Bioluminescent fruit bodies," Grayson said. "And their cousins, incandescent mycelium."

"Huh?" Earl said.

I blew out a sigh. "Glowing mushrooms."

"Y'all think purple toadstools got old Mr. Balls?" Earl asked. "That's crazy."

I nearly gasped. For once, I was in total agreement with my cousin. I shot Grayson a smug glance and folded my arms over my chest.

"Get real," Earl said. "Ever'body knows toadstools wouldn't hurt nobody."

"Why not?" Grayson asked.

Earl snickered. "'Cause they're *fun-guys*. Get it?"

And there goes that *brief alliance.*

I whacked Earl on the arm. "Get back in the wheelchair or you're gonna need that thing for real."

"Party pooper," he grumbled, then disappeared along with his taco breath.

I looked back at the road. Grayson was exiting the highway too soon. "Grayson, Banner Hill is the *next* exit."

"I know." He smiled and shifted gears. "Just thought we'd do one little stop on the way."

Chapter Thirty-Three

"Awe, geez. Not this place," I groused when I caught sight of the huge circus tent.

The monstrous pyramid of fabric was set up in one of those vacant lots used to sell pumpkins during Halloween and fireworks in July. Currently, it was mid-November and they were selling salvation—at least until the Christmas trees arrived.

"I couldn't help myself," Grayson said, pulling up to the massive, white tent. "I felt something stirring in my soul."

I shot him a dirty look. "I told you to stop at four tacos."

Grayson grinned. Suddenly, banging and grunting sounded from the back cabin.

I turned to see Earl slamming the wheelchair into the wall at the end of the passageway that lead to the front cabin.

"You gotta get out of the chair first," I said. "What a dope."

AFTER EARL FINALLY got out of the wheelchair, I'd revived my role as disabled vet. Grayson was pushing me in my Salvation Army wheelchair across the dirt parking lot toward the entry flap of the biggest damned revival tent I'd ever seen.

I scowled at my cousin shuffling along beside us. All of this was his fault. During lunch, he'd talked non-stop about Bertie and his magic healing powers until he'd piqued Grayson's curiosity.

As a result, I'd ended up, yet again, the victim of another of Grayson's hastily planned "field research" tactics.

I was to fake an illness in order to try and get Bertie to "lay hands on me." While I was being felt up, Grayson was going to surreptitiously scan Bertie's electromagnetic field with a detector, or some stupid crap like that.

Whatever.

"Salvation is at hand," Grayson said, raising a hand toward the tent.

"Well, 'salvation' had better keep his hands to himself," I grumbled. I frowned up at the huge, glittery banner draped over the entryway.

Reverend Bertie & the Baptist Evangelical Resurrection Path Seekers!

Below that spangled banner, a smaller, hand-painted one read; *Hurry! November 17-23 Only!*

"Get your miracle while it's hot," I quipped.

Then, suddenly, everything went black. My sight had blinked out again like a porch light in a horror movie.

"I can't see," I said.

"Oh! Are you here for a healing?" I heard a woman's voice say.

"Yes, we are, fine lady," Grayson said from a point above and behind me.

I elbowed him through the back of the chair. "Grayson, I can't see!"

"She's blind?" the woman asked.

"Yes," Grayson said. "Since birth."

"Only Bertie can save her!" Earl sobbed.

"Well please, come this way. We're not open yet, but I'll see if Bertie has time for a true believer."

"We're believers, all right," Earl said. "I been a BERPSer for over twenty years."

"Well, isn't that something," the woman said. "In that case, follow me."

My wheelchair started to roll. Behind me, I heard Earl snicker. "You got some actin' chops, Cuz. Blind. Ha ha! You nearly fooled me!"

THE ROOM WAS STILL and quiet, except for the noisy inhaling and exhaling to my left. I recognized it and the Frito breath as belonging to my cousin, Earl.

"Lettuce pray," a semi-effeminate man's voice rang out.

I felt a hand on my shoulder, then an overwhelming whiff of Old Spice cologne.

"Brother, are you ready to see again?" the voice asked. He was so near I could feel the heat of his breath.

The hand shook my shoulder. "Are you ready?"

"Uh. Oh...yes," I fumbled into the dark void. I turned my head sharply. Something stuck me in the eye.

"Ow!" I cried out.

"Sorry, brother," the man said. "I was just making sure you weren't faking it."

"By poking my eye out?" I grumbled, rubbing my eye.

"Silence," the man said. "Peace be with you. Let the miracle begin."

I felt my ball cap lift off, then a cold, sweaty palm landed on my forehead like a giant tree frog.

"Jeeezus!" the man said, nearly startling me out of my chair. "Jeeezus! We call upon you now to heal our dear brother!"

His hand pushed off my forehead, sending my head craning back. I heard a vertebra in my neck pop. Then a shadow passed over me. I blinked. The world had gone from black to gray. I blinked again.

My vision had been restored!

Hovering over me was a sweaty little man with beady black eyes. He was staring at me from beneath the worst toupee I'd ever laid eyes on.

"Can you see me, brother?" Bertie asked.

"I can see you!" Earl cried out.

I stared at Earl, then back at Bertie. I was too dumbfounded to even be annoyed at Earl.

Geez. Maybe the guy can *perform miracles.*

"Claim your healing!" Bertie said.

"I claim it," I blurted, before Earl could beat me to it. "Brother Bertie, I can see!"

Chapter Thirty-Four

After tipping the toupee-topped faith healer a twenty, I'd insisted that Grayson and Earl wheel me out of the revival tent rather than walking out on my own two legs.

I'd told them it was in order to avoid suspicion and maintain the ruse of me being an old nursing home vet. But the truth was, I was getting a real blast out of making those two haul my butt around like they were my personal *Dumb and Dumber*.

"Ugh," Earl grunted as he lifted me through the side door of the RV and tossed me onto the sofa like a sack of potatoes. "Maybe next time you can get Bertie to heal your *legs*, too."

"One miracle was quite enough," I said, trying to make a joke of it. But inside, I squirmed with unease.

Had it all been a coincidence, or had Bertie actually cured me of my blind spells?

"I told you Bertie was the real deal," Earl said.

"He's *real* all right," Grayson said, hauling the wheelchair through the side door of the RV. "But exactly what kind of *deal* has yet to be determined."

I shot Grayson a *WTH* look. "Wait. You believe in a cannibal *khakua* demon, but not faith healing?"

Grayson shrugged. "No. I believe in faith, to a certain extent. But you're forgetting one important fact, Drex. You faked being blind. Therefore, uh ... no miracle."

"Oh, yeah," Earl said, then frowned.

I sat up on the couch. "But that's just it. I *wasn't*. Faking it, I mean. I ... I had another one of those blind spells."

"What?" Grayson's face registered so much concern it scared me. "Why didn't you tell me?"

I winced. "I did! You just didn't believe me."

Earl shook his head and tutted, "Oh, ye of little faith."

"When did the blind spell come on?" Grayson asked, ignoring Earl. He locked his mesmerizing green eyes onto my dark-brown ones.

I sat up and chewed my lip. "Well, I was reading the tent banner, and—" I gasped. "Just like last time! Oh my God. You don't think my blind spells are related to Bertie, do you? That he has some kind of weird, psycho-kinetic powers?"

"Perhaps," Grayson said, studying me. "But it's more likely hysterical blindness."

"Hysterical!" I yelled. "Who's hysterical?"

"No one, as far as you know," Grayson said. "It could also be triggered by traumatic memories."

I frowned. "But the first time it happened, I didn't even know Earl was coming yet."

Grayson's cheek dimpled. "Back further than that, Drex. Were your parents carneys, perhaps? Were you ever traumatized at a carnival?"

"Not that I can recall. But I *do* have a weird aversion to clowns."

"It'd be abnormal not to," Grayson said. "What about the bad taste in your mouth? Did you experience that again, too?"

Earl snickered. I shot him some side-eye.

"Well, now that you mention it, yes," I said.

"Did you take another Fred Flintstone?" Grayson asked.

"No."

Earl raised his hand. I clenched my molars together. "What, Earl? This is *important*."

"Uh, could a kale smoothie make your mouth taste bad?"

I sneered. "Ha. Ha. I didn't have—"

"Uh, yeah you did." Earl shrugged sheepishly. "When we were at Topless Tacos, I might've dumped that little sample cup they were handing out into your iced tea."

I closed my eyes to keep them from burning a hole through Earl's skull.

"Any tingling like before?" Grayson asked.

I thought about it for a moment and opened my eyes. "No."

Grayson nodded. "What did it feel like when Bertie touched you?"

"Like ikigai."

Grayson's eyebrows raised a notch. "Bertie's touch infused you with a reason to live?"

"No. *Icky guy*. As in his clammy hands gave me the creeps."

Earl gasped. "How could you talk bad about brother Bertie? He's no creep! He's been around for ages!"

Grayson shifted his gaze to Earl. "How *many* ages?"

Earl shrugged. "I dunno. But Granny Selma once told me that when she was a teenager, Bertie rubbed her warts clean off her."

Eew!

"Hmm. I've heard of such accounts," Grayson said. "Never underestimate the power of suggestion. How old is Bertie?"

"Don't rightly know," Earl said. "But Granny was eighty-one when she died four years ago. Bertie would'a had to be at least that old."

Grayson rubbed his chin. "Interesting. He doesn't look a day past fifty."

"Maybe he's related to George Hamilton," Earl said.

"Or Nosferatu," Grayson said.

Earl's eyebrow ticked up. "Nose hair who?"

I scowled. "Bertie, a vampire? Come on, Grayson."

Earl gasped. His eyes grew wide. "Lordy, lordy! That's why Bertie's always in that tent. He don't wanna come out in the daylight for fear a burnin' up!"

"That's a common myth," Grayson said.

"Tents?" Earl asked.

"No. That vampires are sensitive to daylight."

"How do you know all this stuff, Mr. G?" Earl asked, and sat down next to me on the sofa.

I sensed one of Grayson's conspiracy theories coming on, and groaned. I figured I might as well have some refreshments to go along with the show. I scrounged through my purse for a Tootsie Pop and struck gold. A red one. My favorite.

Grayson unfolded the wheelchair and took a seat close in front of us, like a disabled Army recruiter. "Bram Stoker was the first to bring vampires to mainstream attention."

"Wow," Earl said. "Was he some kind a monster hunter like you are, Mr. G?"

"Hardly. He was a business manager for a theater in London. He got paid so badly he had to supplement his income by writing sensational pulp novels."

Earl's eyes grew wide. "How sensational were they?"

Grayson's left eyebrow rose a notch. "The most famous was the one he wrote in 1897, about Dracula."

"That dude from Transylvania!" Earl whispered breathlessly.

Grayson sighed. "Actually, Romania. Stoker based Dracula on Vlad III, a Romanian royal. He was also known as Vlad Tepes, which, roughly translated, means Vlad the Impaler."

"Did this Vlad feller sleep in a coffin?" Earl asked.

"No. Murnau made that up."

Earl's head cocked sideways like a confused puppy. "Murman?"

"No. *Murnau*," Grayson said. "The German guy who wrote the silent film about Nosferatu in 1922. He also invented the idea that vampires disintegrate in daylight."

Earl scowled. "Why would he go and do that?"

"For the same reason all writers embellish their stories."

"To make 'em better?"

Grayson laughed. "No. To keep from getting sued for plagiarism."

Earl nodded thoughtfully. "What about the whole drinking blood part?"

"Yeah. About that …." Grayson took off his fedora. "Old Vlady boy liked to run people through with spikes for his dinner-time amusement. That's how he ended up being called The Impaler. But, as far as we know, he never drank any of his victims' blood. Stoker made that up."

Earl's nose crinkled. "So that's all malarkey, too?"

"'Fraid so."

"But what about all the vampire cults?" I asked. "People all over the world believe in vampires. If there's nothing to it, why would the legend persist?"

"In a nutshell? Bad timing," Grayson said.

"Huh?" Earl and I said in unison.

Grayson gripped the wheels on the wheelchair like he was contemplating doing a wheelie.

What is it with guys and wheelies?

"The year Stoker's Dracula novel debuted, the world was in the grips of a plague of tuberculosis," Grayson said, apparently giving up on the idea. "Back then, it was called consumption. People afflicted with it would cough up blood. And their bodies would waste away until they look like the walking dead."

"That must've been horrible," I said. "But I still don't get the connection."

"The victims looked like bloody-mouthed ghouls," Grayson said. "Add a pinch of superstition and a dollop of hysteria, and you've got a whole new diagnosis—being 'caught in the vampire grasp.'"

I blanched. "What?"

"That's what they called having tuberculosis back then."

I scowled. "You're making that up!"

"I am not. Look it up for yourself. A man named Simon Whipple Aldrich died of it. His gravestone in Rhode Island says, 'consumption's vampire grasp seized his mortal frame.'"

Earl shot up off the couch. "Mr. Whipple was a vampire?"

"Yeah," I said. "That's why he was always squeezing the Charmin."

"Joke if you want," Grayson said. "But people were dropping like flies from the disease. Then a foreign doctor from Eastern Europe arrived in Illinois with a cure."

"Thank goodness!" Earl said.

"Not so much," Grayson said. "His cure was to dig up the first known victim, cut out her heart, burn it, and feed it to her infected brother."

"Did it work?" Earl asked.

I bopped him on the arm.

"No," Grayson said. "Because tuberculosis isn't caused by vampires. In truth, there's only been one verified account of a death related to vampires."

"Shannon Dougherty?" Earl asked.

"No. It was a guy who put cloves of garlic in his mouth to ward vampires off. One got lodged in his throat while he was sleeping and he choked to death."

I shot Grayson a *gimme a break* look. "Any relation to Melvin?"

"So the garlic thing's real?" Earl asked.

"About as real as clinical vampirism," Grayson said.

Earl's eyes grew wide. "I *knew* that clinic I went to took more blood samples than they needed!"

I smirked. Grayson was getting a dose of the medicine I'd been enduring from "Dr. Earl" for nearly four decades. I hope it cured him of ever inviting him along on our investigations again.

"Well, at least we're in agreement about doctors," Grayson said. "Those blood suckers aside, *clinical* vampirism is real enough—at least to those who suffer from it. They truly believe they need to drink human blood in order to survive."

"Where would they get a crazy idea like that?" Earl asked.

Grayson sighed and stood up from the wheelchair. "I thought we just covered that. Books and movies."

I couldn't believe my ears. I grabbed Grayson's arm. "Wait a second. Let me get this straight. Are you saying that *vampires aren't real?*"

Grayson shot me an incredulous look. "No. They're real all right. They just don't drink blood."

I scowled. "Then what the hell was the point of that desensitization program you made me watch? Why put me through all that for nothing?"

"It wasn't for nothing," Grayson said. "It was to help you to conquer your own self-generated fears."

"What about the mirror thing?" Earl asked, making a face into a hand mirror. "Vampires ain't got no reflection, or is that just a myth, too?"

I grinned. The strained look on Grayson's face made enduring the vampire video worth every second.

Grayson sighed. "Look, Earl—"

A loud knock on the side door of the RV silenced Grayson midsentence.

"Hey!" a man's voice called out. "You guys okay in there?"

Chapter Thirty-Five

Grayson, Earl and I exchanged glances. We were in the RV, parked beside the BERPS revival tent, and someone was pounding on the side door.

"Who could that be?" I asked, flinching at the reverberating knocks. "Didn't I pay Bertie enough?"

"Anybody in there?" a man's gravelly voice called out.

"Quick. Get in the wheelchair," Grayson said, pushing it toward me. I hustled my butt into it and reached for the doorknob. "Try to act natural," he whispered at Earl, who was thumb-wrestling with himself. "Or, well, just do the best you can."

Grayson snatched open the door. I rolled my wheelchair next to him, nearly running over his foot.

A wiry, muscle-bound guy was standing right next to the door. Half of him was covered in black leather, the other half in tattoos. "You got engine trouble?" he asked.

"No. We're fine," Grayson asked. "Why?"

"You've just been parked out here for a while." The man adjusted the red do-rag on his head and tried to peek inside.

"My friend here just had a healing by Bertie," Grayson said. "We were just discussing him."

"We were?" Earl asked, looking up from his thumbs.

I shot him a gonad-withering glare.

"Yes," Grayson said. "We were just wondering how old the miracle man is."

"Bertie's ninety-nine," the biker wannabe said. "He turns a hundred on Monday. We're having a big celebration."

"A hundred years old," Grayson said. "Interesting. How long have you been working for him?"

"Been with Bertie for forty years. He stopped me from squandering my life on drugs, sex, and rock-n-roll. I've been working for him ever since."

"Doing what?" Grayson asked.

"I drive that van over there."

The man pointed to a white panel van. The back end was covered in bumper stickers. The side of the van was sported an oversized mural of Bertie dressed in white, holding his hands up below a rainbow. "I pick up people and take 'em to and from the revivals."

"Nice gig," Grayson said. "And a nice rig, too." He held out his hand. "I'm Grayson."

"Rocko," the man said.

I bit my lip.

Rocko. Of course your name's Rocko.

"Nice to meet you," Grayson said. "Bertie looks darn good for a centenarian."

Earl leaned over and tapped Grayson on the arm. "Mr. G," he whispered, "Bertie's a *Baptist*."

"What's the secret to his exceptional longevity?" Grayson asked Rocko, turning his back to Earl.

"Faith," Rocko said. "And daily flossing."

"Makes sense," Grayson said, nodding in agreement. "Flossing's included as one of the critical factors in the *Living to 100 Life Expectancy Calculator*."

Rocko smiled, revealing a nice set of pearly whites. "That's exactly right." He tipped his head to Grayson. "Nice to meet a fellow believer, brother. See you at the revival tonight?"

Grayson grinned. "Sure thing. We wouldn't miss it for the world, Rocko."

Chapter Thirty-Six

I was back in my wheelchair, and the three of us were back on the road, speeding down US 19 toward Banner Hill and my date with a potpie dinner.

Fun times.

"I can't believe Bertie's gonna be a hundred in two days," Earl said, then glanced back at me from the passenger seat. "Bobbie, you got more wrinkles than Bertie does."

I bumped the wheelchair against the narrow passage leading to the driver's cab. "Shut up, Earl. At least my wig looks real."

Earl chewed a toothpick and grinned. "Yeah, you keep on livin' that dream, Cuz."

"Grayson, what do you think Bertie's secret is?" I asked, ignoring Earl.

"Well, it isn't bathing in the blood of virgins," he replied. "Elizabeth Baffrey proved that ineffective back in the 16th century."

"Of course," I said, hoping that agreeing with Grayson would prevent him from elaborating. "So what else could keep Bertie looking so young?"

Grayson adjusted the rearview mirror and locked eyes with my reflection. "I believe Bertie maintains his vitality by sucking the life from his hosts."

My nose crinkled. "What?"

"You know," Earl said. "Like that old lady back in Point Paradise who's always trying to get you to host a Tupperware party."

I looked around for a flyswatter to whack Earl.

"I believe there may be more to Bertie than meets the eye," Grayson said.

I sneered. "Like what? You think he's hiding a tin-foil hat underneath that awful toupee?"

"No." Grayson pursed his lips. "I'm serious. There's definitely something in this faith-healing gig for Bertie. And it's not money. Otherwise, like you said, he'd have a better toupee."

"I *heard* that," Earl said.

While I scrounged around in my purse for a Tootsie Pop, Grayson steered off the exit ramp. He stopped at a red light and stared absently out the windshield. "I have to say, Bertie and his followers' interest in good dental hygiene is intriguing."

My lip hooked skyward. "Earth to Grayson. What the hell are you talking about *now?*"

"Good teeth," he said. "Eternal youth. Regeneration by taking the life forces of others." Grayson pulled a small electronic device out of his breast pocket. "Results from this indicate definite signs of abnormal behavior."

I pulled the blue sucker from my mouth. "A TV remote? What's your addiction to *The X-Files* got to do with this?"

"Nothing." Grayson shot me a glance in the rearview mirror, then readjusted it and steered the RV through the intersection. "I suspect Bertie could be a psychic vampire."

"You mean that feller can read what your blood's thinkin'?" Earl asked.

Where's a damned flyswatter when you need one?

"Not exactly," Grayson said, not missing a beat. "Accounts of psychic vampires have been recorded throughout time. They appear in the religious and occult texts of numerous cultures."

"Really?" Earl asked.

"Yes. The term psychic vampire denotes any person thought to be feeding off the life forces of others, leaving them feeling exhausted or drained of energy."

I glared at Earl. "I thought the term for that was *relatives.*"

"This is no joking matter," Grayson said. "If I'm right about this, we need to act fast."

"Act fast?" I asked. "Why?"

Grayson pulled up to the street in front of Banner Hill and shoved the transmission into park. He turned back to face me, his green eyes deadly serious. "Because, in less than two days, we could be facing a psychic vampire apocalypse."

Chapter Thirty-Seven

"Vampire apocalypse?" I asked, nearly choking on my Tootsie Pop. "What are you talking about?"

Grayson cut the ignition and the old RV sputtered out on the street in front of Banner Hill. "We could be looking at a killer vampire cult that's about to go mainstream."

"That sounds bad," Earl said.

"Very bad." Grayson waved the TV remote gismo at me. "See this?"

"Yes. I'm not *blind*." Then I added sheepishly, "At least, not right now."

"What is that, Mr. G? Some kind a vampire zapper?" Earl asked.

"No. A vampire *detector*," Grayson said.

I sighed.

I'm already in a leotard and a wheelchair. What the hell. I'll bite.

"How does it work?" I asked.

"Good question, cadet." Grayson turned the device until a I could see a little window-like gauge on its face. It looked a bit like a miniature bathroom scale.

"This is an electromagnetic field detector," he said. "We all emit our own electromagnetism."

"You mean like Magneto Man?" Earl asked.

Grayson's eyes made a ninety-degree orbit around their sockets, then stopped. "Well, actually, yes." He jabbed a finger at the small window in the device. "This gauge here detects fluctuations in electromagnetic fields."

"And that detects vampires *how?*" I asked.

"Not just any kind of vampires," Grayson said. "*Psychic* vampires. Electromagnetic field detectors like this one have provided undeniable proof of psychic vampires affecting the electromagnetic fields of their victims while feeding off their energy."

My brow furrowed. "Really?"

"Really. In fact, I detected electromagnetic anomalies when Bertie laid his hands on you. It could explain what Melvin said about the missing vets being gone for a few hours, then coming back looking drained. And it's a bit too coincidental that those veterans started disappearing the exact same week Bertie and the BERPS rolled into town."

I chewed my lip. "Okay. But this energy feeding isn't fatal, is it?"

"No."

"Then how do you account for the fact that four vets have gone missing?"

"Maybe old Bertie sucked their batteries dry," Earl said.

I whacked him in the bicep. "Get real."

"Earl may have a point," Grayson said. "Being older and possibly rendered fragile from combat, it's likely Larry, Harry and Charlie were already in a weakened state. Perhaps Bertie devoured too much of their energy and they died unexpectedly."

"That's impossible," I said.

"Is not," Earl argued. "If Bertie's got Magneto Man's powers, he can make the ocean start swirlin' up. Zapping a few old coots would be child's play."

"Magnetokinesis," Grayson said, rubbing his chin. "Interesting idea. Electromagnetic pulses have been known to cause blackouts, and even silence crickets."

If one will silence this conversation, come on, electromagnetic pulse ....

"Listen," I said, "Say Bertie *is* capable of all that mumbo jumbo. How did our wheelchair-bound victims manage to get from Banner hill to Bertie's BERPS tent?"

A horn beeped. I glanced out the windshield.

A white van emblazoned with Bertie's smiling, graven image pulled into the parking spot in front of the RV. Rocko got out and waved a tattooed arm at us. Then he opened the side door, activated a lift, and lowered an old man in a wheelchair down to the ground.

The old man was the missing Melvin Haplets.

What do you know. Two mysteries solved with one old stoner.

Chapter Thirty-Eight

The three of us stared out the windshield as Rocko pushed Melvin in his wheelchair toward the entrance to Banner Hill.

"Well, that solves the mystery of how the vets got to Bertie," I said. "And where Melvin Haplets disappeared to, as well."

"Interesting," Grayson said. "I need to talk to Melvin." He reached for the door handle.

"Hold on!" I said. "First, explain this business about a killer vampire apocalypse, and why do you think it's going to happen in two days."

"Bad timing," Grayson said.

"I don't care," I said. "We can talk to Melvin in a few minutes."

"No," Grayson said. "I meant that's why I think there's going to be another apocalyptic event similar to the one that happened in the late 1800s."

I frowned. "Don't tell me tuberculosis is making a comeback."

Grayson shrugged. "Okay, I won't. But do you know what the difference is between a cult and a mainstream religion?"

"Uh ...."

"About a hundred years."

My eyebrow ticked up involuntarily. "What?"

"Ten little decades," Grayson said.

Earl scratched his head. "I thought you said a hundred years."

Grayson closed his eyes for a moment, then laid the electromagnetic field detector on the dashboard and turned to face me. "Think about it, Drex. Back in its early days, Christianity was considered a cult by the Jews and Romans. Jesus was worshipped, feared, and misunderstood by millions—as were all prophets in their early days."

Earl appeared stunned to silence by the news. I prayed Grayson would keep talking.

"Go on," I said.

"After Christianity went mainstream, Protestants, Quakers and Baptists were considered cults by early Christians. Actually, come to think of it, some people still consider Southern Baptists a cult, what with the snake handling and whatnot."

"Snake handlin' is *real*," Earl said. "I seen it myself."

"I'm not saying it isn't real, Earl," Grayson said. "What I'm saying is it hasn't been *accepted by the mainstream*. Not yet, anyway."

"Oh." Earl's brow furrowed. "What about that Jim Jones dude, and that Wacko guy? Were they religions or cults, Mr. G?"

"Excellent question." Grayson nodded like a pleased professor. "That's exactly the point I'm trying to make. We call those cults, because *they didn't last*."

I sneered. "Yeah. I guess it's hard to keep the ball rolling when you advocate mass suicide."

"Exactly," Grayson said. "They didn't survive long enough to become anything but a cult."

Earl's brow furrowed. "So, you're sayin' any old crazy thing can be a religion if it sticks around long enough?"

"Well, that's just it. If it's too crazy, it *won't*. Time has a way of uncovering the flaws in an idea, Earl. Anything too weird will eventually self-destruct. But if an idea can hold water long enough, then it has a chance of gaining a foothold ... of going mainstream."

"So, basically, what you're saying is religion is whatever belief passes the test of time?" I asked.

Grayson shrugged. "More or less."

I shook my head. "I'm not buying that."

"Think about it, Drex. Every religion was a cult when it first began."

I frowned. "Maybe a long time ago."

"What do you consider a long time?" Grayson asked. "Less than two hundred years ago, a guy named Joe Smith said an angel named Moroni told him to dig up some gold tablets buried in a hill near his house in New York. Smith translated them into the book of Mormon—and now it's a mainstream religion with over twelve million followers."

I scowled. "Are you mocking religion?"

Grayson looked aghast. "Not at all. I'm just saying that everybody's got to start somewhere."

"So how long we talkin' about, Mr. G, before a cult turns religious?"

"Another excellent question, grasshopper. It's been said that if an idea can outlast its founder for a few generations or so, then it tends to get a green light by society. But even then, if it's too out there, believers have to whittle off some of the crazier edges to survive. You can't get a job at Walmart if you go around wearing a beard and a flowing white robe."

I smirked. "You sure about that?"

Grayson's cheek dimpled. "Okay. I'll concede the point."

"Wait," I said. "You still haven't explained why you think there's going to be an apocalypse *in two days*."

"The hundred year mark," Grayson said. "Bertie's about to turn a century old."

"So?"

"If history repeats itself, that means he's got at least three generations of believers. His 'teachings' could be about to become the next mainstream religion."

"So?"

Grayson blew out an exasperated sigh. "What if Bertie's 'teachings' aren't about saving people, but harvesting their energy instead? What if he's a master of magneto-kinesis, and is teaching his disciples how to drain bodies' electromagnetic systems until they're dead?"

Earl gasped. "Ol' Magneto Man harnessed up the Earth's electromagnetic field and used it to get mountains to tumble down. He beat the tar out of a whole army of folks."

"That's absurd!" I said. "It was just a comic book!"

Grayson stared me down. "If ye had but the faith of a mustard seed, you could move mountains."

My mouth fell open. Could Grayson actually be right?

"Rocko said they were planning some kind of celebration for Bertie's birthday on Monday," Grayson went on. "It could be to announce the launch of a whole army of psychic vampires who've been trained as natural executioners."

"But ... but ...." I stuttered.

"Exactly," Grayson said. "No one believes they're capable of such a thing. It's genius, really. They've been free to travel from town to town, recruiting members and harvesting just enough lives to stay off the radar screen. It's the perfect crime."

"And them bastards get the added bonus of no wrinkles," Earl said.

I couldn't wrap my head around it. "Why in the world would Bertie choose New Port Richey to kick off his cult of doom?"

Grayson shot me a know-it-all smile. "You may not be aware of this, but New Port Richey has been the hub for many a high-stakes political campaign. Why, Ronald Reagan himself spoke at Southgate Shopping Center when he campaigned for the presidency in 1976. George W. Bush stood on his soapbox at the community college during his bid in 2000, and came back for more in 2004, making Sims Park one of his re-election campaign stops. Dan Quayle, Joe Biden and even Sara Palin followed in his footsteps, making stops at Sims Park on their marches toward the White House.

I shook my head in disbelief. "Grayson, even if what you say is true, and Bertie's ready to announce to the world he's got a psychic vampire army, how in the world could we ever hope to stop them?"

Grayson grabbed me by the shoulders. "By feeding them junk food, Drex."

"What?"

"Listen closely and follow along. Psychic vampires feed off the life energy of others, right?"

"Uh ... okay."

"Let's assume they *must* take in the vital life forces of others or they'll grow weak and die."

"I'm with ya," Earl said.

Grayson nodded. "Good. So, according to reports, the best victims for psychic vampires are those who are compassionate, empathetic and generous."

I rolled my eyes. "All right."

Grayson looked me square in the eye. "That could explain why *you* weren't affected by Bertie."

I sat up in my wheelchair. "Excuse me?"

"If we're going to expose these psychic energy suckers, we're going to need to trap them with a nice, juicy victim," Grayson said. "A real happy-go-lucky sap."

If Earl had had a tail, it would've been wagging. "Sounds like a Jim Dandy plan to me, Mr. G.," he said. "Where we gonna find us one of those?"

Chapter Thirty-Nine

"How was the potpie?" Stanley asked, popping his head into my room at Banner Hill.

"All I can say is, good thing I brought a pile of these." I pulled a Tootsie Pop out of my purse.

Stanley laughed. "Those'll rot your teeth out, you know."

I nodded toward the glass of blue water by my nightstand. "Tell it to the dentures."

"Uh, that's why I stopped by. I just wanted to give you a heads up that the tooth fairy is about to make a house call. Better hide the contraband."

"What?"

Stanley glanced down the hallway, then back at me. "Lose the lollipop, pronto. And get your fake teeth into the glass."

"Oh. Right." I scrounged in my purse and pulled out the plastic vampire choppers.

"Here he comes," Stanley said. He wrapped his lips over his teeth and shot me a gummy-looking smile.

The door opened wider. The same guy with the clipboard from yesterday walked in. I plopped the choppers into the glass and mimicked Stanley's toothless grin.

"Good work, Georgie," clipboard man said. "You're fitting in here nicely." He waved a bandaged hand at me. "Not everybody does." He shot Stanley a warning glance. "Watch out for Melvin across the hall. He's a biter."

"Thanks for the heads up," Stanley said.

The tooth fairy left. I stuck the Tootsie Pop back in my mouth and crawled into bed. "I saw Melvin came back this afternoon. Is everything all right with him?"

Stanley's face softened with relief. "Yes. The little man caused us quite a stir this morning. But turns out, he just went a little AWOL. He left this morning without signing out."

"How's that possible?" I asked as Stanley tucked me in with his rippling biceps.

Yeah, I could get used to this, all right.

"This isn't exactly a lockdown unit," Stanley said. "People are free to go in and out from 6 a.m. to 7 p.m. Otherwise, the old chimney smokers around here would stage a mutiny on the Banner."

I smiled. "Oh. Right."

A knock sounded at the door. To be on the safe side, I performed an encore of my gummy smile. "Come in!"

A doctor in scrubs and a surgical mask strolled into my room. Stanley's eyes widened. "Is there another flu epidemic going on, doctor?"

"No," the doctor mumbled through his mask. "I just came in to give Georgie the results of the test we conducted earlier."

"What test?" I asked.

The doctor pulled down his mask, revealing the worst moustache in the Western Hemisphere.

"Grayson," Stanley said. "What are you doing here?"

He nodded toward me. "I needed to let our patient know her toe swabs tested negative for saliva."

Stanley's face puckered. "Huh?"

"Never mind, Stanley," I said. "Long story."

"I also want to talk to Melvin across the hall," Grayson said. "Okay if I pop over there?"

"No can do," Stanley said, shaking his head. "Little man came home this afternoon totally whipped. He went to bed without even eating dinner. And potpie is his favorite."

"Whipped, you say?" Grayson's eyebrows met in the middle of his forehead.

Another knock sounded on the door.

"That would be my associate," Grayson said, and yanked open the door. Earl bumbled into the room looking like Sasquatch in beige scrubs.

"Howdy, y'all."

"What do you need an associate for?" Stanley asked.

Grayson shrugged. "With lights out at 7:15, I figured he and I'd have plenty of time to check out the records of the missing men. I know you don't want to get involved, so I brought Earl to be my lookout. You can count on us to be discreet. Just get us into the file room. We'll blend in like staff. No one will even notice."

Stanley chewed his lip as he thought it over.

"Hey, what's this button do?" Earl asked, and mashed a shiny red button on my bedside.

The wail of an alarm nearly blasted me out of bed.

"Shit!" Stanley hollered. He scrambled to my bed and whacked a button, silencing the alarm.

"Oops," Earl said. "My bad."

Stanley jogged back to the door, glanced up and down the hallway, and then came back in and closed it behind him.

"Look, man," he said, his eyes trained on the door like he was expecting a SWAT team to burst in any second. "Wait here. I'll go get the records. Don't touch anything, okay?"

He took a step toward the door, then eyed Earl suspiciously. "On second thought, Earl, you come with me."

Earl glanced at Grayson. He gave him the nod.

"Be right back," Stanley said. "Larry Meeks, Harry Donovan and Charlie Perkins, right?"

Grayson nodded. "Correct."

Stanley turned to go, then whipped back around on his heels again. "*Please*, don't touch anything while I'm gone!"

"You have our word," Grayson said.

Stanley's mouth pursed with regret. He grabbed Earl by the bicep and led him into the hallway. As the door closed behind them, Grayson turned to me.

"Okay, quick. We need to concoct a plan for exposing Bertie at the revival tomorrow."

I sat up in bed. "Shouldn't we wait until Earl comes back?"

"No."

"Why not?"

"Basic strategy 101, Drex. When you don't know who the patsy in a card game is, it's you."

Chapter Forty

Grayson was eating the sweaty little tub of tapioca by my bedside when the door cracked open. Rasta Stanley and his skunk ape sidekick snuck back inside.

Stanley handed over three files. "Here you go, man. What you hopin' to find in them, anyway?"

"Some kind of connection," Grayson said.

Stanley's brow furrowed. "Connection? You mean to Old Mildred?"

"As far as you know, yes," Grayson said. "We need to figure out why these three men in particular were targeted. Was it their blood type, toothpaste brand, electromagnetic energy, or whatnot."

"What was that last one?" Stanley asked.

"Whatnot?" Grayson asked.

"No. The thing before that."

"Ah. Electromagnetic energy." Grayson nodded. "It's quite possible that Larry, Harry and Charlie could've been emitting energy fields that were particularly tasty to psychic vampires."

Stanley's face dropped two inches. "Psychic vampires?"

"Yes."

Stanley stared, dumbfounded, at the man impersonating a doctor, licking tapioca from his overgrown moustache. Then his eyes shifted to the hairy, itchy-eyed man ogling the controls on my bed like a Ritalin-deprived toddler.

Finally, Stanley turned to me, his eyes pleading for an anchor in the vortex of insanity swirling around him. But given the fact I was posing as an old tranny vet with vampire teeth for dentures, I wasn't exactly the most reliable port in the storm.

Stanley let out a big sigh. "I know nothing, I see nothing," he said, and slowly backed his way out the door.

AFTER STANLEY DID HIS Schultz routine and fled, Grayson and I sat Earl down in the recliner by my bed and hooked him up with headphones and a TV remote set on *Pimp My Ride*.

With Earl floating around in redneck heaven, Grayson and I were free to peruse the files of the three missing veterans without his annoying interference. Even so, we had to be quick. Visiting hours were over in eight minutes.

"Did Larry have hemorrhoids?" Grayson asked, flipping through Harry's file.

"Uh ... yeah," I said.

"So that makes three things so far," he said, scribbling in a notebook.

"Three?"

"Yes," Grayson said, counting on his fingers. "All three men served in Vietnam, they all showed signs of borderline anemia, and they all used Preparation H."

"What does that mean?" I asked.

"Either we've got a Vietnamese khakua with a penchant for cabooses, or we need to do more research."

I grimaced at the unwanted imagery flashing across my mind. "What happened to your psychic vampire theory?"

Grayson looked up from the file. "Who says it can't be both?"

I closed my eyes and sighed.

Awesome. Here we are, Larry, Moe and Curly, searching for Larry, Harry and Charlie. Maybe, if I pray hard enough, the evil twin inside my brain will do a voodoo dance and I'll lapse blissfully into a coma overnight.

Chapter Forty-One

"Rise and shine," a demonic voice whispered in my ear.

I shot up in bed so fast I knocked heads with my human alarm clock.

"Oww!" I yelled. "Grayson, how did you get in here?"

"It's quarter after six, sleepy head. Banner Hill's been open for business for fifteen minutes."

"Well, *I'm* not." I scowled and pulled the covers up to my neck.

"Nice knot on your noggin," Grayson said, rubbing his own forehead. "How'd you get it?"

I touched the lump above my right eye. My gut went slack. "I ... I don't know. I dreamed I got whacked on the head by Old Mildred last night. I mean ... I thought it was a dream ...."

"Interesting," Grayson said, leaning in for a better look. "Do you bruise easily?"

"Not that I'm aware of."

"What do you remember about last night?"

"Aw, geez," I moaned. "Could I at least have some coffee before the interrogation?"

"It's on the nightstand."

I spied the steaming cup. Relief washed over me. I grabbed it and took a big gulp while Grayson studied me like a lab experiment.

"Anything else you remember?" he asked.

I took another slurp and felt the caffeine kick in like heroin. "I remember that after you and Earl left last night, I was reading over the files and—" I shot up in bed. "Where *is* Earl?"

"Don't worry. I sent him to pick up donuts."

I sighed again and took another slurp of coffee.

"So, you were reading the files," Grayson prompted.

"Yes. And ... that's all I remember. I guess I fell asleep."

"Can't blame you there. Those case files weren't the most riveting reading material I've ever run across." Grayson took a sip of coffee, then locked his green eyes on mine. "So, you said you dreamed of Old Mildred again?"

"Yes."

I closed my eyes and tried to recall the dream, but it flitted out of my grasp, like my last boyfriend. I opened my eyes.

"All I remember is that Mildred had a huge hunchback. Then you woke me up." I shivered. "And I feel sweaty, too. All the way to my toes."

Grayson's left eyebrow ticked up. "Interesting. Let's swab 'em."

He pulled out something that looked like a small medicine vial, then screwed off the top. The lid had some kind of applicator thing on it, like a jar of rubber cement.

"Show me the tootsies," he said.

I didn't bother to put up a fight. I stuck my foot out from under the covers. "Go ahead. Knock yourself out."

I'D JUST FINISHED DRESSING and jonesing for a crème-filled donut when Grayson returned with Earl in tow.

"Where'd you get that knot on your noggin?" Earl asked, tossing the bag of donuts to me. "Wrestlin' with your inner demons again?"

"Or *outer* ones," Grayson said. "This could be the work of Old Mildred."

"That hunchbacked old soul sucker?" Earl asked.

Grayson stared at him for a moment, then glanced down at my feet. "Of course," he said, shaking his head softly. "It's been staring me in the face the whole time."

"What has?" I asked.

"Incubus and succubus."

"Inky and sucky *who?*" Earl asked.

"Incubus and succubus," Grayson repeated. "Sex demons."

Earl crinkled his nose. "After Bobbie? I ain't buyin' that."

I closed my eyes and blew out a sigh.

"Incubus appears to sleeping women at night," Grayson explained. "He lies on top of them, trapping them into sex."

"But Bobbie ain't no woman," Earl argued.

"No, but she's pretending—" Grayson shook his head as if to clear it. He gave me a sheepish smile. "Yes, she *is*. A woman, that is."

I supposed I should've been grateful for the acknowledgement, but I just wasn't feeling it. "Grayson, what's this got to do with the men who've gone missing?"

"The succubus is the female version," Grayson said. "She comes to men at night and lures them into salacious behavior. Repeated sexual activity with either kind of demon is thought to result in deterioration of the victim's health, both mental and physical. It can even lead to death."

Earl's eyes grew wide. "You sayin' Old Mildred could be one of these succubus critters?"

"That's exactly what I'm saying."

"But why would she suck my *toes?*" I asked.

Earl laughed. "'Cause, Bobbie. You ain't got what she's *really* lookin' for."

Gross.

"Give me your spy pen," Grayson said. "Maybe we caught the succubus in action."

"Okay."

As I scrounged around in my bedclothes for the pen, someone knocked on my door.

"Come in," I said.

Stanley side-stepped into the room. His face looked grave. "Good. You're all here," he said.

"The pen's missing," I said, glancing over at the nightstand. My gut flopped. "So are the files!"

Stanley shook his head slowly. "And so are two more resident vets."

Chapter Forty-Two

"Two more vets disappeared?" I gasped. I grabbed a paper napkin and wiped the vanilla crème donut from my lips. "How did it happen?"

"Nobody knows," Stanley said. "They just vanished, like the others."

"Dang!" Earl handed Stanley the bag of donuts. "Sounds like that succubus critter sure had her a busy night last night. Donut?"

"Succubus?" Stanley asked, turning to me. His eyes widened in surprise. "How'd you get that bump on your head?"

"I hit it on the bed railing," I blurted, before Earl could say anything.

"Actually, I think it could be the work of Old Mildred," Grayson said, popping the rest of a powdered donut into his mouth. "The old gal may have attacked Drex in her sleep last night."

Stanley's eyes grew wide. "You were attacked by Old Mildred?"

I cringed. "Maybe. Things are kind of blurry. I dreamed about her, then woke up with this knot on my forehead."

"I was afraid this would happen," Stanley said, staring absently at the chocolate glazed donut in his hand. "I told you Old Mildred doesn't care for other women hangin' around."

I wiped my hands on a napkin and reached in my purse for a Tootsie Pop to calm my nerves. "I know this sounds weird, but I think Old Mildred took my spy pen—and the files on the other missing guys you brought us last night."

Stanley shook his head. "But why? What would an old ghost want with those things?"

"Good question," Grayson said, pulling out the little testing vial he'd swabbed my toes with earlier. He held it up to the light. "But one thing's for sure, Drex. You weren't dreaming. There's definitely saliva on your toes."

A shiver of disgust ran down my spine. On the one hand, at least I wasn't crazy. On the other hand, *someone sucked my toes last night!*

"Hmm," Grayson said, studying the vial. "I wasn't expecting that."

"What?" I asked.

"According to the test results, Old Mildred is a pothead."

"LET ME GET THIS STRAIGHT," Stanley said after I told him my recurring dream and Grayson showed him the test vial results. "Someone's actually been sucking your toes while you're asleep?"

"Yep. A succubus," Earl said. "Wait a minute, y'all. Wouldn't a succubus suck a *bus?*"

I winced to stop an eye roll. "Ignore him, Stanley. Those two vets who went missing last night—was Melvin one of them?"

"No." Stanley helped me into the wheelchair. "Why? You don't think *he's* the one sucking your toes, do you?"

The thought of the pasty, Brooklyn comb-over champ gumming my big toe made me nearly dry heave. "Ugh! I hope not!"

"There's no way to tell who the culprit is from this," Grayson said, pocketing the test vial. "I only used a six-panel preliminary saliva test. I'll need another sample in order to conduct a DNA match."

I winced. "*Another* sample?"

"Listen, man," Stanley said, "I get what you're trying to do here. But I can't be part of it."

"Too late for that," Grayson said. He opened the door to my room, stuck his head out, and glanced up and down the hallway. "I really need to talk to Melvin," he said, turning back to face us. "I need to find out what he knows about the BERPS, and if he saw or heard anything last night."

"You can't man," Stanley said, pushing me out into the hall. "Melvin got up early and left with some tattooed guy."

"Don't touch that!" I hollered.

Stanley and Grayson's heads swung my way. Earl jerked his hand away from my bedside as if he'd been shocked with 10,000 volts.

"Sheez," I growled at my cousin. "Keep your mitts off the buttons!"

I returned my attention to Stanley. "Why was Melvin in such a hurry to leave this morning? Did you see what kind of vehicle the guy was driving?"

"No. But I think we should make an appearance before anyone comes looking for us, too."

Stanley took the reins on my wheelchair ushered me into the main hall toward the breakfast room. There wasn't another person in sight.

"Where is everybody?" Grayson asked.

"It's Sunday morning," Stanley said. "Around here, that means you either get in a van to go to church, or you head to the rec room there for an exercise class."

Earl peeked into the rec room and laughed. "Anybody wanna work up a sweat to old Regis & Cathy Lee DVDs?"

"In leotards or not?" Grayson asked.

"Ugh!" I grumbled. Someone needed to take charge of this lame operation. From the looks of it, it was going to have to be me.

"Stanley, you go grab the files on the other two missing men and meet us at the RV," I demanded. "Grayson, you take the helm on my wheelchair. And Earl? For the millionth time, stop touching that!"

Chapter Forty-Three

"What's the plan, Mr. G?" Earl asked as Grayson rolled me down the sidewalk in front of Banner Hill, toward the RV parked on the street.

"Nothing's set in stone, as far as you know," Grayson said. "But with two more vets missing this morning, we need to act fast."

"Agreed," I said in my best commanding tone. "We need to put our heads together on this."

Earl picked up a fallen oak branch, stuck an end in his armpit and shot it like it was an Uzi. "You can count on me!"

My eyes had just completed their orbit in my sockets when we reached the RV. Stanley came trotting up, holding his duffle bag.

"You got the files?" I asked.

"Yeah, man. But I think the tooth fairy is getting suspicious."

"Tooth fairy?" Grayson asked, looking intrigued.

"The guy who checks the dentures at night," I said.

Earl laughed. "Woo, boy, I love me some spy talk! Can I have a secret code name, too?"

"Sure," I said. "Ignoramus."

I looked up at Stanley from my wheelchair. "You in? We could really use whatever insider info you might have about Banner Hill and the guys who've gone missing."

Stanley winced and bit his lip. "Uh ... geez."

"Please," I said, touching his arm. "We may be the only hope these guys have."

Stanley's board-straight posture went limp. "Okay. But can you drop me off at home afterward?"

I nodded. "Absolutely. Now, let's load up."

"Where are we going?" Stanley asked.

I glanced around and noticed everyone was staring at me with expectant looks on their faces.

Crap. Am I really in charge now? What have I done?

"Uh ...." My gut gurgled. "We need protein. You know, to fuel our brains. Those donuts didn't cut it. I say we hold a strategy meeting at Topless Tacos. Everybody in?"

"Yeah, sure," Stanley said. "I could eat."

"Tacos sound good," Earl said. "What time do they open?"

"Eleven," Grayson said.

I glanced at my cellphone. It was 9:38. "Oh. Well, if you drive slow, Grayson, we should get there just as they open."

Grayson snorted. "If I drive *that* slow, we'll be pulled over for causing a public hazard."

"Uh, looks like we got a problem, Houston," Earl said.

"Ugh! What now, Earl?" I grumbled.

He nodded toward the back of the RV. "Looks like somebody done stole the back tire, Mr. G."

Our eyes shifted to the gaping dark hole under the chassis where the back left tire used to be.

"Great," I said. "What do we do now?"

Earl grinned. "Not to worry. Sit tight. I got us a plan."

BEFORE I COULD OBJECT, Earl had disappeared, off on a self-described "secret mission" to obtain a new tire for Grayson's RV.

Knowing Earl's penchant for both auto mechanics and James Bond films, I gave him about a fifty-fifty chance he'd return alive.

Meanwhile, Grayson, Stanley and I sat around on a bench outside Banner Hill, looking like time travelers who'd arrived thirty years too early to our retirement party.

"I don't understand it," I said to Stanley. "Why has nobody reported any of these vets missing?"

"They *have* been reported missing," Stanley said.

"To who?"

"To Ms. Gable. From what I hear, she's got Officer Holbrook investigating."

"That cop we saw at Topless Tacos?" Grayson asked.

Stanley nodded and fiddled with the end of one of his dreadlocks. "Yeah."

"What do you know about Rocko?" I asked.

Stanley's brow furrowed. "Who?"

"The tattooed man who drives that Bertie and the BERPS van. He's the one who dropped Melvin off here yesterday afternoon."

"Oh. That guy." Stanley shrugged. "Nothing, really. He just started turning up this week to take people to that revival thing."

"Doesn't anybody monitor their comings and goings?" I asked.

Stanley shrugged. "Hey, if it's church related, it kind of gets the green light around here. No questions asked."

Grayson shot me an *I told you so* look. I pursed my lips.

"The tattooed guy's name is Rocko," I said to Stanley. "It seems awfully suspicious that he began showing up the same time the vets started going missing, isn't it?"

Stanley opened his mouth to answer. The roar of a loud muffler appeared to come out. It pierced the sleepy, mid-morning slumber surrounding Banner Hill, and was quickly followed by the blast of a horn tooting out the musical notes to the first line of *Dixie*.

I suddenly wished I was in the land of anywhere but here.

"Who's that?" Stanley asked.

"Earl," I said. "That's his truck, Bessie."

Earl parked the massive, black monster truck on the street in front of Grayson's RV. Comparing them side by side, the two vehicles were almost the same size. However, Bessie came equipped with a 540-horsepower Hemi engine and tractor tires taller than me. With enough rope tied to its trailer hitch, that truck could yank the teeth out of King Kong.

Earl hoped out of the cab and waved to us. Then he bounced a new tire out of Bessie's tail gate and disappeared with it on the other side of the RV.

"Okay, start from the beginning," I said to Stanley. "When did the vets first go missing?"

Stanley glanced around, then lowered his voice. "First I heard of it was Wednesday morning, four days ago. That's when Larry Meeks disappeared from room 2G. But whatever happened to him went down on Tuesday night."

"Why do you say that?" Grayson asked.

"Wednesday morning, his bed was made up."

"So?"

"Larry *never* made up his bed. Said it hurt his arthritis."

"So, you're saying he never slept in his bed Tuesday night?"

Stanley nodded. "Which was weird, because the day before, I couldn't get him out of it. Said he was too tired to get up."

"I remember that from his file notes," I said. "You recommended a blood analysis. The results showed he had mild anemia."

"That's right."

"What about Harry Donovan?" Grayson asked.

"Pretty much the same routine. Harry ate dinner Wednesday night, and was still up when denture check rolled around."

Grayson cocked his head. "What's up with this whole tooth patrol thing, anyway?"

Stanley shrugged. "Draper insists on it. Anyway, Harry disappeared the next morning."

"Was his bed still made up?" I asked.

"No. I tucked Harry in that night myself. The guy was white as his sheets."

"And Charlie?" I asked.

Stanley stared at his hands. "Pretty much the same thing. Ate dinner Thursday evening, then disappeared overnight."

I glanced down at the files Stanley had pulled from his duffle bag. "These new guys, Tom Hallen and Joe Plank. Were they at dinner last night?"

"Sure. Nobody misses potpie night."

My gut gurgled involuntarily. I set my purse on the bench and scrounged around for a Tootsie Pop. Grayson took the opportunity and grabbed the files from my lap.

"These new guys. Did they have bloodwork done in the days preceding their disappearance?" he asked as he flipped through their records.

"Not that I know of," Stanley said.

I plucked the sucker from my mouth. "Wait, I just realized something."

"It's about time," Grayson said. "Tootsie Pops are a mental crutch, Drex."

I shot him some side eye. "No. These men. They're all *DNR*s."

"Democrats, Not Republicans?" Earl asked, wandering up.

"No!" I frowned. "They're all on their last legs, and they know it. They've all signed DNR forms—as in Do Not Resuscitate."

Chapter Forty-Four

With all four of us crammed into Bessie's front cab, we looked like hillbillies heading to a Sunday hootenanny. Stuck between Earl and Grayson, there was no escape.

"This is kind a like *The Expendables*," Earl said, shifting the monster truck into third, making me duck right to avoid his giant elbow.

Why do I always have to sit by the gear box?

"What are you talking about?" I asked, bracing my foot against the floorboard in case more evasive maneuvering was required.

"That movie," Earl said. "Them vet fellers that went missing. Maybe they knew they was probably gonna die."

Grayson took his nose out of the file he was reading. "Well, given that the youngest one of the bunch is seventy-two, that's pretty much a given."

Earl shook his head. "That ain't what I mean."

"What, then?" I asked.

"These fellers what disappeared from Banner Hill. What if they believed they was on a secret mission—one they wasn't likely to come back from?"

Like when you went out to get a tire for the RV?

"Hold on a second," Grayson said. "You may be onto something." He shuffled through the files. "Tom and Joe were in Vietnam at the same time. From 1960-62. So were Larry, Harry and Charlie."

I shot Grayson a look. He tapped a finger to his temple. "Eidetic memory, remember?"

My brow furrowed. "Is it possible they were all members of the same troop, fighting the Viet Kong together?"

"It's possible," Grayson said. "Now they could be banding together to fight a new enemy."

"*King* Kong?" Earl asked.

I elbowed him in the ribs. "What if they all have that Peoria thing, Grayson?"

Grayson's left eyebrow disappeared under his fedora. "Peoria?"

"You know. That blood disease. What did you call it?"

"Porphyria." He glanced at the files. "There was no mention of it in their paperwork."

"What if the enemy they were all fighting was Old Mildred?" Stanley asked. "What if she took them to some other world with her?"

"Hmm," Grayson said. "An intriguing possibility. There does seem to be some evidentiary commonality, what with the purple light you reported, Stanley. The light also appeared right as Balls was attacked, too."

Stanley flinched. "Something attacked someone's balls?"

"I knew it!" Earl said. "It's the Attack of the Purple Pe—"

I jabbed Earl in the ribs again. "Shut up and drive. We are *not* going down that road again."

THE CUTE WAITRESS AT Topless Tacos had already taken our orders. When I find something good, I tend to stick with it, so she already knew mine by heart—Mahi tacos and nacho salad.

While the four of us waited in hungry anticipation around the shiny red table in the corner, we discussed Bertie's potential as the leader of a new psychic vampire cult hell bent on world domination.

Well, at least it wasn't boring.

I took a slurp of Dr Pepper and looked up. Through the glass storefront, I saw a white van pull into the lot. As it parked, I was treated to the smiling face of Bertie and his rainbow BERPS.

"Uh-oh. We've got company," I said.

Earl whistled. "Speak of the devil."

"Not so fast," Grayson said. "That has yet to be scientifically proven."

Stanley's face twisted with worry. "What do we do now?"

Grayson leaned in across the table and whispered, "Improvise."

We all nodded uncertainly, then turned and stared out the plate glass window. Rocko climbed out of the van, clad in his customary black leather and full-sleeve tattoos. He put on a pair of sunglasses, adjusted his red do-rag, and swaggered across the parking lot up to the front door.

He flung it open and glanced around. The cocky confidence plastered on his face withered into disappointment.

"Where're all the topless chicks?" he asked, whipping off his sunglasses.

The feminist in me smirked.

"False advertising," Grayson said.

"Figures." Rocko's shoulders slumped. "Hey. I know you. Yesterday. Parking lot. You're the RVers, right?"

Grayson tipped his fedora. "Nice to see you again, Rocko. Please, join us if you like."

"Thanks. Let me just make a pit stop at the head, first."

Rocko ambled out of earshot. I leaned in close to Grayson. "What are you doing, inviting the enemy to the table? How are we going to discuss bringing Bertie down now?"

"Elementary," Grayson said. "We fight fire with fire."

"We're gonna burn the place down?" Earl asked. "Ain't that illegal?"

"Not arson," Grayson said. "To slay a *psychic* vampire requires a *psyche* approach."

My nose crinkled. "I don't get it."

"Just follow my lead." Grayson looked around the table at Earl and Stanley. "No mention of Bertie or psychic vampires, got it?"

"Got it," Earl said, and saluted.

"I didn't see nothin', I won't say nothin'," Stanley said.

"Shh. Here he comes," Grayson whispered. He motioned for Rocko to sit beside him.

"Tough day at the office?" Grayson asked the former biker turned van driver.

I suddenly felt a migraine coming on.

"Last day of a revival is always the hardest," Rocko said. "I could use a beer."

"Let me buy you one," Grayson said.

Rocko shook his head. "No. I gave all that up for the BERPS."

"Me, too," Stanley said. "Wine is a whole lot less gassy."

Grayson shot Stanley a quick *can it* look. "What?" he asked, holding up his hands. "It's true."

"So, Rocko," Grayson said, turning on the charm, "What do you like most about your life on the road with Bertie?"

What is this? An interrogation or a date?

"The opportunity to travel, I guess," Rocko said. "Meet new people."

"Nice." Grayson slapped on a grin. "Sounds like you're a religious man and a free spirit."

"Yeah, I guess." Rocko broke into a smile. "I like to think so."

"Perhaps you can help us, then," Grayson said. "My friends and I were just discussing the difference between a religion and a cult."

Grayson glanced our way. We all smiled and nodded like idiotic bobble-heads.

"Cults are bad," Rocko said.

"That's right," Grayson said. "You know how you can spot the difference?"

Rocko bit his lip. "Uh ... cults serve Kool-Aid?"

"Well, yes," Grayson conceded. "That, and the fact that cult leaders are bullies. They're always acting better than everybody else. You know, like they've got some special powers nobody else has."

Rocko nodded. "Uh-huh."

Grayson scooted his chair closer. "Cults don't like you to think for yourself, either. If you don't follow the rules, or if you say something bad about the group, a cult leader will tell you you're a disbeliever, and that you're going to burn in hell."

Rocko's face reddened. He shifted in his seat. "Really?"

"Absolutely. Cult leaders are slick," Grayson said. "And they're total control freaks. You see, they keep members under their thumbs by telling them that all kinds of horrible things might happen if they even *think* about leaving the cult."

Rocko chewed his lip. "Bertie's always telling me I should get my tattoos removed."

"What?" Grayson gasped. "These beautiful works of art?"

"Is that one supposed to be Woody Woodpecker or Miss Piggy?" Earl asked, nodding at Rocko's forearm.

Grayson shot my cousin a *shut it* glare, then turned back to Rocko. "Cult leaders are also cheapskates. The skinflints don't even want their workers to be able to have a place of their own."

The veins in Rocko's temples looked like tree roots. "I been workin' for Bertie for forty years. All I got to my name is a sleeping bag stowed in the back of the van."

"That's not fair," Grayson said. "Cult leaders also—"

"Wait a minute," Rocko said. "Are you saying *brother Bertie* is a cult leader?"

"Me?" Grayson gasped, then shot us a surreptitious wink. "How would I know, brother?" He put a hand on Rocko's shoulder. "All I'm saying is, that if the shoe fits, somebody's likely to get kicked in the ass with it. I just don't want it to be *you*."

Chapter Forty-Five

"Well, looks like it's all over but the cryin'," Earl said, and nudged me on the elbow. We stared across the table at Rocko. Grayson had reduced him to rubble.

"I gave Bertie the best years of my life," Rocko sobbed. "And for what?" He grabbed Grayson's bottle of beer and glugged half of it down.

Grayson wrapped an arm around Rocko's shoulder. "Don't beat yourself up, brother. We've all been there."

"That's right," Earl said. "I used to believe in Bertie, too. I sent him a pile of emails about poor Sally, but he never even bothered to write back."

"Sally?" Rocko asked, sniffing back a tear.

Earl nodded. "The two-headed turtle I found in Wimbly swamp last year. She's a red-eared—"

"Amen, brother," Grayson said loudly. He shifted his eyes to me and nodded once. "What about you?"

I flinched. "Uh ... I found out my father isn't my father."

"Amen. Everybody's got troubles," Grayson said.

Stanley glanced over at me, his eyes wild with stage fright.

"Brother Stanley?" Grayson prompted.

Stanley licked his lips. "Uh ... I can't go to Jamaica without somebody sticking a joint in my mouth."

Grayson nodded. "That happens to everybody, son."

"Amen, brother," Rocko said. "Kingstown. Those were the good old days."

"All right, men. One for all, and all for me. We've got work to do." Grayson straightened his shoulders and puffed out his chest, morphing from mentalist to Army man in half a second flat.

Impressive.

"Five men have gone missing from Banner Hill," Grayson said as if he were laying out the tactical maneuvers for an impending war. I could almost see the American flag flying behind his head as he spoke.

"These heroic veterans fought on foreign soil so we could be free. Now, it's up to us to return the favor. We need to find out what happened to them, and set our MIAs free—if they're still alive. Can I get an amen?"

"Amen!" Earl and Rocko cheered.

Stanley and I glanced at each other, then chimed in lamely. "Amen."

"We'll fight our enemies wherever we find them," Grayson preached.

"Amen!" Rocko and Earl cheered.

"Amen," Stanley and I muttered.

"If Bertie's the bad guy, we'll shut him down. Amen?" Grayson crooned.

"Amen!" Rocko and Earl roared.

"Amen," Stanley and I said.

Grayson shot Rocko a determined, tight-jawed stare. "No man should have to do another's bidding, brother."

Rocko nodded his tear-stained face. "Yes, sir."

Grayson leaned in across the table. "Now, listen closely, everyone, and do exactly as I say ...."

Chapter Forty-Six

"You all in, brother?" Grayson asked Stanley, as Rocko loaded me and my wheelchair into the back of his rainbow Bertie van.

"I gotta go see the voodoo priestess first," Stanley said, chewing his lip. "Bertie's some bad juju. I'm gonna need a spirit animal or something for backup."

"Good idea," Grayson said. "Best to cover all the bases. This is the Bible Belt, after all, and a lot of people around here know how to use it."

I cringed.

Worst mixed-metaphor ever.

I sighed and resigned myself to my fate. I was half-bald, and half-heartedly on a half-baked mission with a pile of half-wits, headed for a showdown with Bertie and his half-assed toupee.

What more could a girl ask for?

After loading me into the back, Rocko and Grayson climbed into the front of the van. Grayson turned to face me from the passenger seat. "You got the EFD?"

I patted the electromagnetic field detector duct-taped to my waist underneath my shirt. "Tucked and ready."

"Got your vest?"

I winced. "Bullet proof vest? I didn't think—"

"No. Wool," Grayson said. "It's supposed to get cold tonight."

"Oh. Yes, Dad."

"Good. You know the plan?"

"I know it." I squirmed in my wheelchair and pulled out the Tootsie Pop I'd stashed in a side pocket. I pointed it at Grayson like a toy gun. "You can count on me, Sarge."

"Wow," Rocko said. He turned the ignition and the van shuddered to life. "Sounds like we're preparing for war."

"In a way, we are," Grayson said. "You said it yourself, Rocko, 'Cults are bad.' We can't let this go unchallenged."

"Right." Rocko backed the van out of the parking lot of Topless Tacos. I could tell by the reflection of his face in the rearview mirror that Grayson's Kool-Aid was kicking in, big-time.

I waved to Earl and Stanley, who were sitting in Bessie, ready and waiting to tail us to the revival tent.

"Did you know that most major foreign wars were fought over religious intolerance?" Grayson asked Rocko.

"No, sir," Rocko said, pulling out into traffic.

Grayson patted him on the shoulder. "That's what makes America so great, brother. We don't fight over theological differences. We fight over socioeconomic ones. Economics is our religion."

"Huh?" Rocko grunted.

I let out a jaded laugh. "If that's true, then why do so many people go to church, Grayson?"

Grayson shrugged. "To live longer, of course."

I plucked the sucker from my mouth. "Are you saying you believe in eternal life?"

Grayson turned his head to face me again. "Studies show that regular church attendance increases life expectancy. Frequent attendees live an average of 83 years. Non-attendees about 75."

I frowned. "Maybe. But they spend all those extra years in church, so it's a wash."

A dimple formed in Grayson's cheek. "Fair enough. Now ditch the Tootsie Pop, cadet, and get ready to rumble."

Chapter Forty-Seven

The inside of Bertie's revival tent was a fire-hazard waiting to happen. Packed to capacity, people had squeezed into every folding chair in the place, then lined the fabric walls two- and three-people deep.

The electric buzz of the pulsing crowd was palpable. And, for the first time, I began to think Grayson's theory about Bertie being a psychic vampire might actually be plausible. If Bertie really could feed off the energy of others, tonight would be an all-he-could-eat buffet.

With Bertie's van-man Rocko with us, we were quickly ushered up to the front row. I have to say, it was cool getting the red carpet treatment. But the envious stares we garnered as Rocko parted the sea of humanity in the tent made me seriously question some folks' charitable intentions.

Once we reached the front row, Grayson parked me at the end of a long line of other folks in wheelchairs. The swell of anticipation was contagious. I even felt my own pulse quicken as I watched people shift nervously in their seats, putting on or pulling off the jackets and hats they'd worn to fend off the chill of the cold front that had blown in that afternoon.

Above the constant, murmuring hum of the throng behind me, a belch blasted out. I craned my neck around to give the impossible ingrate some side-eye. It was Earl, grinning at me like the cat who ate the canary carbonara.

"Just making a joyful noise unto the Lord, Cuz," he said.

"Earl, you're such a cretin!" I shouted.

As the words left my lips, the tent grew silent as a grave.

My last word, "cretin," echoed through the sudden hush like the call of an angry cricket. I shrunk back into my wheelchair, mortified.

I had no idea my voice sounded that shrill when I screamed!

Like a mortified turtle, I slowly stuck my head up and glanced around. The room was still silent. But nobody was paying any attention to me. All eyes were on the stage directly in the front me. I turned to look, too.

A man was walking across the raised wooden platform. He stopped at the microphone set up center-stage. He tapped it three times, sending staccato sound bites blasting through the tent.

"Brothers and sisters, are you ready for a miracle?" he yelled.

"Yes!" the crowd roared back like thunder. Then the chanting started. "Bertie! Bertie! Bertie!"

A moment later, Bertie stepped out onto the stage in a suit I'd seen somewhere before.

On Colonel Sanders.

The hordes went wild.

Bertie smiled, raised his right hand, and pranced around the stage like a rock star. Then, in a move that made my jaw drop, he did a reverse moon-walk, stepped up to the mic, and put his hands together.

The room went so quiet you could hear a pinhead drop.

"Lettuce pray," Bertie said, and bowed his head.

Grayson whispered in my ear. "Ready for your close up, cadet?"

I swallowed against the rising bile in my gut. "As ready as I'll ever be."

TEN MINUTES LATER, a sing-along with Bertie had whipped the crowd into a hypnotic frenzy. Bertie was playing to the believers, pointing here and there yelling, "Be healed!"

Suddenly, a plus-sized woman in a small-sized tank top and rainbow-striped leggings stood up and yelled, "Halleluiah!" She plowed down the aisle of believers behind us, then ran toward the stage.

Right as she passed by Grayson and me, she doubled over, as if some invisible force had punched her in the gut. She convulsed, babbled incoherently, and fell to the floor in front of me, writhing and rolling around like she was trying to put out a fire.

"Bertie's got her in his energy-sucking grasp!" Grayson said. "We've got to do something!"

Before I could stop him, Grayson scooted around the back of my wheelchair and knelt by the woman's side. He looked up at me. "Hurry, Call nine—"

I kicked him in the buttock. "Shh! Leave her be. She's just fallen out in the spirit."

The woman grunted and kicked out wildly. Grayson jerked to standing, his face scarlet. He lowered his eyes and scurried back to his position behind my chair.

"Shouldn't somebody at least cover her up?" he whispered into my ear. "Her spirit isn't the only thing that's fallen out."

I didn't want to look.

My spirit was willing, but my flesh was weak. I got an eyeful that will haunt me until I reach the Pearly Gates.

I shivered with disgust, then looked up and saw something even more horrifying.

Up on stage, a line of people was forming to be healed by Bertie. The person at the very front of the que was as big as a bear—and his name was Earl Shankles.

I closed my eyes, willing this all to be a nightmare I'd wake up from soon.

"What's he doing up there?" Grayson asked.

"I don't know," I said, shaking my head. "As far as I can tell, Earl's gone rogue."

Chapter Forty-Eight

The crowd was swaying to the beat of *I'm a Believer*. Earl was inching his way toward Bertie, who was standing center-stage. Earl's eyes appeared glazed over, as if he were hypnotized, or in some kind of trance. But then again, they often did ....

"Come, brother," Bertie coaxed.

Earl took a few more zombie-like steps, the stopped two feet in front of Bertie.

"What's your name, brother?" Bertie asked.

"E ... Earl."

"And what brings you to seek a miracle tonight?"

"I'm not here for me," Earl said.

The crowd oohed and aahed.

"What faith from this kind and generous spirit!" Bertie said, offering a giant grin to the hordes. He turned back to Earl. "Pray, son, then who are you here for?"

"Sally," Earl said.

Bertie's face fell like an anvil off a cliff.

"You!" he squealed, scrambling away from Earl. "Security!" he shrieked. "Get him! It's that freak with the two-headed turtle!"

Two burly biker-men rushed the stage and grabbed Earl by the arms. I could tell by the bad forearm tattoo that one of the men was Rocko.

I started to get up. Grayson's hands pressed down on my shoulders. "Don't blow your cover," he said. "Earl will be all right."

I stared up at the stage, helpless to do anything.

"But Bertie, you're Sally's only hope!" Earl yelled as they hauled him away.

Grayson's hand squeezed my shoulder. "Time for Plan B," he whispered in my ear, then shoved me forward so fast I nearly fell out of the wheelchair.

"I bear testament to Bertie's powers!" Grayson yelled.

Bertie's panicked eyes landed on us. Seeds of recognition set in. He pulled himself together and straightened his bolero tie. "Brothers!" he cried out. "So good to see you again! Come up here where everyone can see you!"

As Grayson wheeled me up the disability ramp toward the stage, Bertie told the throng of believers our backstory.

"Brothers and sisters," he said, "these two came to see me yesterday, on a mission to restore this poor soul to health."

The crowd murmured acknowledgements. Grayson wheeled me up to Bertie. He laid his clammy hand on my shoulder.

"Mind you, this poor crippled man didn't ask to be healed of lameness. You see, until yesterday, he was also blind, weren't you?" Bertie squeezed my shoulder. Hard.

"Yes!" I chirped. "I was blind, but now I see!"

The hordes erupted in cheers.

"Okay, calm down," Bertie said. "Now I'm going to lay hands on this man and he's going to *walk!*"

A second round of applause and yelling broke out.

Under the cover of the cacophony of cheers, Bertie leaned over, slapped his froggy palm on my forehead and said, "I don't know what your game is, but I know you're with that two-headed turtle freak. If you really can walk, I suggest you do it when I tell you to, or you're gonna need that wheelchair for real."

Bertie raised up, grinned, and waved at the crowd. "Be healed, brother! Get up and walk!"

I stood up. The crowd went wild.

"Walk!" Bertie said.

For the first time in my life, I was a believer. Stage fright was *real.* My mind was scrambled. My legs wobbled so badly I could hardly take a step. Half paralyzed with fear, a sudden thought made me nearly collapse back into the wheelchair.

Is it stage fright, or is Bertie sapping my psychic energy?

"Excellent," Bertie said in a tone that sent a shiver down my spine. "Take him to the recovery room."

A biker dude pushed me back into the wheelchair. I landed with a thud, then craned my neck around, trying to see Grayson.

I spotted him in a dark corner of the stage. Two security guards had him pinned down. I turned back to face the crowd. I zeroed in on a guy taking money from the collection plate. His face seemed familiar, but my mind was too scrambled to recall his name.

"Help," I said, half-heartedly. Knowing help was nowhere nearby.

"Make sure he doesn't get away," Bertie whispered to the bodyguard as he wheeled me away.

I had a bad feeling about this. And, even worse, I had a bad taste in my mouth.

Again.

Chapter Forty-Nine

I was blind. Again.

But this time, I couldn't tell if I was having another spell of lost eyesight, or if it was because wherever I was being held against my will was as black as pitch.

It was cold, too. Like, meat-locker cold.

I shivered and felt the telltale tug of the ropes binding my wrists and ankles to the wheelchair. The goon who'd tied me up had warned me to keep quiet or he'd gag me, too. I'd obeyed. What other choice did I have?

After he secured my arms and legs to the chair, he'd put a hand over my eyes and rolled me down a passageway behind the stage. I heard the click of a door handle, then movement as he'd drug me backward into a cold, dark room. He'd spun my chair around so my back was to the door, then removed his hand from over my eyes.

"Don't make a sound," he'd demanded before he shut the door. As it closed, it clanged heavy and metallic.

Maybe it *was* a meat locker.

A sudden thought sent shivers down my spine.

Cripes! Maybe this is where they store the bodies!

Blind and alone, I fought against the rising panic in my throat. The goon hadn't gagged *or* blindfolded me. Was that a good sign or a bad sign? I strained my eyes open as wide as they would go. I still couldn't see squat. To top it off, my mouth tasted like Lincoln had come to life from a roll of pennies and taken a dump on my tongue—just like the other two times I'd gone blind.

I have to get out of here!

I tried scooting with my torso, hoping it would move the wheelchair. But it wouldn't budge. My mind swirled with panic. Were bodies hanging on hooks all around me, empty husks sucked dry of life-giving energy by Bertie and his believers?

I didn't want to wait around to find out.

"Help!" I yelled into the darkness.

"Help me!" Someone cried out from across the room.

"Oh my God!" I said. "They got you, too?"

"Yes! Save me!"

"Who's doing this to us?" I asked.

"Brother Bertie!"

My gut flopped. "Crap! I knew it!" I called back. I squirmed against the ropes binding me to the wheelchair.

"Help!"

"I'm trying, but I'm tied up!"

The rancid, metallic taste in my mouth intensified. I wanted to spit, but was worried it'd end up all over me. I didn't want to die like that.

Suddenly, I heard the door crack open behind me, then footsteps. Someone was approaching—*to kill me?*

"Who's there?" I squeaked.

"Bertie!" the other hostage called out.

"Shut up!" a man's voice yelled behind my back. A hand of unknown origin clamped onto my shoulder. If it had been Grayson, I would've felt the electricity of his touch. It if had been Earl, I'd have smelled his Frito breath.

A clammy hand landed on my forehead.

No doubt about it. It was dirty Bertie himself.

My mind scrambled. Had Bertie turned on the lights when he came in, and I was blind again? Or was he operating in the dark, hoping I wouldn't recognize him?

"What do you want with me?" I asked.

"The question is, what do *you* want with *me?*"

Suddenly, hands were all over me, patting me down. One hand stopped on the EFD gizmo taped to my side. The other hand stopped on my right boob.

I heard Bertie gasp. "Brother, when did you become a sister?"

"It's a long story," I said.

"What's this thing?" he asked, ripping off the EFD taped to my side. "Is this some kind of remote control recording device?"

"No," I said.

"A bomb?" The pitch in his voice rose. "Are you trying to blow me up?"

"No!" I pleaded into the dark. "I ... I just wanted to record your electromagnetic field disturbance."

"My *what?*"

"Your psychic energy fluctuations, okay?"

"Really?" he said. "How does this thing work?"

"The monitor detects electromagnetic changes," I offered hopefully.

"Is this the monitor?"

"I ... I don't know. I can't see. I'm having one of my blind spells again."

"So ... you haven't ... *seen* anything?" he asked.

"Uh ... no."

Bertie grabbed the wheelchair, spun me around and began shoving me forward.

"Are you going to kill me now?" I squealed.

"Kill you?" Bertie asked.

"Yes." I blinked back tears. Suddenly, the gray outline of the room came into view.

"Hell, no," Bertie said. "Just don't sue me, okay? I didn't know you had boobs!"

I glanced down at my lap. The EFD monitor lay between my knees, where he'd tossed it. The indicator was all the way past the red zone.

"Help me!" the voice called out to my left.

"Shut up!" Bertie shouted.

I hazarded a sideways glance and caught sight of a shiny, white, coffin-looking thing.

What the hell?

"You're ... you're going to let me go?" I stuttered.

"What?" Bertie said. "Of course. Why wouldn't I? I thought you were some kook out to discredit me."

"No way. I'm a believer," I lied, hoping it would save my skin.

As Bertie reached the door, my eyesight was hazy, but clearing. He stopped pushing the wheelchair, then scooted around it and flung open the door. Even with my limited sight, I could see he was red and sweaty from the ordeal.

"Sorry about this," he said as he pushed me toward the door. "I'll untie you in the hallway. This has all been just a silly misunderstanding."

"Sure," I giggled hysterically. "That works for me."

Suddenly, a dark shadow appeared in the open doorway.

Not another blind spell! I thought, and closed my eyes hoping to ward it off.

"And just where do you think you're goin'?" Earl's voice boomed into the room.

Aw, no!

My wheelchair came to a screeching halt, nearly catapulting me out of it. I flung open my eyes.

Earl's burly, bear-like silhouette blocked the oversized doorframe. I locked eyes with him, hoping to tell him we were in the clear, if he'd just—but then I realized he wasn't looking at me.

Earl was staring at a point near my right elbow.

I shifted my eyes in that direction. The shiny barrel of a pistol was pointing right at my cousin's beer gut.

Aw, shit!

"New game plan. Get in here and close the door behind you," Bertie barked.

I shook my head.

I could scarcely believe it.

It was just too bad to be true.

Chapter Fifty

The metal door clicked solidly behind us. My vision had cleared enough to see that Bertie was holding us at gunpoint in a long, narrow room with metal walls.

The room was empty except for a shiny, white, pod-like contraption in the corner that appeared to be some kind of flash-freezing unit. Next to it was a rectangular object covered with a beige tarp. It was about the size and shape of a double-door freezer. If this *was* a meat locker, it was in need of fresh meat.

"Lord-a-mercy! Is that your *coffin?*" Earl asked, pointing at the long, cylindrical machine in the corner.

"No!" Bertie said. "It's not a coffin. It's a hyperbaric chamber."

"Oh! Like the one Michael Jackson and Bubbles slept in," Earl said.

Bertie's already red face went crimson. The tendons on his scrawny neck stuck out like a lizard's dewlap.

"See?" Bertie screeched. "This is why I can't have nice things! People think I'm a freak!" He aimed the gun at Earl's belly. "Now get over there. Get in the cage!"

"What cage?" Earl asked.

A vein in Bertie's temple began to pulsate as if it were about to erupt. "The one under the tarp over there. Now do it!"

Earl strolled over to investigate what was under the rectangular stretch of tarp.

As he bent over to pick up the edge of the fabric, someone cried out from underneath it.

"Help me!"

The woman I'd heard earlier!

"You got somebody else in there, too?" Earl asked. "That's illegal, you know."

"Shut up and get in!" Bertie said.

Earl lifted the tarp, revealing a huge, wrought-iron cage. Inside, half naked and frazzled, was the biggest damned parrot I'd ever seen.

"Dirty Bertie!" it squawked at an ear-splitting decibel.

"For the last time, shut up, Polly!" Bertie yelled. He blew out an angry sigh and muttered at me. "Gift from a grateful believer. Been the bane of my existence for nearly fifty years."

"Why are you doing this to us?" I asked.

"Because the last thing I need is more bad publicity," Bertie said. "Everybody thinks it's a miracle from God that I look this good at one hundred. If they find out that it's because of the chamber there, the mystery surrounding my persona will be ruined. I'll just be another blow-hard hack."

"Just tell 'em you eat Kale," Earl said, stepping into the cage. "Like all them celebrities do."

Bertie thought it over. "But then, I'd have to eat kale."

"That's the down side," Earl said, closing the cage door behind him.

"Listen, I'm sorry about this," Bertie said. "But I can't have anyone knowing about the hyperbaric chamber. And I'm too damned old to start eating kale now. My colon would blow a gasket."

"I heard that," Earl said, rubbing his stomach. "If I had to choose between life and kale, I'd be hard pressed to decide myself."

"Thanks for understanding," Bertie said, locking the bird cage with a padlock. "I'll have to wait until the crowd's gone before we can dispose of you two."

"Dispose?" I asked.

"Mind if I eat the sunflower seeds while we wait?" Earl said, picking up the parrot's food cup.

Bertie shot him a look. "Eat the damned bird for all I care."

"Thanks." Earl smiled at Bertie, then glanced over at me. My exasperated expression made him blanch.

"What?" Earl asked, and popped a sunflower seed into his mouth.

I COULD SEE AGAIN, but it was mostly red.

I'd been tied to a wheelchair for what seemed like hours now, forced to watch Earl eat sunflower seeds and try to teach a half-buzzard parrot named Polly how to say, "two-headed turtle."

Oh, the humanity.

"How'd you find me?" I asked Earl, just to get him to stop saying two-headed turtle.

"Rocko," he answered, spitting out a seed hull. "He let me in the back door."

I chewed my lip. "I wonder what those other two bodyguards did with Grayson."

Earl shrugged. "Maybe they got him caged up with another parrot somewheres."

I shook my head. "If Grayson doesn't show up soon, our only hope is to talk Bertie into letting us go by swearing on our lives to be discrete. Can you do that?"

"Two-headed turtle," the parrot said.

I slumped back in my wheelchair. "You're right, Polly. It's hopeless."

Chapter Fifty-One

I'd almost dozed off, content in the fact my life would soon be over, and I'd never have to hear the words "two-headed turtle" ever again.

The door handle squeaked. I jerked back to full consciousness.

The door flew open. Bertie stepped inside, flanked by two of his bouncer goons.

"How about a nice ride in the country?" Bertie asked.

"That sounds cool," Earl said. "Can we stop for hamburgers on the way? I'm starvin'. Sunflower seeds just don't—"

"Shut up!" Bertie screeched. He nudged one of the men. "Put some duct tape over his mouth."

Right. Now *you shut him up.*

"Can't we work something out?" I asked as the two thugs took Earl from the cage, duct-taped his hands together, then plastered a strip over his mouth.

"Sorry," Bertie said. "Like I said before, I can't have anyone knowing I sleep in a hyperbaric chamber. They'll think I'm some kind of sideshow freak, like they did my father."

"You're not a first-generation healer?" I asked.

"No. My father and grandfather were also what the old timers called 'electric people.'"

"Electric people?"

"Yeah. You know. People who stop watches if they wear 'em. Or make street lights go out when they walk by."

"But there's more to your gift than that," I said. "The device I brought with me. It says you're able to alter people's electromagnetic fields. Is that how you heal them?"

Bertie shrugged. "I don't know. I never questioned it. But maybe there's something to that. I remember folks used to call my grandfather the 'Magneto Man.'"

"We're ready, boss," one of the bodyguards said.

I looked up. The other tattooed muscle man was hauling Earl toward the door. My cousin glanced back and shot me what I figured he meant as a reassuring face—the part that wasn't covered in duct tape, anyway. I smiled and nodded back.

God speed, cousin.

"Let's go," Bertie said, and shoved my wheelchair out the oversized metal door. Only when we joggled over the threshold did I realize we'd been inside the metal trailer of a semi-truck. It'd been parked up against the raised walkway that led to the stage.

When we turned a corner and rolled out onto the stage, it was shocking to see how dramatically everything had changed. The crowds were gone, along with their kinetic energy. The tent was an empty hull. Only a few side lights and exit signs illuminated the stale, dull air within it.

"All this will be gone after our big celebration tomorrow," Bertie said.

"Your hundredth birthday," I half-whispered.

He gave me a sad smile. "That's right. Too bad you won't be around to see it. It's gonna be spectacular."

"The ushering in of a new vampire cult," I said.

Bertie's face shifted from mild empathy to not-so-mild anger. "What?"

"That's what my partner, the private investigator believes. He says you're a psychic vampire."

The two bodyguards turned and looked at me. I might not have known all the tricks Grayson did, but I was a fast learner. And, as a former mall cop, I knew what it was like to put your life on the line for barely over minimum wage.

"Be careful, guys," I warned. "That's *really* how Bertie stays so young. He doesn't heal people. He sucks the life energy out of them, instead."

The two goons exchanged glances. "Bullshit," the one closest to me said.

"Fine. But don't say I didn't try to warn you. That's what Bertie's planning to do with me and my cousin. We're his next energy meals, ready to eat."

The guys' faces registered a hint of skepticism. Whether it was about me or Bertie, I couldn't ascertain.

I turned to Bertie. "Why aren't you hauling us away in the big semi-truck?"

He frowned. "What do *you* care? It uses too much gas."

I nodded. "Oh, sure. I guess all that money you save goes to give these guys a good salary and benefits."

The goons frowned.

"Have you seen the cost of health care plans?" Bertie said. He looked over at the guys. "I'm working on it, I promise."

"Still?" I laughed. "You've had a hundred years already."

"Shut up!" Bertie yelped. He jabbed a gnarled finger at one of the guys. "You. Duct tape her mouth."

"We didn't bring the tape with us," the goon said.

"Ugh!" Bertie groaned. "Do I have to do *everything* myself, you half-w—"

The two men were glaring at Bertie.

The old man backtracked quicker than Bo Jangles.

"Don't get me wrong, fellas," Bertie said. "You guys do good work. Tell you what, I'll get the tape myself." Bertie took a step toward the side of the stage, then turned around. "On second thought, let's just go. Load 'em up in the van."

"I hope you're getting paid extra for homicide," I said to the guy pushing my chair.

"Time and a half," Bertie said.

"Oh. Sure. Just like San Quentin," I quipped.

Bertie's face twisted with rage. "Come on, you two. Let's go!"

BEHIND MY BRAVADO OF sarcasm, I was trembling like Jell-O in a 9.7-Richter earthquake.

When Bertie and his goons rolled me out into the dirt parking lot behind the massive revival tent, my teeth began to chatter. Whether it was from fear or the stark, chilly breeze, I couldn't say for sure. In the cloudy night sky above our heads, tree branches rustled like tissue-paper ghosts, swirling to the rhythm of the unseen wind.

"Keep moving," Bertie barked.

The guard who had Earl by the arm shoved him forward. My wheelchair lurched.

Ahead, in the distance, the white van glowed surreally in the light of an overcast moon. On its side, Bertie's larger-than-life image—once comical—now appeared sinister, like a ghoul beckoning us to our fate.

An icepick of fear stabbed me in the back.

I knew that once they loaded us on board, we were doomed.

I closed my eyes and prayed for a miracle.

Chapter Fifty-Two

Earl was bound and gagged with duct tape, yet he didn't seem to sense the peril we were in. His trusting nature was the opposite of mine. Sometimes, I was envious of it. But not at this exact moment.

Bertie and his two bodyguards were taking us to his van to be "disposed of." Earl wasn't even putting up a struggle. He must've really believed it when Bertie had said we were going for "a ride in the country."

I opened my mouth to yell, "Run, Earl!" but I didn't get the words out. The guy pushing my wheelchair hit a muddy pothole. I lurched sideways with the chair and the armrest knocked the words right out of me.

"Ung," the goon pushing me grunted.

"What's wrong?" Bertie asked.

"Nothin'. Just stuck in a hole."

As the guy shoved at chair trying to get out of the hole, I pleaded with our captor. "It's not too late to call this off, Bertie."

"I'm afraid it is, sister," Bertie said. "I can't let anything jeopardize my big party tomorrow."

Suddenly, as if on cue, strange jungle drums began to echo in the darkness, just beyond the reach of the lamp posts' yellowish, conical beams of light.

Bertie's face creased with concern. "What the hell?"

Somewhere in the near distance, a voice broke into a tribal chant, filling the thick air like a portent from an old Tarzan movie.

"Hooga-shaka. Hooga-shaka."

"Stay away!" Bertie yelled. Clearly spooked, he grabbed his gun from his pocket and pointed it at me. "Stay away or the girl gets it!"

"Girl?" the goon pushing my wheelchair said. He stopped in his tracks.

"Bertie's crazy," I whispered.

"Hey Walter, I think the old man's losing it," he yelled to the other guard who had ahold of Earl. "Thinks this old buzzard here's a woman."

Walter looked me up and down, then stomped his feet. "I *knew* this would happen! I've still got three years on my car payments!"

"Hush!" Bertie screeched.

The three men clammed up momentarily. In the silent void that followed, a ghostly woman's voice echoed in the breeze. "Let them go-oooo, Bertie."

Bertie froze. "Is that ... is that you, Ma?"

"Uh," the voice fumbled. "Yes, Bertie. I am your mother. Let them go-ooo."

Bertie's face puckered. "I can't, Ma! They ... they think I'm a freak, like Dad!"

"Freaks need love, too, Bertie, baby," the woman cooed.

Bertie's eyes darted around wildly. "If that really *is* you, Ma, call me what you always called me when I was a kid."

"Uh ... can you give me a hint?" the voice asked softly.

Bertie winced. "BB. Remember?"

"Ah, yes. Beautiful Boy," the voice sang.

"No," Bertie whined. "Bastard Brat. I hate you, Mommy!"

Bertie raised his gun and fired into the darkness. The blast's recoil sent his frail frame tumbling onto the soggy ground beside me. As he fell, the front of his toupee flapped up and over, then clung to the back of his skull like a road-kill possum.

Bertie glanced up at me. His sinewy face registered sheer terror. He dropped the gun and scrambled to secure his toupee. As he knelt on the ground and folded his fake hair back onto his moon-like pate, the goon in charge of me hustled over and kicked the gun out of his reach.

"No guns, Bertie," he said.

Bernie looked up at him with the face of an angry child. "But—"

A man's deep voice echoed from the darkness to my right, silencing Bertie. "I call upon you, great animal spirit!"

All of us craned our heads in that direction and peered into the chilly, night air. Suddenly, an African warrior stepped into the ghostly light of the lamppost.

It was Stanley!

Dressed only in a bear-claw necklace and an animal skin, he waved his arms like an orchestra conductor and yelled, "Harness the wind, spirit animal! Defend the innocent!"

A sudden blast of arctic wind gusted across the parking lot like an invisible tsunami. Overhead, a tree limb cracked. I looked up. Above me, a five-foot long, horned beast was hurtling at us from the sky like a rogue asteroid.

I screamed and ducked.

A second later, I heard a sickening thud.

"Unkgh!" Bertie grunted, as the creature landed squarely atop his back. The impact knocked Bertie off his knees, flattening him in the dirt like a dehydrated belly-flop.

"Get thee off my behind, Satan!" Bertie screeched, clawing at the fork-tongued monster riding his spine. He glanced up at me, wild eyed, and yelled, "Help! Get it off me!"

Tied to the wheelchair, I couldn't exactly offer much assistance other than to cheer the beast on.

"What should we do?" I heard Walter yell. I looked over at Bertie's bodyguards just in time to see them exchange glances, then take off running—in the opposite direction.

Frozen in horror, I was fated to watch, helpless, as Bertie writhed on the ground beside me, wrestling in the mud with a monster every bit as ugly as the devil himself.

Chapter Fifty-Three

"Somebody help!" I finally managed to yell, my eyes still glued on Bertie and the beast wrestling in the mud beside my wheelchair.

Stanley, who'd been standing frozen with his mouth open, suddenly thawed. He ran over to Earl and ripped the duct tape from his mouth, then he sprinted up to me.

"You okay?" he asked. "What happened?"

"You didn't see?"

"No. I only heard a thud and—"

"Augh!" Bertie grunted.

Stanley and I turned and looked down at the ground, where my wheelchair had been blocking his view.

The reptilian creature had Bertie in a headlock. The old man's toupee was gone, a casualty of the melee.

"Dear lord, what *is* that?" I asked.

"An iguana," Stanley whispered, a stunned look on his face.

I looked up at him. Stanley's eyes grew wide. A proud grin popped onto his face. "My spirit animal. It came!"

Earl came hobbling over for a look.

"Lord-a-mercy!" he said, getting an eyeful of Bertie and the beast. "Them's the worst dang hair plugs I ever seen!"

HAVING BESTED BERTIE, the iguana slithered off into the night. As for Bertie, after his heavyweight match with Iguanodon Jr., he was so worn out he couldn't even sit up.

"I guess there's no need to restrain him," Stanley said as he untied me.

"Nope. That feller's spent his last dime," Earl said.

I glanced around. "Where's Grayson?"

"So *now* you ask about me," Grayson said, stepping out of the darkness. By his side was Nina, the skinny black nurse from Banner Hill.

I shot him an angry look. "Why didn't you help us escape from Bertie?"

"That's *my* fault," Stanley said. "In order to summon my spirit animal, Nina said someone had to play the bongos." Stanley shrugged. "I don't know how."

Grayson grinned and banged on the bongos strapped to his waist. "See? I told you I was multi-talented."

I gave Grayson a begrudging smile. "Where'd you get the spirit animal idea, Stanley?"

"From Nina." He nodded toward her. She's not just a nurse. She's also a voodoo priestess."

Nina folded her hands and bowed her turbaned head. The clatter from the bone necklaces around her neck made me shiver with awe.

"Wow," I said.

"And a powerful priestess she is," Stanley said. "She helped me summon the great spirit of the iguana."

"Actually, that was a zombiguana," Grayson said.

"You put a dead iguana in a trance?" I asked Nina. "That's amazing!"

"No," Grayson said. "Zombiguana is the term I invented to describe iguanas trapped in a metabolic stupor."

My nose crinkled. "What?"

"Iguanas aren't native to Florida," Grayson droned on, ruining the magic of the moment with his dry, boring facts. "Therefore, their bodies aren't adapted to cold temperatures. Anything approaching the forties causes iguanas to half-freeze. With a strong enough wind, they drop from their tree perches like overripe mangos."

"You're making that up," I said, shooting Stanley and Nina an apologetic smile.

Grayson shook his head. "When are you ever going to trust me, Drex? Zombiguanas are a real phenomenon. In fact, last year, the National Weather Service started issuing warnings about falling iguanas."

Bertie let out a moan. "Need ozzie ...."

We all turned and stared at our forgotten nemesis. The poor old geezer was lying face up in the dirt, weakly waving a hand at us.

"What are we going to do about him?" Stanley asked me. "You want to press charges? He *did* hold you at gunpoint."

"His mama didn't love him, and he can't wear a watch." Earl said. "Ain't that punishment enough?"

"It all depends on his involvement with the missing vets," Grayson said. "At this point, we've still got no proof he's guilty of anything but poor taste in head rugs. The only card we've got left is to wrangle a confession out of him."

A sadistic grin crept slowly onto my lips. "I think I've got an idea on how we can do just that."

Chapter Fifty-Four

The door to Bertie's semi-trailer clicked closed behind me, trapping him inside.

The sadistic grin on my lips grew a little wider. "Give Bertie half an hour in there with Earl and that parrot, and he'll spill the beans, guaranteed."

AS IT TURNED OUT, BERTIE broke in under three minutes. Frantic banging from inside prompted Grayson to open the door.

"Please," Bertie groaned. "Can't ... can't—"

"Fine," Grayson said.

He walked over and knelt beside the old man. Bertie was leaning against the wall by the hyperbaric chamber, holding a pillow over his head like giant earmuffs.

"Ready to answer some questions?" Grayson asked as I walked up beside him.

Old Bertie must've been in bad shape. He didn't even react to the fact that I could walk. Instead, he stared at Grayson, wide-eyed as a strangled chicken.

"Please," Bertie panted. "Must ... chamber ...."

"Chamber?" Grayson asked. "You need a chamber pot, old man?"

I gasped. "I think he means he needs his hyperbaric chamber!"

Bertie nodded, his face turning the color of a blue Tootsie Pop. "In by nine ... or die," he gurgled, then slumped sideways. His torso collapsed to the floor.

I glanced at my cellphone. It was 8:56.

"Hurry!" I yelled. "Stanley, you get his feet. Grayson, you get his arms. We've got to get him into that hyperbaric chamber!"

"Dirty Birtie," the parrot squawked as we lifted Bertie into the chamber. Freed from its cage, Polly was promenading around like a penguin that'd barely survived Mardi Gras.

"I don't understand," I said to Earl. "Why didn't Bertie just climb into the chamber himself?"

"He tried to, but Polly wouldn't let him. She kept chasing him around, worryin' that old feller half to death."

"Why didn't *you* help him?"

Earl balked at the idea. "I thought he'd get all rejuvenated up in there then suck my vital juices!"

I turned and stared at Bertie. Inside the chamber, he looked like a long-distance space traveler whose cryonic capsule had sprung a leak.

"Anybody know how to operate this thing?" I asked.

"I think I can figure it out." Stanley studied the buttons for a minute. "Okay. I think I got it. Seal the lid."

"It may be too late," I said, and nodded at Bertie. His coloring had gone from blue-raspberry to grape.

Stanley grabbed Bertie's wrist. "Aw, man. No pulse. He's already gone."

My heart pinged with sadness for Bertie. Sure, he'd been a jerk. But I knew all too well what it was like to feel like a freak.

"Let's get him out of this thing and back to wherever he usually spends the night," I said. "I know he wouldn't want to be found here like this."

"First, let's say a prayer for his soul," Nina said.

"Say a prayer for yourselves!" a man's voice rang out.

We all whipped around to face the door—and found ourselves staring down the barrel of a sawed-off shotgun.

Chapter Fifty-Five

"You killed him!" Rocko yelled.

He aimed his shotgun at us as we stood around the hyperbaric chamber, staring at Bertie's blue face.

A collective gasp echoed through the semi-trailer. We all simultaneously raised our hands and took a step back from Bertie—all except Grayson, that is.

"No, Rocko. Bertie killed himself," Grayson said, taking a step toward him.

"What?" Rocko's angry face softened a notch. "Bertie committed Suicide?"

Grayson pursed his lips. "Well, in a way, yes."

"I don't believe it," Rocko said, shaking his head.

Neither did I.

I shot Grayson a *what the hell* look. He opened his palms and took another step toward Rocko.

I blanched. Either Grayson was being heroic and trying to save us, or he was sealing our doom.

"Hear me out," Grayson said. "Brother Bertie believed he would die if he didn't get into that hyperbaric chamber by nine p.m. He didn't make it because he didn't make it."

"What?"

Rocko's face crinkled in confusion. The rest of us followed suit and stared at Grayson.

"His belief is what killed him," Grayson said. "Faith is a powerful, mystical thing that can't be quantified."

"Actually, he died at 8:59," Nina said.

All eyes shifted to the woman dressed in African voodoo garb.

"What? I'm a nurse," Nina said. "I noted his vitals on my watch. It's a habit of mine."

"Your watch could be wrong," Grayson said.

I tugged on Grayson's sleeve. "That's hardly the point to be arguing right now," I whispered, nodding toward Rocko.

The leather-clad ex-biker was standing in the doorway looking utterly shattered. He was blocking our only exit from the semi-truck trailer. He still held the shotgun, but at the moment, it hung limp in his hand, pointed at the ground.

"Lettuce pray," Earl said, breaking the silence. "Come on over, Rocko. Let's join hands in a circle."

I stared at Rocko, wondering who he would shoot first. Then, just like that, I got the miracle I'd prayed for. Rocko laid the sawed-off shotgun on the floor and ambled over to us.

Stunned, I joined the circle holding hands around Bertie's dirty body as it lay in state in his hyperbolic chamber.

We all stood as one, in silent reverence for the man who could've been a psychic vampire, a scam artist, a healer, or merely suffering from dementia.

I glanced around. Our group included one voodoo priestess, one dreadlocked warrior, one fake paraplegic, one tattooed biker, one fedora-topped physicist, and one bear-sized redneck. As different as we all were, we were united in one thing—paying our final respects to the hundred-year-old faith healer who, sadly, never figured out how to resurrect his own hair.

The irony that our circle looked like some kind of bizarre cult ritual wasn't lost on me. Earl's words only added to the surreal nature of the moment.

"Dear God, whoever and wherever you are, take our brother Bertie with you," Earl prayed, his eyes shut tight, his face pinched with sincerity. "Ol' Bertie tried hard to do what he thought was best. He couldn't heal old Sally, but Grandma Selma swore he got rid of her warts. Amen."

"Amen," we all echoed.

"Oh, and P.S., God?" Earl said, squeezing his eyes shut once more. "Is it all right with you if I keep Polly?"

Chapter Fifty-Six

Bertie looked at peace tucked into his bed inside his cozy travel caravan. The guys had washed and dressed him in a fresh, white suit. Nina and I'd done our best to resurrect his mangled toupee.

I made the final adjustments, tugging the fake, silver-white cap of hair over the doll-like row of hair plugs dotting his pale forehead.

"There," I said. "He's ready."

Rocko came over and gazed sadly at Bertie. "I mean, the guy could be a tool sometimes. But why did he have to die?"

"Some things just are beyond our understanding," Grayson said.

"Like two-headed turtles?" Earl asked.

"Yes." I slipped an arm around my cousin's waist. "Like two-headed turtles."

"I guess we'll never know what happened to those missing vets now," Earl said.

I turned to Rocko. "Do you think Bertie could've been involved? Could he have used his semi-trailer to haul them away?"

"If he did, I never saw anything," Rocko said.

"I hear you," Stanley said, nodding his head. "Pleading the Schultz."

"No." Rocko let out a sigh. "The old guy had his secrets, but I really don't think he was a murderer."

"Dirty Bertie!" Polly screeched as Earl brought her in to pay her last respects.

"His untimely death was certainly inconvenient," Grayson said. "We may never know now if Bertie was a psychic vampire or not. However, we may still be able to clear his name about the missing veterans."

"How?" Rocko asked.

"By proving *you* did it," Grayson said. He reached for his Glock, but didn't pull it out.

"Me?" Rocko said.

"You had ample opportunity when you picked up the men in Bertie's van. Maybe you transported them to the revival, or maybe you took them for your own ulterior motives."

"Like what?" I asked.

Grayson studied Rocko's face. "Selling their body parts. Exacting revenge for their ex-wives over unpaid alimony. I can think of a dozen viable money-making reasons."

Rocko rolled his eyes. "If I had any money, you think I'd be living in the back of a van with Bertie's face on it?"

Grayson's brow furrowed. "Good point." He turned to Stanley. "There's still the possibility Old Mildred's ghost got the men. If she's responsible, Bertie would be innocent of any wrongdoing."

"Bertie!" Polly screeched. "Dirty Bertie!"

Rocko winced and twisted an index finger in his ear. He shot a sour face at Earl. "You sure you want that bird?"

"Me and Polly are friends now," Earl said. "We understand each other, don't we girl?"

Polly sidled up to Earl's leg and squawked, "Two-headed turtle."

Earl beamed like a proud papa. "Yep. I'm sure."

"Then she's yours." Rocko clapped a hand on Grayson's shoulder and nodded toward the caravan door. "Brother, I want you to go clear Bertie's name, if you can."

I glanced over at Bertie's corpse. "What about—"

"I'll notify Bertie's family," Rocko said. "You guys take off. If you hang around, it'll just stir up questions about vampires and stuff we don't need to get stuck having to answer."

Grayson nodded and shook Rocko's hand. "Thanks, brother. You can count on us. If Bertie's innocent, we'll prove it."

Rocko knelt beside Bertie. A tear slid down his cheek. "To think, he was so close to turning a hundred."

"He made it," Grayson said.

Bertie looked up at Grayson. "What do you mean?"

"Some Asian cultures mark the start of someone's life as the date of conception, not birth. In those terms, Bertie lived well past the century mark."

Rocko nodded and wiped his eyes. "Thanks for the reminder, brother."

Grayson smiled. "That life isn't the number of years you live, but the life you put into those years?"

"Well, sure," Rocko said. "That, and that Asian chicks are hot. After all this blows over, I'm moving to Thailand."

BESSIE'S ENGINE ROARED and the revival tent faded into the darkness. Relief washed over me.

It was extremely short-lived.

"We need to talk about our stakeout plan for Banner Hill tonight," Grayson said.

My gut flopped for the fourteenth time that day. "What?"

Wedged between Grayson and Earl in the front seat of his monster truck, there was no physical escape from the madness. I was going to have to talk my way out of it.

"It's too late," I argued, scrambling for excuses. "It's already past nine-thirty. That's midnight at Banner Hill. The doors are already locked!"

"I can get us in," Stanley said. He'd called shotgun and had a window seat to our human sardine act.

"Won't they suspect something?" I asked hopefully.

Stanley shook his head. "No. I told the other guys working tonight that I was taking you to see your brother. Said we might be back late tonight. They're expecting us."

"Well done," Grayson said.

"No way am I going back there tonight," I said, digging in my heels. "Haven't we had enough crazy for one night?"

Grayson took my hand, put his lips to my ear, and whispered the magical words I'd been longing to hear. "If we solve this case tonight, you don't have to spend another night in Banner Hill."

I blew out a sigh. "Fine. I'm in. What's the plan?"

Chapter Fifty-Seven

"Where you guys been all evenin'?" Melvin asked after poking his head out of his room across the hall from mine.

"Sorry if we disturbed you," Stanley whispered, pausing my wheelchair in the hallway in front of my room. He leaned over and patted me on the shoulder. "I really need to grease the wheel on your chair, Georgie."

Stanley straightened his back and wagged a finger at Melvin. "And you, young man. You should be in bed. It's after ten o'clock."

"I was worried," Melvin said, giving his rumpled comb-over a swipe with his gnarled hand. "I thought maybe they'd come and got Georgie, too."

"Who?" Stanley asked.

Melvin glanced both ways down the hall. "The vampires," he whispered. "I heard y'all talking about 'em this morning. You want a clove?" He held up a head of garlic.

"There's no such thing as vampires," Stanley said. "Now get back in bed."

Melvin scowled. "Have it your way. But I ain't taking no chances." He popped a garlic clove in his mouth, then disappeared behind his door.

Stanley rolled me into my room. "See? I told you that old coot was crazy. Get ready for bed. I'll be back in a few minutes to set things up."

I WAS IN BED IN MY hospital gown, dunking my vampire teeth into the glass of blue water beside my bed, when I heard a light tap at my door. The door squeaked open. Stanley entered, pushing a laundry cart.

Operation "Get Old Mildred" was about to begin.

Stanley closed the door behind him, then laid his hands on a bag stuffed with dirty laundry. It began to squirm like an oversized larva. Stanley untied the drawstring. Grayson's head popped out like some tragic, not-meant-to-be-funny scene in a low-budget horror movie.

"Seen any toe-sucking parasites?" Grayson asked, inching the laundry bag down to his waist. He reached into it and pulled out his black fedora. He popped it atop his shaved head.

"No," I managed, stifling a laugh. "But Melvin across the hall asked about vampires again." I shook my head. "I just don't get it. What's up with everybody's infatuation with vampires?"

Grayson birthed himself from the bag, pulling its sides down to his knees, then kicking it free. He sat up on the cart and pulled a static-cling sock from the side of his black shirt. "Every culture since time immemorial has had some kind of legend about a blood-sucking monster."

"Yeah," Stanley said. "They're called politicians. Now keep it down, *please*. We don't want to disturb the other residents."

"Right." Grayson hopped off the cart.

"I'll be back in a few with the second load," Stanley whispered, pushing the cart and its deflated laundry bag out the door.

"Thanks, Stanley," I said. "We appreciate you helping us."

"I know nothing, I see nothing," he said, then smiled and shut the door behind him.

"The Egyptians had Sekhmet," Grayson said. "The Greeks, Ambrogio."

"What are you talking about?" I asked, adjusting my bed covers.

Grayson cocked his head at me. "Vampires, of course."

"Of course."

"If any of the old legends are true, the creatures mentioned in historic lore would have to be thousands of years old by now."

I fluffed my pillow. "And your point is?"

Grayson rubbed his chin. "Suppose this blood-sucking creature ran out of relatives to care for it? What better place for it to hide out than in a nursing home?"

"Huh?"

Grayson nodded his head. "It's ingenious, really. The perfect solution."

I sighed. "Again, Grayson. What in the world are you talking about?"

"Sticking elderly vampires in nursing homes, Drex. Think about it. Dinner is easy to catch—like sucking seniors in a barrel." Grayson smiled. "*Meals on wheelchairs*. Brilliant!"

I blew out another sigh and pulled the blanket at the end of the bed up and over my legs. "I thought you said Bram Stoker *invented* vampires."

"The modern version with capes and bad sideburns, yes. But we could be dealing with a much older creature from ancient mythology. A pre-vampire, yet nevertheless blood-sucking, parasitic being. As you might recall, most of the missing men suffered from anemia."

"Yeah. I remember." I sat up and chewed my lip. "This Ambrosia dude and Seek'em creature. What did they look like?"

"Sekhmet was a warrior goddess. Egyptians drew her as having the likeness of a lioness," Grayson said. "Ambrogio was actually a regular guy. An Italian mortal who Apollo turned into the first known human blood sucker."

"Why'd Apollo do that?"

"Because they both wanted the same chick, Selene."

"Ugh!" I groaned. "Guys!"

Grayson laughed. "Long legend short, Ambrogio was cursed by Apollo so the only way he could touch Selene was to drink her blood. Doing so also had the rather inconvenient side effect of killing her."

"Most contact with males usually does," I deadpanned.

Grayson's cheek dimpled. "Anyway, Selene died and legend says she became the Goddess of Moonlight. She now forever more shines down on the children who carry both Ambrogio's and her blood—their progeny of vampires."

I frowned. "Great. Let's hope Ambrogio wasn't too lucky with the ladies."

Grayson shrugged. "He *was* Italian."

"Ugh!" I groaned. "It's all just nonsense." I scrounged around in my purse for a Tootsie Pop to calm my nerves. Grayson's words had spooked me. It was going to be a long night.

"Remember the TV show *The Night Stalker?*" Grayson asked out of the blue.

"No."

"How about the *Twilight* saga? Or *Buffy the Vampire Slayer?*"

"Yeah." I stuck an orange Tootsie Pop in my mouth. "Want one?"

"Sure." Grayson took the green sucker I'd handed him. "It may seem trivial, but TV shows like those have kept the idea of vampirism alive."

"So what?"

"Just postulating, but what if our belief in vampires keeps the reality of them possible?"

My nose crinkled. "You mean like our thoughts turning random particles into real matter—that quantum physics stuff you're always talking about?"

Grayson's green eyes shone in a way I'd never seen before. "Precisely, cadet." He sighed, and his eyes dulled again. "But sadly, more and more, poor vampires are being dumbed down to cartoonish freaks, just like poor Bertie was."

"What do you mean, cartoonish freaks?"

"You know. The 'Count' on *Sesame Street*," Grayson said. "Count Chocula. Even *Spongebob Squarepants* has an episode with Nosferatu in it. The poor, mighty vampire was reduced to a hash-slinging slasher who made the lights flicker at the Krusty Krab whenever he showed up. You have to admit, that's a pathetic end for Murnau's fearsome creation."

Grayson stuck the Tootsie Pop in his mouth and tipped his fedora back on his shaved head. I smirked.

If Kojak and Super Mario had a baby ....

He glanced at his cellphone. "What's keeping them? It's well past ten o'clock. The unexplained phenomenon we're waiting on could appear any minute."

I grinned. "You talking about Earl or Old Mildred?"

Grayson laughed.

Suddenly, a weird *scree, scree* sound echoed down the hallway. The hair on my arms pricked up.

"That doesn't sound like the laundry cart," Grayson whispered.

"Oh my lord, Grayson! That's the sound Stanley described—the night Charlie Perkins disappeared!"

The sound stopped at my door. Grayson pulled his Glock, then sprinted over and hit the light switch, plunging the room into darkness.

"You're going to shoot at a ghost?" I whispered.

"Shhh!" Grayson hissed.

Slowly, the door creaked open.

In the dim glow of the hallway night lights, a gnarled, black, withered hand snaked its way inside. It clamped hold of the edge of the door.

I gasped.

A gravelly voice wafted into the darkness. It sounded like it said, "Old Mildred ...."

Chapter Fifty-Eight

I lurched up in bed and clawed around in my purse, desperately searching for something—anything—I could use to defend myself from the gnarly-handed ghoul creeping into my room.

Scree, scree.

The door creaked open wider ....

Scree, scree.

The hand reached out, revealing a boney arm ....

Scree, scree.

Then a shoulder ....

My fingers found purchase and wrapped themselves tightly around my makeshift weapon. I snatched it from my purse and hurled it toward the black silhouette skulking through the door.

At that exact moment, Grayson flicked on the lights.

I watched, in horror, as my bottle of Flintstones vitamins bounce squarely off the forehead of an old black man pushing a mop and bucket. The guy, dressed in blue janitor coveralls, crumpled to the ground like a heap of old clothes.

"Oh my God!" I squealed and scrambled out of bed. "I'm sorry, I'm sorry, I'm sorry!" I said as I ran over to him.

He gave no response.

Grayson knelt beside him and checked his neck for a pulse.

"Is he dead?" I squeaked.

"No. I think he'll live." Grayson locked his green eyes on mine. "Nice throw, DiMaggio. Now, help me get him up."

We pulled the old janitor to sitting, then lifted him into my wheelchair. He sat there limp as a ragdoll for a moment, then let out a groan.

"Are you okay?" I asked. "I'm so sorry!"

"I ... I think so," he said, rubbing the rising knot on his head. "What'd you go and do that for?"

I cringed. "I thought you were Old Mildred."

At the mention of her name, the old man's eyes grew wide. "You know about Old Mildred?"

"Yes."

"And it seems you do, too," Grayson said, studying him.

"That I do," the geriatric janitor said. "Been here near as long as she that runs the place."

"Gable?" Grayson asked.

"No." The old man chuckled. "Gable just a baby. I'm talkin' 'bout Ms. Draper, the owner. Mildred was her sister."

"Her sister?" I gasped, offering him a glass of water. He turned his nose up at it.

"Never touch the stuff." The old man perked up and smiled. "But I'll take one of them Tootsie Pops, if you got another."

"Sure. Hold on." I ran over and grabbed my purse off the bed.

"Old Mildred was somethin' special," the janitor said as I searched for a sucker amid the wrappers, coupons, and Walmart receipts crammed inside my pocketbook. "She lived here back in the '80s."

"What do you mean, 'something special'?" Grayson asked.

The old man shrugged and took the Tootsie Pop I offered, unwrapping it as he spoke. "She was a simple-minded gal, that Mildred. What folks back then called 'retarded.' Ms. Draper had her livin' here, amongst the old folks, until she up and died in 1988. Ever since then, ol' Draper wouldn't let no other woman stay here overnight, on account a what happened to Mildred."

"What happened?" I asked.

"Well, I don't like to be spreadin' no rumors."

The janitor popped the sucker in his mouth. Grayson and I exchanged glances.

"We're here on official—" Grayson began. I stepped on his toe.

"We won't tell anybody. We promise," I said.

"Well, all right then," the old man chuckled. "Legend has it, one night poor old Mildred bit off more'n she could chew. Found her dead in her bed, with somebody's big toe stuck in her throat. She been wandering these halls ever since."

"Wow. That's quite a story," Grayson said. "Have you ever seen Old Mildred yourself?"

The old man shrugged. "Sure. From time to time. She always partial to showin' up right around Thanksgivin'."

"Why do you think that is?" Grayson asked.

"Her anniversary, I guess. Mildred died here the day before Thanksgivin'."

"Oh." I frowned. "How sad."

The old man nodded. "Sure was. Draper never forgave herself. She was supposed to be watching her, you see? But she'd gone off to see some beau she was sweet on. That woman ain't never dated nobody since, as far as I know."

"Has Mildred ever ... uh ... killed anyone?" I asked. "Her ghost, I mean."

The old man's gray eyebrows rose and inch. "What? Why you askin' me that?"

"Five men have gone missing from here this week," I said.

"Huh," he grunted. "Well, I'll be."

"Does everyone here know about Old Mildred?" Grayson asked.

"Mostly," he said. "Word gets around, you know. But if'n you asked, wouldn't nobody admit to it. You can't say word one around Ms. Draper about Old Mildred. She'll fire you faster'n' double-aught buckshot."

"Have you heard any rumors about the men that've disappeared?" Grayson asked.

The old man shook his head. "Not that I recall."

Grayson pursed his lips. "Did you notice anything suspicious during any of your shifts this week? You see, each man went to dinner, but none of them made it to bed. When the staff went to get them for breakfast, they were gone. Their beds hadn't been slept in. They were still made up with military precision."

"Don't see how it could be Old Mildred," the janitor said. "When she was alive, she never made her bed. No, sir. She been haunting these halls for over thirty years. And ain't nobody just up and disappeared in the night before."

He stood and grabbed his mop. "Well, I best be gettin' back to my rounds. Thanks for the lollipop, Miss."

"You're welcome." I cringed out a smile. "Sorry again about ... well, you know."

"Don't you worry your head none about it." He tapped his boney knuckles on the thin, white tufts of hair atop of his skull. "Head's the hardest spot on old Sampson Jones."

Chapter Fifty-Nine

After bidding Sampson and his poor head-knot farewell, I crawled back into bed while Grayson shuffled through the drawer on my nightstand.

"What are you looking for?" I asked.

"A spoon to eat your tapioca pudding cup."

"It's behind the glass with the fake dentures."

Geez. If a random stranger wandered in on this conversation, we'd be committed.

Grayson grabbed the spoon and held it up. "Got it!"

I leaned back in bed. "I wonder, does Draper know about the disappearance of the vets? If she does, you think she's covering it up? You know, to protect the memory of her sister Mildred?"

"Unlikely." Grayson shrugged and worked on peeling the lid off the pudding. "Why would she care about the reputation of a ghost?"

"What if she's protecting a *live* person, not a ghost?" I asked. "Sampson mentioned Draper had a boyfriend ...."

A sudden thought made me gasp. "Grayson! What if the 'beau' Draper snuck off to see the night Mildred died was *Bertie?*"

"Hmmm." Grayson frowned. "The timing's right. But what about—"

The door creaked open. Stanley entered, dragging Earl by the arm.

"I thought I told you to put him in a laundry bag," Grayson said.

Stanley shot Earl a look. "I couldn't get him to go in it."

Earl stuck his chin out and pouted. "I'm claustrophobic. Just like Polly."

Right. And you've also both got brains the size of walnuts.

"You didn't bring that stupid bird with you, did you?" I asked.

"No." Earl jerked free of Stanley's grasp. "*He* wouldn't let me."

"Thank goodness someone has some sense around here." I glanced back over at Grayson. "What were you—"

"No time left for talking," Grayson said setting the half-eaten pudding cup back on my nightstand. "We're already running behind. Okay, troops, take your positions. And keep alert."

Grayson stashed his fedora in my closet and donned the white lab coat hanging inside. "I'll check out the hallways with Stanley," he said. "Earl, you hide in the bathroom, like we planned. Be ready to spring into action if Old Mildred stops by for another round of digital digeridoo."

Earl's brow furrowed. "Of what?"

"Toe sucking," I said.

"Yes, sir," Earl saluted. "You can count on me."

Stanley and Grayson disappeared out the door. I laid back in bed and let out a sigh. "Great. Just what I need. Another night with ikigai."

Earl shot me a look. "You ain't no prize yourself, Cuz."

Chapter Sixty

Sometime in the night, I was startled awake by the sound of heavy breathing.

I flinched with panic, and clamped my eyes shut. Slowly, I cracked one open.

Where is the sound coming from?

The door leading to the hallway was closed. That meant the rasping sound was coming from ...

... inside my room!

At the foot of my bed!

Right where the eerie, green light to the .... My gut went limp.

Crap! You've got to be kidding me.

I jumped out of bed and padded to the bathroom. In the glow of the green night light by the sink, Earl was sitting sprawl-legged on the floor. His head was slumped over the toilet bowl. He looked like a drunk-ass gorilla after too many Halloween Jell-O shots.

The weird, rasping sound was being caused by Earl snoring into the toilet bowl. Like an echo chamber, it was sending them bouncing off the wall tiles.

I bit down on my molars. Hard.

It took every bit of willpower I had not to slam the lid and flush.

Instead, I took a deep breath, then jabbed my big lump of a cousin in the ribs with my big toe.

Earl sprang to life like a mummy in a movie. One of his meaty hands shot out and grabbed my foot.

"Aha! Gotcha, you toe-sucking pervert!" he yelled.

"Shhh!" I hissed. "It's just me, Bobbie."

"*You're* the toe-sucking perv—"

"Hush!" I whispered. "You fell asleep."

"Oh."

I leaned over and slapped his face. "There, that ought to help you stay awake."

He rubbed his cheek. "Thanks, Bobbie."

"Don't mention it." Guilty pleasure washed over me. I fought back a grin. "Now stay alert!"

"Yes, ma'am."

I crawled back in bed and pulled the covers over me. My fingers were still stinging from slapping Earl, but I didn't care. I was happy in the satisfaction that, no matter what else happened, this stupid stake-out hadn't been for nothing.

I'D BARELY GOTTEN MYSELF settled back in bed when I heard the knob on the hallway door begin to turn.

I held my breath.

The door cracked open.

If I hadn't taken Grayson's desensitization training, I'd probably have peed my pants.

A short, hunchbacked creature crept into my room.

This was no dress rehearsal. This was the real deal.

I LAY IN BED, FROZEN with fear, as the hideous creature entered and slowly closed the door behind it. The room was pitch black, save for the eerie green glow of the bathroom nightlight.

In the darkness, I heard what sounded like dragging footsteps as the hunchbacked ghoul made its way to the foot of my bed.

Heavy breathing filled the air, along with a horrid stench.

Then something so utterly crazy happened that I nearly blacked out from my mind not being able to process it.

Somewhere in the dark, Michael Franks' *Popsicle Toes* began to play.

Holy crap! The other two nights—they hadn't been dreams after all!

The covers lifted at the foot of my bed. A cold, clammy hand brushed my ankle.

Earl! Where are you? I screamed inside my head. *You're supposed to grab Old Mildred!*

My haywire brain raced in tempo with my heart. My pulse thrummed in my eardrums.

Should I yell for Earl or not? Would I be foiling his surprise attack?

Then I heard it.

That telltale, echoing rasp of breath.

Earl had fallen asleep with his head in the toilet.

Again.

Chapter Sixty-One

I was caught in the grips of the undead.

A shadowy entity had ahold of my left foot.

Paralyzed with fear, I lay helpless in bed as my leg rose in the air like Linda Blair's—under the control of some otherworldly demon.

Fear shot down my spine like a bullet of ice. Toxic vapors enveloped the room. A wave of nausea swept through me.

I blinked into the green-black darkness. The dark silhouette at the foot of my bed disappeared. Then, just as suddenly, reappeared.

A slimy sensation, like a cold-water slug, slithered across the bottom of my foot.

Then came a disgusting slurping sound.

I nearly dry-heaved.

It was Old Mildred, all right.

And she was sucking my big toe ....

Chapter Sixty-Two

"Forgive me, Jesus," I heard a voice call out in the dark.

Ack! Old Mildred's fixing to kill me!

I lurched up in bed. A hollow, metallic sound gonged, then reverberated off the walls.

"What's happening?" I screeched.

Suddenly, the lights flipped on, searing my retinas with a blinding white flash.

I squinted through the stars in my eyes. I couldn't believe what I saw.

Earl standing at the end of my bed holding a dented bedpan.

A second later, Grayson and Stanley rushed into the room.

"What's going on?" Grayson yelled.

"I kilt Old Mildred," Earl whimpered.

Grayson and Stanley stared at the floor at the foot of my bed. I crawled across the covers for a look.

For the second time in ten seconds, I couldn't believe my eyes.

Crumpled on the floor, half buried by a Santa-sized laundry sack, were a pair of hairy, pasty legs clad only in white socks and the same cheap black slippers I'd been issued.

"Looks like Old Mildred wasn't a hunchback after all," Earl said.

"Or a shaver." Grayson heaved the sack from atop the body, revealing the open back of a hospital gown and a flabby, white, pimply bare ass.

Grayson groaned. "I may never eat tapioca pudding again."

"Who is it?" I asked.

"Only one way to find out."

Grayson squatted down and started to turn the body over. Suddenly, the door flew open as if it had been kicked by a mule.

"Hold it right there!" a man's voice yelled.

All eyes shifted from the body on the floor to the man at the door—then to the barrel of the gun in his hand.

"Don't move," he said.

I recognized the weapon as a Glock. I recognized the face as the man I'd seen at the revival ... the one stealing cash from the collection plate.

Where do I know him from?

His name was on the tip of my tongue ....

Chapter Sixty-Three

"Holbrook!" Stanley said. "What are you doing here?"

The cop we'd seen at Topless Tacos rushed into the room and closed the door behind him. He waived the pistol at Earl and Grayson. "Hands on the walls. Now!"

Grayson cleared his throat. "I know this looks a bit odd, officer, but we were just—"

"Shut up!" Holbrook hissed. He glanced down at the mangled heap of legs and laundry lying on the floor. "What did you do to him?"

"Him?" Earl asked. "I thought Old Mildred was a woman."

"Shut up!" Holbrook said. "All of you. Get in the bathroom. Now!"

He jabbed his gun in Grayson's ribs.

"Easy! Okay!" Grayson said. He held his hands up and marched into the bathroom. Earl and Stanley followed suit.

I started climbing out of bed to join them. Holbrook closed the bathroom door. He grabbed a chair and was dragging it across the floor when he turned and glanced at me.

"Not you, old man. You stay there."

My heart lurched in my throat.

Why? Am I the next one on your list of vets to "disappear?"

"I ... I ...." I stuttered.

"What?" Holbrook said, staring at me. He tucked the Glock into his waistband. "Stay in bed. Sorry about the disturbance."

As Holbrook turned his back on me and wedged the chair under the bathroom's doorknob, I realized he hadn't recognized me. No wonder. When he'd seen me at Topless Tacos, I'd been a woman with shoulder-length red hair.

"Go back to sleep," Holbrook said, dropping a pill into my water glass. The liquid turned blue. "Drink this. You won't remember a thing."

He handed me the glass. I smiled weakly and took a sip of the bitter brew.

"There you go," he said. Then he turned, bent down, and wrestled with the giant laundry sack on top of the guy with the hairy legs. "I'll be back in a minute for him," he said, heaving the sack onto his back. "Sorry about the toe thing. He's always been a bit funny that way."

Holbrook turned to leave. My mind raced. What was Holbrook going to do to my friends he had locked in the bathroom? Were *they* going to end up on his missing persons list?

I had to stop him! I reared back and heaved the water glass at Holbrook. It cracked against the side of his head.

"Ow!" he yelled as he stumbled. He slapped a hand against the wall for balance, then turned and glared at me.

"Take that, DiMaggio!" I yelled, standing up in my bed.

Holbrook's eyes doubled in size. He turned back toward the door, but it was too late. I leapt on top of him and his hunchback sack, slamming him sideways into the wall.

"Get off me, you crazy old man!" he yelled, trying to shake free of me.

I held on for all I was worth. "Stop!" I screeched as Holbrook regained his balance and lumbered, Frankenstein-like, out the door and into the main hallway of the nursing home.

"Get off!" he yelled again, and dropped the sack. He tried to claw at me, but I clung to his back like a super-glued turtle shell. I knew it was up to me alone to stop him. Everyone else in the place was either locked up or in a wheelchair.

"Why are you doing this?" I hollered, feeling the cold air on my backside as my hospital gown flapped in rhythm to Holbrook's lurching steps.

"I could ask you the same thing, old man!" Holbrook yelled back.

Then, suddenly, he froze.

I followed his blank stare down to the end of the hallway.

What I saw through the glass exit doors made me wish I had on clean underwear.

Or, at least, underwear.

Chapter Sixty-Four

An eerie purple glow was emanating just outside the glass exit doors of Banner Hill. It was the strange, violet glow Stanley had warned about. The purple glow that made people disappear ....

Holbrook saw it, too. He stopped in his tracks, heaving to catch his breath. "Get off," he wheezed.

"Not happening," I said.

"Shit," he hissed, and began turning around, grunting with each awkward, jerky step.

I held tightly to his back. My plan was working. The burden of carrying me was wearing Holbrook out. I squeezed my thighs around his sides even tighter.

"Come on, old man!" he yelled. "You're killing me. Let go!"

Holbrook took a few steps down the hall, then turned right.

I knew what that meant. He was heading for the side exit. If he made it, I figured I was a goner. But what else could I do to stop him? If I let go of a hand to poke him in the eye, he'd surely sling me off. If I fell off, he's surely stomp me to death! I dug my nails deeper into his shoulders.

"Argh!" Holbrook yelled, then staggered determinedly down the short hall to the side exit door. He laid a hand on the push-bar and gasped. "You've got some grip for an old man."

"He takes Kung Fu lessons," a voice quipped behind me.

Grayson!

I craned my neck around. Grayson and Earl were standing right behind me. One was armed with a Glock. The other with ... a bedpan.

"How'd you get out of the bathroom?" I asked.

Grayson winked. "You're not the only one who knows Kung Fu."

"Ugh!" Holbrook groaned. He shoved open the exit door and lumbered off into the night, carrying me on his back like a worn out rodeo bull.

"Drop and roll, Drex!" Grayson called out.

I let go and tumbled into the grass. Holbrook took off. Grayson sped past me, leaping over me as he ran after him.

"You okay, Cuz?" Earl asked, holding out a hand to help me up.

"I think so." I did a quick survey of my body parts. "Yeah. I'm okay. Let's go!"

I ran in the direction Grayson had gone. Earl followed right behind me. Fifty yards out, in the dim haze of a lamp post, I saw Holbrook hobbling toward a Grand Safari stationwagon parked in the lot.

Its lights blinked on. Its engine roared to life.

Someone was there waiting for him.

Holbrook jumped in. The stationwagon took off, burning rubber.

"Over here," Grayson called out.

Earl and I ran over to the RV. Grayson was standing beside the passenger door, shaking his head.

"Let's go!" I yelled. "They're getting away!"

"No can do," Grayson said, and nodded toward the rear of the RV.

"Crap!" I yelled. "Who the hell keeps stealing our tires?"

"Looks like it's gonna be Bessie to the rescue," Earl hollered. "Follow me!"

"Where's Stanley?" I asked as we raced toward my cousin's monster truck.

"He stayed behind to check on your secret admirer," Earl quipped.

"Who was it?" I asked, not sure I wanted to know.

"We didn't have time to stick around and find out," Grayson said, opening the passenger-side door.

I started to climb in, then realized I was wearing a hospital gown—and not much else.

"You first," I said.

"I already called shotgun," Grayson said, offering me a hand up.

"But—"

"And I already saw your caboose." He waggled his eyebrows. "And might I say, *choo-choo.*"

I pinched the back of my gown together and climbed in. Once Grayson's butt hit the seat, Earl punched the gas pedal to the floor. The g-force could've made me lose my dentures—if I'd been wearing any.

As we tore through the parking lot, I realized I'd never been so embarrassed—or proud—in my entire life.

I was a real-life private-eye trainee—on a real-life, high-speed chase.

And Grayson thought I had a nice caboose.

Chapter Sixty-Five

As it turned out, tailing the twenty-foot long stationwagon wasn't that hard. It had the turning radius of a small cruise ship.

"Not the best choice for a getaway vehicle," I said.

"I don't think it was chosen for that purpose," Grayson said.

"What do you mean?" Earl asked.

"Look at the thing. It's as big as a hearse."

"So why did they choose it?" I asked.

Grayson shot me a look. "I thought I just covered that. Because it's as big as a hearse. Nobody would suspect there were bodies inside."

I cringed with fear and disgust. Then I held on for dear life as Earl's monster truck chased Holbrook's sheet-metal land cruiser all the way into New Port Richey's old downtown strip.

As we sailed by a couple of blocks, the quaint, striped awnings and wrought-iron railings of the old buildings reminded me of New Orleans. Then I remembered we were chasing a guy who sawed people up for body parts.

"Hurry!" I said, staring at the road ahead.

The stationwagon's brake lights flashed in the distance about a quarter mile ahead of us. Earl stopped at an intersection.

"What are you doing?" I yelled.

"Looking both ways," Earl said. "You can't never can be too careful."

I glanced over at Grayson. He was preoccupied, staring out the window at a mural. It was hard to miss.

The drawing was nearly as large as the building itself, and depicted a crowd of people in brown, old-timey bathing suits taking a dip in a body of water—either a lake or the ocean.

Earl hit the gas. I lurched sideways into Grayson.

"Lucky them," I said as the mural disappeared from view. "Those old timers probably drowned before they had to live here."

"Don't be so fast to judge," Grayson said, pushing me back to my center position on the bench seat. "Back in the 1920s, New Port Richey used to be a magnet for the rich and famous. In fact, it was once dubbed 'The Hollywood of the East.'"

"Yeah, right. I guess now it's just part of "The Redneck Riviera.'"

Grayson shook his head. "Is this as fast as she'll go?" he hollered at Earl.

"Lord, no," Earl said. "I just didn't want to scare y'all." Earl punched the gas pedal and plastered us to the back of the seat. The tractor-sized tires hummed like a swarm of bees, and we made a city block in two seconds flat.

"We're gaining on them," I said.

"That's the point," Earl said.

We were maybe twenty yards behind them when the Grand Safari ran the stop sign at the intersection. Earl slammed on the brakes. I nearly hit my head on the windshield.

"What the?" I groused. "Earl, you can't stop at every—"

Hoooonnnk! A deafening horn blasted us from the left. A split second later, a huge semi-truck blew through the intersection.

I settled back in the seat. "Good call, Earl."

A second later, the taillights of the stationwagon lurched sideways. The sound of breaking glass and twisting metal filled the air.

"Lordy! They've done crashed," Earl said.

Earl drove us up to the scene. The stationwagon had clipped a corner, spun around, and crashed into a cigar shop. The store was decorated with a mural of a straw-hat sporting, stogie-chomping gator. Smoke billowed from the car's crumpled hood, lending the surreal effect that the gator's cigar had somehow come to life.

Someone groaned inside the car.

"I think it's time to call the police," I said.

Just then, behind us came the blip of a siren and the flash of blue lights.

"No need," Grayson said. "They're already here."

Chapter Sixty-Six

"Well, tests don't lie, but I can barely believe it," the patrol officer named Daniels said. "None of you tested positive for alcohol. Not even *you*, Holbrook."

Daniels had lined us all up against the wall opposite the now mangled mural of the cigar-smoking gator. He was shaking his head in wonderment that all of our breathalyzers came back clean.

"The tow truck is on its way," Daniels said. "Now, will somebody tell me what in the world is really going on here?"

Grayson and Holbrook exchanged glances. "I was doing an investigation at Banner Hill nursing home," Holbrook blurted. "This man is a lunatic. He's impersonating a doctor!"

"I'm the one conducting an investigation here," Grayson said, tugging the collar of his white hospital coat. "You've got a dirty cop there. In fact, I believe he's the mastermind behind a body-snatching ring."

Holbrook shot his fellow officer a *see what I mean* look.

The confused cop shifted his gaze over to the rest of us—Earl, me, and Ms. Gable, who'd been behind the wheel of the stationwagon.

"Somebody *else* want to help me out here?" Daniels said.

Another car pulled up beside us. Stanley got out, paid the driver, and tugged a giant laundry sack out of the back seat. Then he reached in and pulled out Melvin Haplets.

"What's *he* doing here?" I asked.

Stanley shrugged. "Turns out old Melvin may be Old Mildred instead."

"What?" I gasped.

Officer Daniels winced as if he'd just had an aneurism. "*Now* what?" He shook his head and pointed his weapon at the new arrivals. What've you got in the bag, bad Santa?"

"Uh ...." Stanley stuttered.

Grayson cleared his throat. "Excuse me, officer. If my theory is correct, that bag contains evidence of Holbrook's trafficking in human body parts."

Stanley dropped the sack like it was made of molten lava. "It *does?*"

"Looks like they got us," Melvin said to Holbrook. "The gig's up."

"Shut up!" Holbrook hissed. "Don't tell them anything!"

"Like what?" Melvin asked. "That you're my nephew?"

Holbrook's face crumpled. "Look," he said to Daniels. "It's not body parts."

"*What* isn't?" Daniels asked.

"What's in the bag," Holbrook said. "It's not body parts."

"What is it then?" Daniels demanded. He turned to Stanley. "You," he barked. "The guy who brought the bag. Open it."

"Me?" Stanley asked.

"Yes, you."

Stanley winced, then untied the drawstring. Resigned to his fate, he closed his eyes and cautiously reached a hand inside the bag. When he pulled it out, he had ahold of a tube of Preparation H and a brown prescription bottle.

"Medical supplies?" Daniels asked. "What are you doing with these?"

"*Me?* I know nothing!" Stanley said.

"Stealing them," Melvin said. "What else?"

I peeked inside the bag. The missing men's files were there, tucked among a mountain of pill bottles, bedpans, cotton swabs and tubes of denture cream. I stared at Melvin. "Why did you take all this stuff?"

Melvin shrugged. "To sell at the flea market. Have you seen what they want for a decent condo around here? Social Security don't cut it."

"How long has this been going on?" Daniels asked.

"Only a week," Melvin said, sounding disappointed.

"But Melvin," Gable said, "you've been at Banner Hill for years. Why start stealing now?"

"Ask *him*." Melvin nodding toward Holbrook. "Christmas is coming. He told me this girl he met on line wants him to buy her a boob job."

"What?" Gable screeched.

"It's a lie, honey," Holbrook said. "I ... I was conducting my own investigation into the missing office supplies."

From the look on her face, Gable wasn't buying a nickel's worth of Holbrook's BS. "No you weren't. I knew it! You're a two-timing fleabag!"

"Don't play dumb, Gable," I said. "You're in on it, too. I saw you waiting for him in the parking lot. You drove the getaway vehicle."

"I ... I didn't know anything about this, I swear!" Gable choked back a sob and glared at Holbrook. "You told me we were going on a romantic getaway!"

"We'd have made it, too," Holbrook said, "if you hadn't crashed the damned car. Why weren't you wearing your glasses?"

Gable pouted angrily. "You told me I looked sexier without them. And contacts bother my eyes. They make me squint." She demonstrated, giving us a spot-on impression of Miss Piggy—constipated on macaroni.

"I bet it was a lot easier to sneak supplies past her with her glasses off, eh?" I said to Holbrook.

Holbrook's shoulders slumped. "Look. I was just trying to cover for my crazy klepto uncle. Melvin kept stealing things. I didn't want him to lose his room at Banner Hill. I swear I didn't know what was in the bag."

"Then why did you take it with you?" I asked.

"Okay. Everybody just hold it," Daniels barked. "Without more evidence, it'll be hard to pin charges on *any* of you. My money's on Holbrook. Any of you have any other evidence against him?"

"Yes!" I cried out. "He tried to poison me!"

Daniels looked me up and down. Bald and in a hospital gown that barely covered my bottom, I couldn't blame him for being skeptical.

"Apparently, you survived," he said. "Got anything else?"

I did. But it was a long shot. "I saw Holbrook stealing money from the collection plate at Bertie's revival."

Daniels' face hardened like quick-setting plaster. He turned his angry eyes to Holbrook. "You dirty scum! Stealing from the Lord!" The cop marched over to Holbrook and slapped a pair of cuffs on him. "You're going to jail, you lowest-of-the-low!"

"If I may," Grayson said, raising a finger. "I still think theft is just the tip of the iceberg when it comes to Holbrook. Officer, we've got five vets missing from Banner Hill nursing home." He grabbed the prescription bottle from Stanley and rattled it. "This prescription is for Charlie Perkins. One of the missing men."

Daniels shook Holbrook by the collar. "What do you have to say for yourself now?"

Holbrook glared at Grayson. "I want an attorney."

"Actually, now that I think about it, Ms. Draper, the owner, has been missing for a week, too," Grayson said. "Holbrook might've done something with her, as well."

Gable spun around and slapped Holbrook hard across the face. "How could you? She's just a little old lady!"

"Look who's talking," Holbrook said. "You said she's the worst boss you ever had!"

"You work at Banner Hill?" Daniels asked Gable.

"Yes."

"Why didn't you report the disappearances?"

Gable winced. "Ms. Draper left on vacation with strict orders for me not to call unless the place was burning down, or she'd fire me. And I *did* report the missing men. I told Officer Holbrook."

Daniels shot Holbrook a disgusted look. "I think we can all figure out why *he* didn't report it." He shoved Holbrook toward his patrol car. "Didn't want anybody snooping around Banner Hill, did you, you disgrace to the uniform!"

Daniels shoved Holbrook into the back of his vehicle, slammed the door, and turned to face the rest of us. "All right, you bozos. Let's go."

"To the police station?" I asked.

"No. To Banner Hill. I want to see for myself what the hell's going on there."

Chapter Sixty-Seven

The horizon was tinging pink as we pulled up on the street in front of Banner Hill in the wee, pre-dawn hours. On the eastern side of the building, I thought I saw a flash of purple light shimmer, fairy-like, then disappear around the corner.

Could that be Old Mildred saying goodbye?

I shook my head to clear it. After a crazy night with no sleep, I figured I was so tired I was hallucinating. What I'd seen was merely a reflection coming from the lights atop the other patrol car officer Daniels had called in for backup.

I glanced in Bessie's rearview mirror. Holbrook and Melvin were cuffed in the back of Daniels' patrol car. Gable had ridden up front with Daniels. Her helmet of brown hair was in tatters.

As for me, Stanley, Grayson, and Earl, after threatening to call out the troops if we did anything suspicious, Daniels had followed behind us as Earl drove his monster truck back to the nursing home.

Earl shifted Bessie into park. A moment later, a pink Cadillac with vanity plates DRAPER1 pulled up in front of us. A scrawny little old lady in a pink knit suit and matching leather pumps climbed out of the driver's seat.

"What's going on?" she asked, smoothing her silver, salon-styled hair. She glanced over at the patrol car, still loaded with passengers. "Ms. Gable!" Draper screeched. "What are you doing in a police car? Are you under arrest? You're fired!"

"But!" Gable said, and scrambled out of the car.

"Now hold on," Officer Daniels said, coming around the car and taking Draper by the hand. "I don't believe there's any call for that. Ms. Gable is just helping me out in an investigation."

"Oh," Draper said. Then something clicked inside her brain. Her face puckered. "An *investigation?*"

"Yes," Daniels said. "Into five residents who've allegedly gone missing at your nursing home. We want to do a formal head count. Match up records with residents—and stolen medications."

"Someone's been stealing medical supplies?" Draper's face snarled like a psychotic Pekinese. She turned and glared at us as we climbed down out of Bessie. "Officer, I know everyone on staff. That man over there is no doctor. And that woman is no resident of Banner Hill!"

Gable cleared her throat and smiled sheepishly at her boss. "Well, Ms. Draper, while you were gone, I—"

"She assisted us in our investigation," Grayson said. He straightened his shoulders, stepped up to Draper, and showed her his tin P.I. badge.

"Oh," Draper said. Her snarl faded to a sneer. "I see. Well, thank you. But how did *you* get involved, Mr.—?"

"Grayson. Nick Grayson. Ironically, we were alerted to the disappearances by the nephew of one of your residents, Melvin Haplets."

I glanced over at the patrol car. Holbrook's face went white. "I'm gonna kill that nitwit," he muttered.

"Melvin Haplets?" Officer Daniels asked. "Isn't he one of the men I have cuffed?"

"Yes, sir," Gable said.

Stanley stuck an elbow in my ribs and whispered, "I *told* you Melvin was crazy."

"You, Stanley Johnson!" Draper barked, wiping the smirk off Stanley's face. "Stop horsing around with that man—woman—whatever it is! Get busy helping Officer Daniels. We're going to search Banner Hill from top to bottom. If we don't find those missing vets by nine am, I'll kick all your rotten heads in!"

Chapter Sixty-Eight

An hour later, under the eagle-eye command of Tyrannosaurus Draperi, all the residents' rooms at Banner Hill had been thoroughly searched.

During the raid, two things of note were found. One small cache of dirty magazines under a resident's mattress, and a tackle box hidden inside Melvin Haplets' closet. Inside it, he'd stashed away enough Viagra and Preparation H to, well, I really didn't want to think about it.

"I leave town for a week, and everything goes to hell," Draper said, shooting Gable some serious side-eye.

"I'm sorry," Gable said, looking as if she wanted to disappear behind the reception desk she was standing beside. "I was a fool for love. I didn't realize Holbrook was just using me for cheap rent and free medical supplies."

Draper nodded, then walked over and wrapped a scrawny arm around Gable's plump shoulders. "Aw. There, there, dearie. It happens to the best of us."

Draper's soft side took me by surprise. "You've been scammed before?" I asked.

She shot me a sour look, then turned and walked down the hallway.

"What a tyrant," I whispered to Gable and Grayson.

Halfway down the hall, Draper spun around on her pink heels. The look on her face turned my gut to ice-water. "I heard that!"

She took a step toward me. Gable and I both gasped. I expected to be beheaded, or at least court-martialed. But the old lady took a few steps and stopped, then leaned up against a doorframe, as if she'd lost her balance.

"Are you all right?" I called out, sprinting toward her. Grayson and Earl followed right behind me.

"Hush!" Draper hissed. She pressed her dangly old ear against the door and sniffed. "Humph!" she grunted, then stepped back and tried the handle. It was locked.

She turned and stared at the three of us like we were useless lumps. "Stanley!" she screeched. "Unlock this closet door at once!"

I realized Stanley was nowhere to be found—unless ....

Crap! Draper's caught Stanley "rearranging the supply closet!"

"Grayson, do something," I said, hoping my eyes conveyed what my lips could not.

"Allow me," Grayson said, ignoring me. He pulled a tool from his pocket and quickly picked the lock. "Step aside, ma'am. This may not be what you think it is."

Draper laughed cynically. "You think I was born yesterday?"

"No, ma'am," Earl said. "I'd say at least a good eighty or a hundred years ago."

Draper glared at Earl, then pushed Grayson out of the way. She flung open the door. "Aha! Just what I thought!" she said.

We all stuck our noses in for a peek. But what we saw wasn't just what *I'd* been thinking.

Not by a longshot.

Chapter Sixty-Nine

Through a thin veil of marijuana smoke, I made out the wild eyes, dirty faces, and singed hair of three half-starved old men. Dressed in filthy clothes, they must've been held prisoner in the supply closet for days—if not weeks!

"This is Stanley's work," Draper said. "It has to be. He had the key—and the stash."

"Stanley?" one of the three men asked, then laughed. "No, man, we're waitin' for Vlad."

Grayson's green eyes grew wide. "Vlad the Impaler?"

The three homeless-looking guys exchanged glances, then nearly rolled on the floor laughing.

"No, man. Vlad the *Inhaler*."

The three men broke into another round of giggles.

"Hey!" the third man called out. "You guys got any munchies? I'm starving!"

Officer Daniels came running up. He took one look in the closet and blanched. "What's going on here?"

"Looks like we found three of the missing men," Grayson said. "But two are still unaccounted for."

Daniels stared at the men. "Who did this to you? Who has a key to this room?"

"Oh! Oh!" one of the old men grunted and held up his hand. "I do! I do!"

TRYING TO INTERVIEW the three stoned old geezers was like trying to pop corn without a lid. New kernels of truth kept springing up when and where we least expected them.

After feeding the men spam omelets and plenty of weak coffee, their story began to emerge, bit by bit, like a dismembered corpse from a bog.

"Let me get this straight," Officer Daniels said. "Nobody did *anything* to you?"

"No, man," Larry Meeks said, scrambled eggs trapped in his scraggly beard. "We all went to Oldstock."

"Oldstock?" Daniels asked.

"Yeah," Harry Donovan said. His bloodshot eyes gleamed with fond memories. "It was *wild*."

"What's Oldstock?" I asked.

"Oh, oh!" Charlie Perkins grunted. "I know this one!"

Harry and Larry smiled and nodded. "You tell 'em, Charlie."

Charlie beamed at us with eyes so dilated they appeared solid black. "Oldstock was a dream," he said. "Every band from the '60s was there. Well, everybody that's still alive, that is."

"Oldstock," Earl said. "I heard of that. It's the remake of that hippy fest, Woodstock."

"Right," Larry said. "About the only thing that's changed is the price of admission. We had to sell our plasma to get enough money for tickets."

Grayson and I exchanged glances. That explained the anemia and sapped energy.

"Yeah, but it was worth it," Charlie said.

"Right on, man." Larry fist-pumped the air. "That was *our* music."

"Your music?" I asked.

"The music we all fought together with during Vietnam," Harry said.

"So you all served together?" Grayson asked.

"Yeah," Harry said. "Back in 1960 when we joined, there weren't even a thousand troops deployed in that blamed old second Indochina war." He sighed. "Even fewer came back. Those of us who did, well, we kept in touch over the years. As our wives died, we all moved to Florida and ended up here at Banner Hill."

"But where are the other two men?" Grayson asked. "Tom Hallen and Joe Plank?"

"Vlad's got Tommy," Larry said.

"Vlad. You mentioned him," Grayson said. "I thought you were joking."

"No. Vlad's real, man," Harry said. "He's our weed connection."

"He drove us to the Greyhound station so we could catch a bus to the concert," Larry said. "We got back early this morning. He could only hold three of us in his Smart car. We're waiting for him to drop off Tommy, now."

"Yeah," Harry said. "He's runnin' late, man."

Larry's Jitterbug phone rang. "Hey, that's Vlad now. Says he's at the front door with Tommy. Somebody should go get him."

"Oh! I will! I will!" Charlie said.

THE EERIE PURPLE LIGHT emanating from the dashboard of the Smart car proved that Vlad wasn't an alien or a ghost.

He was a Lyft driver.

As Tommy Hallen climbed out of the passenger seat, his buddies cheered and slapped him on the back. Grayson tapped on the driver's side window and waved a twenty at the man inside. He rolled down the pane of glass.

"I'm curious," Grayson said. "Why do people call you Vlad?"

"Because that's my name," he said in a thick, Eastern European accent. "Vladmir Popescu. I'm from Romania."

"Interesting," Grayson said. "Mind if I show you a video?"

"Sorry, man. I only drive."

"No. I mean, I want to find out if you ever gave this guy a ride."

Vlad shrugged. "Okay, fine."

Grayson opened his laptop and played Vlad the mysterious audio of Albert Balls arguing with a woman over too-big a swig of alcohol. Then of his feet in checkered tennis shoes.

"I recognize the voice," Vlad said. "That's Al, all right. I usually give him a ride when I pass by the plasma center. But that night, he wouldn't get in. I told him it was his last chance, but ...."

"Ah. Thanks," Grayson said. "That explains everything but the disappearance of—"

"Hold up a minute, Larry said, looking over Grayson's shoulder at his laptop. Grayson had paused the video on the last few seconds, when Balls' face had appeared. "That guy in the video. He's the jerk who stole my Viagra and took off with Joe and that chick from the band!"

The four old geezers exchanged teary eyed glances. "Good old Joe," Harry said.

"Good old Joe," the men repeated. Then they saluted and said in unison, "Another soldier who went down rockin'."

Grayson's cheek dimpled. He turned to me and whispered, "I guess there are worse ways to go."

Chapter Seventy

After taking our testimonies, Officer Daniels and his colleague released us on our own recognizance. Left to our own devices, we went straight to Topless Tacos for one last meal before we left town.

"Gros orteil," Grayson said out of nowhere, after we sat down at our favorite table.

We all looked up from our menus.

"Where?" Earl asked. "Is that somethin' new on the menu?"

Grayson's cheek dimpled. "In a way, yes." His eyes shifted to mine. "It's French for 'big toe.'"

"I don't get it," Earl said.

"That's what Draper's sister died from," I said, cutting Grayson off before he could say more. "Mildred choked to death on a big toe."

"I heard Old Mildred choked on a clove of garlic," Stanley said. "That's why Draper won't allow it in the kitchen."

"Huh," I grunted. "Either way, that could explains why Draper instigated the tooth fairy patrol."

"So, is Old Mildred real or not?" Earl asked.

"Doubtful," Grayson said.

"Then maybe I don't need this after all," Stanley said.

He pulled out the little voodoo pouch he kept in his hip pocket. He studied it for a moment, then looked up at me. "Where'd you hear that Mildred choked on a big toe?"

"From Sampson, the night janitor," I said.

Stanley's eyes grew wide. "I've heard of him. He used to work at Banner Hill."

"Used to?" I asked.

"Yeah," Stanley said. "Until he died last year."

Grayson and I locked eyes for a moment, then Grayson reached over and grabbed the amulet from Stanley's hand. He untied the string and emptied it onto the table.

A huge clove of garlic tumbled out.

"What does it mean?" I asked.

Grayson shrugged. "Hell if I know."

I looked over at Stanley. He shook his head. "I see nothing. I know nothing."

Earl picked up the clove of garlic and popped it into his mouth. He chomped down on it, then met our blank stares with a quizzical furrow of his brow. "What?"

AFTER THE LAST TACOS were devoured, Stanley left with a Lyft driver Grayson had ordered using his cellphone. We all waved as he disappeared with Vlad in his Smart car.

"Well, I guess I better get going myself," Earl said. "I'll give you two a lift back to Banner Hill."

"Sounds good," Grayson said.

Grayson's cellphone began vibrating on the table. "Must've left it on silent for the stakeout last night," he said. He picked it up and clicked the green answer button. "Hello?"

Grayson smiled and mouthed the words, "It's Rocko." He put the phone on speaker and set it in the center of the table.

"Brother Grayson!" Rocko's voice boomed over the phone.

"Yes, I'm here," Grayson said. "What can we do for—"

"Did you ... uh ..." Rocko stuttered. "Uh ... have you happened to see Brother Bertie around?"

"What?" Grayson said.

"I ... I got up this morning and ... the semi's gone, man. It's just ... *gone!* And so is Brother Bertie."

"Well, that's an interesting development," Grayson said, in the understatement of the century. "We'll keep you posted if we see anything."

"Thanks, man. But hey, if you do find him, you're on your own. My plane leaves for Thailand in three hours."

"I see. Well, good luck and God speed," Grayson said, and hung up.

"Bertie's disappeared?" I said.

Grayson shot me a look. "Brilliant deduction, cadet."

"You think old Bertie played possum?" Earl asked.

Grayson's left eyebrow flat-lined. "What's a marsupial got to do with any of this?"

"He meant did Bertie fake his own death," I said.

Grayson shrugged. "Huh. Who knows?"

Earl grimaced. "Dang it. Now I'm all worried."

"Why?" Grayson asked.

Earl pouted. "You think Bertie will want Polly back?"

I closed my eyes.

That's what you're worried about?

"I highly doubt it," Grayson said. "Where is that parrot, anyway?"

"In a box under the passenger seat." Earl glanced out the window toward his truck. "I guess I should probably let her out, huh?"

"Yes. You do that," Grayson said. "And then head on home. We can get a ride from here."

"WISE MOVE," I SAID as we watched Earl through the plate glass window of Topless Tacos. He'd climbed into the cab of his monster truck, and was now in the midst of what appeared to be a pillow fight gone horribly awry.

"He'll survive," Grayson said.

"I know. But what about Bertie?"

"That's who I was talking about."

I stared at Grayson. "You don't think Bertie's actually come back from the dead!"

"Resurrection," Grayson said, mulling the word over. "If you think about it, traveling prophets and con artists have been with us throughout history, Drex. Counterfeiters. Fake royals. Snake-oil salesmen. Amway distributors."

My brow furrowed. "Are you saying Bertie is the reincarnation of some historical crime figure?"

"Not necessarily. Maybe he played with a possum and never died in the first place."

I smiled to myself. Mixing up metaphors was becoming part of Grayson's charm.

He took off his fedora and rubbed the stubble growing back on his head. "A really good confidence man would never get caught in the first place," Grayson said. "Who knows how many scammers are out there were never detected?"

He rubbed his chin, then looked into my eyes. "Here's a thought, Drex. What if con artists are always the same people, just in different garb?"

"What do you mean? Like immortals?"

Grayson shrugged. "Maybe. What if Brother Bertie is part of some small band of alien creatures with incredible lifespans, masquerading on Earth, adapting to whatever scheme keeps them from being noticed?"

"I guess it's possible," I conceded. "Are you planning to go after him?"

Grayson smiled and shook his head. "No. I've got a feeling we've seen the last of Bertie and his crew of soul-sucking BERPS. They're probably already in hiding somewhere, planning their next reincarnation."

I blew out a sigh. "I still say somebody just stole his semi." I popped the last bite of taco in my mouth and nearly choked on a sudden thought.

"Grayson! That truck that blew through the intersection last night. I bet it was the thieves stealing Bertie's semi!"

"Okay. So how did Bertie himself disappear?"

I frowned and slumped back in my seat. "Maybe Rocko or some of Bertie's goons loaded him up in it to take him to a funeral home."

Grayson smirked. "Oh ye of little faith. So you no longer believe Bertie healed you of your blind spells?"

I sat up straight. "No. I've got a theory about that, too."

Grayson smiled. "What is it?"

I stared into Grayson's eyes. "Viagra."

Grayson nearly choked on his iced tea. "Okay," he hacked. "Let's hear it."

I leaned in over the table. "You said before that Viagra was one of the things that could've caused my temporary blindness."

"Yes, I did. But how—"

"Hear me out. Melvin and Holbrook were putting pills in the water glasses of their victims at Banner Hill, so they wouldn't remember them sneaking into their rooms to steal their stuff. What if Melvin spiked my water glass with Viagra to ...." I swallowed against the bile rising in my throat. "To try and put me in the mood."

Grayson's cheek dimpled. "Okay, but—"

"The dreams I had about Melvin *weren't* dreams. I think he slipped me Viagra every night I was in Banner Hill. Mystery solved."

Grayson folded his arms across his chest. "What about the first time it happened, on our drive to New Port Richey?"

I chewed my lip. "I thought about that. You remember that woman who was in the corner booth at Sargent's Pizza? The one who looked like a hooker?"

"No. I don't recall."

I rolled my eyes. "*Sure* you don't. Anyway, maybe our waiter was planning a little somethin'-somethin' with her. What if he spiked her drink—or his—and accidently delivered it to me instead?"

Grayson cocked his head and unfolded his arms. "I suppose it's possible. But more likely, he didn't wash the glasses very well and you caught somebody's second-hand mickey. That place was nothing but a pick-up joint, for sure."

"Why do you say that?"

"Because any respectable place would've had liver and onions on the menu."

"No. *That's* what explains the bad taste in my mouth."

Grayson smirked. "And here I was blaming poor Betty and Bam-Bam."

Chapter Seventy-One

While we waited on the Lyft driver to come and take us to Banner Hill, Grayson paid the check, then tapped a few keys on his computer.

"Huh," he grunted. "Did you know that foot fetishism is the most common sexual fixation relating to body parts?"

I nearly choked on the Tootsie Pop in my mouth. "As opposed to what? Wait! Don't answer that."

"According to some sexpert at *Cosmo*, toe sucking is called *shrimping*." Grayson looked up at me. "It makes sense, if you think about it."

"I don't want to think about it!" A thought made me cringe. When I'd first met Melvin, he'd asked me to call him Shrimpy.

Ugh! There goes ever eating seafood again.

"Sucking toes is totally gross," I said.

Grayson looked up from his computer. "Why? Melvin's got his oral fixation, you've got yours."

I scowled. "What are you talking about?"

"Those Tootsie Pops of yours. Those who suck on straws shouldn't break a camel's back."

Ugh!

With a Tootsie Pop lodged in my mouth, it was difficult to defend my position. I settled for shooting Grayson a scowl instead.

He smiled. "But I suppose the ultimate oral fixators are incubus and succubus."

I raised a snide eyebrow. "Not vampires?"

Grayson shot me a look. "I think we just proved they don't exist, Drex."

I blew out a sigh. "Right. What was I thinking?"

WHEN WE GOT BACK TO Banner Hill, we were in for a rude surprise. We'd both forgotten about the RV's stolen back tires. Now all four were gone.

"I guess I'll call Earl," Grayson teased.

"No!"

"Triple A?"

"Better."

While Grayson dialed, I climbed into the back of the RV. Gizzard was waiting there in her terrarium.

I picked up one of the miniature Jim Beam bottles from the couch where Balls had emptied it. I rinsed it out, and fixed the anole some fresh vitamin water.

"Thanks, little Gizzard," I said as I filled her water dish.

"For what?" Grayson asked, coming in behind me.

"For being our spirit animal," I said. "If you think about it, one of her iguana relatives saved us. Even if it was a zombie."

Grayson smiled. "That, it did."

I plucked the sucker from my mouth and studied Grayson. "Do you really think I have an oral fixation?"

He shrugged. "Sometimes a Tootsie Pop is just a Tootsie Pop. And a taco is just a taco."

I smiled. "Now *that's* a belief I can get behind."

Grayson took a packet of mealy worms out of a cupboard and dropped a few into Gizzard's terrarium. "You know, I've been thinking about what you said, about vampirism being the ultimate oral fixation."

I groaned. "Please, can we give this whole vampire thing a rest?"

"I don't mean vampires as blood suckers or soul suckers. But as *oral robbers*."

My brow furrowed. "Oral robbers?"

"Yes. Those who steal with their mouths—not by way of fangs, but with words."

"I don't understand," I said.

Grayson turned his back on me and reached back into the cupboard. "What if I told you I was thinking of letting you go, Drex?"

My gut fell four inches. "What? Why? What did I do wrong?"

He turned back around. "Did you feel an internal shift?"

"Internal shift?" I said. "I feel *destroyed*. Like I want to throw up! Why are you doing this?"

"To prove my point."

"What point? That I'm no good?"

"No. That in a way, we're all oral robbers—*with our words*."

"Huh?" I whined.

Grayson studied me clinically. "All I did was utter some particular arrangement of tones through my vocal chords. You interpreted them as words, and applied your own meaning to them."

I was hurt. And on my last nerve with Grayson's stupid analogies. "Come on, Grayson! Just tell me. Am I fired, or what?"

Grayson locked his green eyes on mine. "My words formed images in your mind that sent chemical and hormonal secretions into your bloodstream, causing emotions that shifted your entire world view."

I glared at him. "Fine. I'll pack my bags and leave with the Triple A guy."

"See?" Grayson said. "Now you're insecure about your whole future, based on a couple of words that came out of my mouth."

"You'd be undone, too, if you just got fired and had to go back to Point Paradise and work with Earl!"

"That's just it," Grayson said. "You don't have to. I didn't fire you. I only asked you, 'What if I told you I was thinking of letting you go?' You did the rest yourself."

I blanched. "So ... I'm not fired?"

"No. Like I said before, it was all to prove my point. Every word we say is a psychic vampire, Drex, striking others with the power of suggestion that either drains or boosts the energy of its intended target."

"Oh," I said, feeling a wave of confused relief wash over me. "In other words, we all live and die by the thoughts and words we chose to believe?"

"Exactly," Grayson said. "Unless coronary artery disease gets us first."

Chapter Seventy-Two

With four new tires on the RV, we were finally ready to leave New Port Richey behind and head out on our next adventure.

I glanced over at Nick Grayson, the man in black. The man who murderized metaphors. The man with my future in his hands.

Why do I put my faith in this man? I wondered. Then I remembered. Because every time I think Grayson's nothing but a lunatic, he says something so profound it blows my mind.

I sat back and smiled. By my own admission, ours was a conflicted, ironic, and so far, platonic partnership. I might occasionally wish Grayson was dead, but something about that man made me feel alive.

Plus, for once, we'd finished a case with my wig still intact. I flipped down the visor and checked my shoulder-length auburn hair in the vanity mirror. I tugged the wig a tiny bit to the left.

Perfect.

"Ready to hit the road?" Grayson asked.

I nodded. "Ready. Where to next, chief?"

"Excellent question, cadet."

Grayson's cheek dimpled as he leaned over to open the glove compartment. His shoulder brushed mine, and a tingle of electricity passed through me.

If he felt it, too, he didn't let on. Instead, he pulled out a brochure and snapped the compartment shut.

"Look what I found at the Dilly Dally Motor Court," he said, handing me the brochure. "Someone stuck a bunch of these behind the refrigerator in the lobby."

I stared down at the brochure for the Skunk Ape Research Center in Ochopee, Florida.

"Do you think it's a sign from the universe, or a conspiracy?"

"Conspiracy?" I stuttered.

"Yes. You know, like someone doesn't want us to go there."

Grayson's calm, green eyes studied me, giving nothing away.

"I ... uh ...." A sharp hiss of static from the ham radio underneath the dashboard saved me from perjuring myself.

"Oh gee double-oh seven to Mr. Gray," the transmission crackled. "Come in, Mr. Gray. Over."

I smiled and shook my head softly as Grayson picked up the mic. Goofy, buck-toothed Operative Garth had either saved my bacon—or was about to throw me into the frying pan.

"Gray here," Grayson spoke into the mic. "Come in, oh gee double-oh seven. Over"

"Heard about Melvin and the bogus missing vets. Sorry about the bum lead. Over."

Grayson shrugged. "It happens. Anything new and interesting on the grapevine? Over."

"Yeah. Possible skunk ape encounter down in the Everglades. Over."

"Well, I'll be a monkey's uncle," Grayson said. He grinned and plucked the brochure from my hand. "A sign from the universe, it is."

The End

Ready for More *Freaky Florida Mystery Adventures?*

Find out where Bobbie and Grayson go from here in their next crazy adventure, *Ape Shift*.

For a sneak peek at the cover, click here. It's on my website!

https://margaretlashley.com/library/#DrexFiles

Get a Free Gift!

Don't miss another sneak preview, sale, or new release of *Freaky Florida Mystery Adventures!* Sign up for my newsletter for insider tips. I'll send you a free copy of the hilarious *Chronicles of Florida Woman* as a welcome gift!

https://dl.bookfunnel.com/ikfes8er75

Or, if you prefer, follow me on Facebook, Amazon or BookBub. They'll let you know when my next book is out!

Facebook:

https://www.facebook.com/valandpalspage/

Amazon:

https://www.amazon.com/-/e/B06XKJ3YD8

BookBub:

https://www.bookbub.com/search/authors?search=margaret%20lashley

I hope you enjoyed Oral Robbers! If you did, it would be freaking fantastic if you would post a review on Amazon, Goodreads and/or BookBub. You'll be helping me keep the series going! Thanks in advance for being so awesome!

https://www.amazon.com/dp/B081VS4S77

More Freaky Florida Mysteries

by Margaret Lashley
Moth Busters
Dr. Prepper
Oral Robbers
Ape Shift
More to Come!

"The things a girl's gotta do to get a lousy PI license. Geez!"

Bobbie Drex

About the Author

Why do I love underdogs? Well, it takes one to know one. Like the main characters in my novels, I haven't lead a life of wealth or luxury. In fact, as it stands now, I'm set to inherit a half-eaten jar of Cheez Whiz...if my siblings don't beat me to it.

During my illustrious career, I've been a roller-skating waitress, an actuarial assistant, an advertising copywriter, a real estate agent, a house flipper, an organic farmer, and a traveling vagabond/truth seeker. But no matter where I've gone or what I've done, I've always felt like a weirdo.

I've learned a heck of a lot in my life. But getting to know myself has been my greatest journey. Today, I know I'm smart. I'm direct. I'm jaded. I'm hopeful. I'm funny. I'm fierce. I'm a pushover. And I have a laugh that lures strangers over, wanting to join in the fun.

In other words, I'm a jumble of opposing talents and flaws and emotions. And it's all good.

I enjoy underdogs because we've got spunk. And hope. And secrets that drive us to be different from the rest.

So dare to be different. It's the only way to be!

Happy reading!

Made in the USA
San Bernardino, CA
05 April 2020

66814305R00168